Praise for
FICTION RIVER

"[Fiction River] is one of the best and most exciting publications in the field today."

—Keith West, *Adventures Fantastic*

"Fiction River is off to an auspicious start. It's a worthy heir to the original anthology series of the 60s and 70s. ... It's certainly the top anthology of the year to date."

—*Amazing Stories* on *Fiction River: Unnatural Worlds*

"Editor Dean Wesley Smith has compiled an outstanding volume of time travel stories, no two alike. I highly recommend it."

—*Adventures Fantastic* on *Fiction River: Time Streams*

"A sugary Christmas treat for those who love romance."

—*Publisher's Weekly* on *Fiction River: Christmas Ghosts*

"*Fiction River [Special Edition]: Crime* edited by Kristine Kathryn Rusch leads off with strong new tales by three familiar EQMM contributors: Doug Allyn with a gangster whodunnit, Steve Hockensmith with a con game story, and Brendan DuBois with a fresh variation on the old brothers-who-took-different-paths ploy. A sampling of other contents, including experimental short-shorts by Melissa Yi and M. Elizabeth Castle and a clever turn on the greedy-relatives-want-inheritance by Kate Wilhelm, suggest high quality throughout."

—*Ellery Queen Mystery Magazine*

FICTION RIVER

Year One

Unnatural Worlds
Edited by Dean Wesley Smith & Kristine Kathryn Rusch

How to Save the World
Edited by John Helfers

Time Streams
Edited by Dean Wesley Smith

Christmas Ghosts
Edited by Kristine Grayson

Hex in the City
Edited by Kerrie L. Hughes

Moonscapes
Edited by Dean Wesley Smith

Crime (Special Edition)
Edited by Kristine Kathryn Rusch

Special Edition

FICTION RIVER

Crime

Edited by
KRISTINE KATHRYN RUSCH

Series Editors
DEAN WESLEY SMITH & KRISTINE KATHRYN RUSCH

Fiction River Special Edition: Crime

Copyright © 2014 by WMG Publishing
Published by WMG Publishing
www.wmgpublishing.com
Cover art © copyright 2014 by Chan Yee Kee/Dreamstime
Book and cover design copyright © 2014 by WMG Publishing
Cover design by Allyson Longueira/WMG Publishing
Editing and other written material © copyright 2014 by Kristine Kathryn Rusch
ISBN-13: 978-0-615-93516-4
ISBN-10: 0-615-93516-8

Fiction River is an imprint of WMG Publishing, Inc.

Contents

Happy Birthday, Fiction River

Dean Wesley Smith

Fiction River has a birthday with this volume. We now can officially blow out the first candle and move on into the second year. For any magazine or series, that's amazing.

Seven Fiction River anthologies are now out full of great original stories written by some of your favorite professional writers. And all seven books are all still in print and available. (Which was one of the main reasons we did Fiction River in this anthology format.) We wanted readers who discovered Fiction River and all the great stories inside each volume to be able to read these books at any time, in any format. So we put out all seven books in electronic format, in trade paper, and in audio.

So why do Special Editions? The answer is really simple, actually.

First, we wanted to mark the end of each year. That's one reason this volume is called "Special" because it doesn't fit in the regular bi-monthly pace of Fiction River, or in the numbering system. This book is the mark that says, "Year one is completely out to readers. Seven books full of great original fiction in all genres."

There will be a Special Edition #2 one year from now as well. And so on into the future.

The second reason is that when we started this we wanted the room to do more fiction. And while six books per year offered us a lot of room, it just felt short for some reason. So the idea of adding in a special edition between two regular volumes came about and just stuck. It allowed us one more book full of stories.

Of course, seven books per year still doesn't feel like enough room for all the great stories we can find, but we're happy for now.

At this birthday point, I want to stop for a moment and once again thank all the fine readers who supported this idea back on Kickstarter. This book ends just about all rewards we offered during that campaign. But we sure hope that many of you who supported this project will continue on with us, either subscribing or buying the books in your local bookstore or online retailer.

Thank you all.

And also a grand thank you to all the readers who have subscribed or bought Fiction River over this first year. We hope you also will stay with us.

Kris and I and all the wonderful people at WMG Publishing promise to continue to bring you the top short fiction that we can find over the coming years.

So Happy Birthday Fiction River.

Now everyone, crowd around and blow out that single candle. Then let's get back to work and let these fine readers dig into some of the best crime stories Kristine Kathryn Rusch could find written by some of the top crime writers working today.

This is a very special volume. In far more ways than just one.

—*Dean Wesley Smith*
Lincoln City, Oregon
Sept. 2, 2013

Introduction

Miss Scarlet in the Library with a Crime Story

Kristine Kathryn Rusch

Most people who don't read the mystery genre have a skewed perception of what the genre is. They believe that all mysteries are puzzle stories—Miss Scarlet in the Lib'ry with a Wrench. They know about Sherlock Holmes and Miss Marple; they're familiar with *Murder She Wrote* and *Elementary*. They believe that every mystery story has a bloodless corpse at its core, and a brilliant amateur detective who can ferret out the killer with a single glance.

The mystery genre needs a new name.

I propose crime fiction.

Crime fiction encompasses what mystery has become. We can't really say that it's evolved past the body in the lib'ry, because the American father of the mystery is Edgar Allen Poe. He wrote about crime—*The Tell-Tale Heart*, which is about a guilty murderer, *The Cask of Amontillado*, a revenge story in which someone gets buried alive, and of course, that "first" detective story, *The Murders in the Rue Morgue*, which Poe himself called a tale of "ratiocination." (Boy, am I glad *that* label didn't stick.)

Crime: murders, revenge, guilt—when bad things happen to good people or, even better in my opinion, when bad things happen to bad people. Crime encompasses everything from the cozy mystery, which is generally upbeat and bloodless, to noir, which is generally bleak and blood-filled.

We have both cozies and noir stories in this, our seventh anthology in the Fiction River series. As Dean explained in his foreward, this is our first special edition. I wanted to do an extra push on this edition because, honestly, I adore crime fiction in all its forms.

All of the previous Fiction River anthologies had a crime story or two, but those stories were usually in a different genre: Urban fantasy detectives in *Unnatural Worlds*, evil mass murderers in *How To Save The World*, time-hopping criminals in *Time Streams*, kidnappers in *Christmas Ghosts*, magical murder in *Hex in The City*, and dead clones in *Moonscapes*.

But this volume focuses on the here and now, or in some cases, the then and now. The *real* world, as the case may be. Crime-ridden and imperfect. Some stories have heroes who come to the rescue. A few have detectives who use their talents to solve crimes. A few stories have no heroes and no happy ending, just the darkness that can be real life.

Each story features a crime, but not all the crimes in this volume are murders. Some crimes are small—traffic stops, cheating at cards—and others are so vast that they envelope an entire culture.

Several stories have twists that you can see coming, and others are so subtle that you'll have to stop and think about what kind of crime actually occurred. The stories surprise in other ways. Just by changing gender, for example, an old tale becomes new again. The stories also jump all over in time—from the Great Depression to the 1960s to the Reagan Era—and back to the present.

I'm particularly proud of the mix of storytellers who've joined us for this volume, from newcomer Karen Fonville to award-winner Kate Wilhelm whose work spans genres and decades.

When I invited the writers into this volume, the only parameter I put on them was that the story needed to be a *crime* story.

I had expectations, though. I invited a mix of cozy writers and noir writers, writers known for dark fiction and writers known for light fiction.

What I got surprised me. Freed from rules, the writers explored new territory. The cozy writers wrote dark tales; the noir writers wrote light tales. It all balanced, even though not in the way that I expected.

This volume has become exactly what I hoped it would be: a snapshot of the modern mystery genre. Or, as the title says, the modern *crime* genre.

I had a great deal of fun compiling this special edition of Fiction River. I hope you have as much fun reading it.

—*Kristine Kathryn Rusch*
Lincoln City, OR
September 2, 2013

When we came up with the idea for a crime volume of Fiction River, I knew I had to ask Doug Allyn to participate. He is, in my opinion, one of the best short story writers of his generation. I'm not alone in this. His first published story won the Robert L. Fish Award from the Mystery Writers of America. He has won mystery's highest honor, the Edgar award, twice. He also has four Derringer awards for novellas, and he's won the Ellery Queen Readers Award an unprecedented ten times.

About "Hitler's Dogs," he says that the story came from a casual conversation with another award-winning author, Clark Howard. "We were kicking around our experiences as young delinquents, and one of us used the term 'wild dogs.' It occurred to me later that it was true, in many ways, gangs do resemble wolf packs. Perhaps it's the best thing about them..."

———

Hitler's Dogs

Doug Allyn

The weight of the casket caught me by surprise. Fat Jack was no daisy, but with five pallbearers on the job—except there weren't five. Not really.

Directly across from me, Beef Malenfont was built like a barrel with a keg for a head, topped by a Marine brush cut. Sturdy as a Mack truck, Beef was definitely toting his share.

But beside him, the Gimp was on the south side of sixty, grizzled and gray with a bum foot. Gimp was probably leaning on the box to keep himself upright.

On my right, Benny the Banker was as round as a bowling ball, too squat to be much help. The new kid on the end was tall and blonde with shoulder-length hair. Tailored suit. Looked like he was carrying his percentage, but that meant Fat Jack's bulk was basically split three ways.

And nothing in this world is heavier than a dead friend.

As we shifted the casket from the bier onto the gurney, Benny stumbled, knocking me off balance, and we nearly dropped the damned thing.

It wouldn't have mattered, I suppose. Fat Jack wouldn't feel it and the only mourners were his sister Moira and an ancient aunt, who couldn't remember who she was, let alone who Jack used to be.

Back in '06, when the rapper Proof got capped in a Detroit club, they say 5,000 people jammed the Fellowship Chapel for his wake.

Fat Jack Cassidy had been loan sharking in Warsaw Heights for thirty years. Locals saw him every day. Some nodded or said hello. Some crossed to the other side of the street.

But at the end, not a soul turned out to see him off. Not at the church, not at the graveside. No one.

Which was a very bad sign.

Afterward, our subdued little group gathered at Jack's grubby storefront office in the Heights.

The door was locked. No problem. Popping locks was the first skill Fat Jack ever taught me. I had us inside in under five seconds, showing off a little. Moira found the bottle of single malt Jack kept in the bottom drawer of his desk. Gimp passed out paper cups from the water cooler and Moira filled 'em up. But no one drank.

We were all eyeing each other uneasily. Waiting for someone to say something, I suppose. I realized someone was missing.

"Where's Toto? Jack's dog?"

"He died last year," Benny said. "Jack was bummed for weeks. He loved that lop-eared mutt."

"Well?" Beef said, raising his cup. "Here's to Fat Jack."

"What the hell, Beef?" Gimp said. "It's a wake. Is 'here's to him' the best you can do?"

"What do you mean?"

"It's the last toast we'll ever drink to the man. Say something nice about the guy, for chrissake."

"I can't think of nothin' nice."

"Fine," Benny the Banker said. "Here's to Fat Jack. He was good to his dog."

"So was Hitler," the kid cracked.

"Fat Jack wasn't no Hitler," Benny said, bristling. "We all know thugs who'd cap their mother for ten bucks. If Jack busted some mope's finger for bein' a slow pay, that mope should count his blessings. Ain't that right, Doc?"

"Depends on which finger it was," I said, holding up my scarred left hand. "I'm already short a pinky. As for Hitler, he actually *was* nice to his dogs. Shepherds, I think. Ever wonder what Hitler's dogs would've said about their boss?"

Dead silence. The others were staring at me.

"I give up," the kid said at last. "What would Hitler's dogs say?"

"Probably something like, 'Hey, too bad about World War II and all, but Adolph always took good care of us.' And Fat Jack took care of *us*. Didn't he."

It was a rhetorical question. I waited anyway. Nobody said anything.

"Jack's word was a lock," I went on. "If he promised something, he delivered. If you got jammed up, he had your back, and bail money if you needed it. He might piss and moan, but he never stiffed a friend."

"As long as you earned your keep," the kid said.

"The Heights ain't no charity ward, sonny," the Gimp said. "Jack expected people to carry their weight, but he always held up his end. Doc's right, the man wasn't no saint but he was always straight with us."

"For all the good it did him," Moira said bitterly. "At the end, when he had trouble, where were his so-called pals?"

"Whoa up, Moira," Beef protested. "I was doin' ninety days over at county."

"You've been out for two weeks, Beef," Moira said. "Today's the first time I've seen you. And Doc? How long have you been gone? Five years?"

"Don't lay Jack's death on me, lady, or anybody else in this room," I said. "It's on whoever took him out."

"Cops said it was an accident, Doc," Beef said. "He got clipped by a hit and run driver."

"Since when do Warsaw Heights cops give a rip about guys in the life?" I asked.

"Jack was one less thug to worry about," the kid chipped in.

"Nobody asked you," I said. "Who the hell are you, anyway?"

"I'm you," the kid said, not a bit intimidated. "I took your old slot in the crew. I'm Jack's paperboy, Bobby Zee." He offered his hand.

I ignored it. "What's the Zee for?"

"Zelinski. What's the Doc for? Doctor Feelgood?"

"More like Doctor Kevorkian," Benny cracked. "Doc puts people to sleep. Permanent."

"You talk too much," I said.

"Jack called him Doc because he went to college awhile," Beef put in. "Big freakin' deal."

"Where?" Bobby Zee asked.

"Here in Detroit," I said. "I dealt X and high-end weed on the U of D campus. A new class of customers every hour."

"Took classes, too," Gimp added. "Aced 'em all."

"What was your major?" the kid asked.

"Philosophy," I said. "Man's search for the secret of life."

"Did you figure out the secret, hotshot?" Beef asked.

"Yes," I said. "Life's short."

"Shorter for people in our line of work," Bobby Zee said.

"Short for everybody," I said. "Nineteen or ninety, when your time's up, you'll want a little more. A year. A day. Five more seconds. And don't talk to me like we're pals, sonny. I don't know you."

"Bobby's okay, Doc," Moira said quickly. "Jack brought him into the crew last year."

"And now he's dead," I said. "Can I talk to you a minute? Alone?"

* * *

I followed Moira into the file room that served as her office, a windowless box that she swept for bugs twice a day. Jack never did business over a phone. Simple orders were whispered on busy street corners. More complicated setups were planned in this office. If these walls could talk, we'd all be doing life without parole.

Moira sat on the corner of her desk with her arms folded. I leaned my back against the door jamb to be sure we weren't interrupted. And found myself staring at Moira. Couldn't help it.

She and Jack couldn't have looked less alike. Moira Cassidy was slender, almost gaunt, with haunted eyes. Black Irish to the bone, her hair was dark as a raven's heart, her complexion had a faintly blue tint, like fine china. A hard line of a mouth. She wasn't conventionally pretty, but she was...magnetic. For me.

She was wearing black for mourning. It suited her. Moira seldom wore makeup, and in her heavy horn-rimmed glasses, you might pass her on the street without a second glance. But to me—she was eyeing me. Her dark eyes like laser scalpels.

"Still single?" I asked. "I'm surprised some wild boy hasn't carried you off by now."

"Not likely. How's your family, Doc? Got a little wifey and a couple of rug rats stashed somewhere?"

"No," I admitted. "No family."

"I never had the chance for one," Moira said. "Whenever a boyfriend got serious, Jack ran him off."

"He was looking out for you."

"He didn't want to lose his bookkeeper," she snapped. "Enough with the Auld Lang Syne, Doc. Why did you come back?"

"For Jack's funeral. How much did it cost?" I asked.

"Forget it. Jack had insurance."

"Get a refund. Even with the lid closed, I could smell funk around the casket."

"Damn," she winced, looking away. "I didn't notice. I've gotten used to it."

"Used to what?"

"The smell of death. Jack had morbid diabetes, Doc. Necrotic sores on both legs. He needed surgery but he kept putting it off. The stench was on his clothes. Dry cleaning only made it worse. I should have bought him a new suit."

"To bury him in? Jack would have broken out of that box to slap the crap out of you."

"Probably," she agreed with a wan smile.

"You should have called me sooner, Moira. He might have listened to me."

"They wanted to amputate his legs at the knee. He wouldn't do it for you, me or the baby Jesus. You couldn't have saved him, Doc."

"Maybe not from his illness, but that's not how he died. Somebody ran him down in the street, Moira. Like a dog."

"They did him a favor."

"Then maybe I'll look them up. To say thank you."

She caught the edge in my tone, and nodded slowly.

"That's the real reason you're here, isn't it? To square things for Jack?"

"Somebody has to."

"Why you? It's been five years, Doc. You can't come waltzing back like you still belong."

"Jack was my friend."

"He was nobody's friend," she said bitterly. "Not even mine. You were smart to get out when you did."

"I didn't have a choice. Are you angry with me about something?"

"Jesus H. Christ," she shrugged helplessly. "Do you have to ask? It's like seeing a ghost, Doc. No word in all these years? I thought you were dead."

"I was in trouble when I left. I didn't want it to blow back on you."

"On Jack, you mean."

"No. On you, Moira. I practically grew up in this office. Saw you every day with your game face on. Like now. A lot of edge to you. I used to daydream about you. Did you know that? How you'd look by candlelight."

"Candlelight?" she snorted.

"Maybe over dinner? Someplace with linen tablecloths, silverware, soft music. I always thought you'd be beyond beautiful. By candlelight."

"You always were a crazy kid."

"You're only a few years older."

"I'm a thousand years older, Doc. Old enough to see what you were becoming. Doc Bannan, Fat Jack's teenage killer. You scared the hell out of people, Doc. Including me. You still do."

I didn't say anything. My right hand unconsciously covered my maimed left, with its missing finger. "I'm not the wild kid who left, Moira. I've been some places, learned a few things."

"Like what?"

"Like there's no way to get even for a death, Moira. No way to make it right. Ever."

"Then why—?"

"There has to be payback. A reckoning. Who killed Jack, Moira?"

"I don't know, Doc. Truly."

"Who were his enemies?"

"Are you kidding? Open the phone book. My brother was a loan shark, he collected street tax and protection. He didn't have a friend in the world unless you count those clowns out front. And you. What difference does it make now?"

"Maybe none. If somebody was settling an old score, it might be over. But if somebody's moving in on Jack's action, maybe they're just getting started. You could be next, Moira. Or one of the crew. Beef, most likely. He's the most dangerous."

"Or you," she pointed out.

"Actually, I'm kind of hoping for that," I said. "What about the crew? If Jack's been sick, has anyone been angling to move up?"

She hesitated, reading my face. Then took a deep breath.

"Beef," she said. "He's been pushing Jack to step aside, let him take over."

"Jack wasn't willing?"

"Beef's tough enough, but not smart enough. Can't control his temper, can't stay out of jail. When Jack turned him down, Beef got loaded, got into a brawl, wound up at county. He's been out a couple of weeks, but hasn't been around."

"What about this new kid? Bobby Zee?"

"He took your old job, Doc, but he's nothing like you were. A talker, not a fighter. Works the U of D coffee shops dealing uppers and X. That's his speed."

I nodded, absorbing that.

"Last question," I said. "Word about Jack's illness must have gotten around. Have any Detroit crews been trying to muscle into the Heights?"

She looked away, avoiding my eyes. "I was hoping you wouldn't ask about that."

* * *

The party was in full swing when we rejoined the others in the front office. The first bottle stood empty on Jack's desk. A second was already half gone.

"What's up, Doc?" Bobby Zee grinned, doing a bleary Bugs Bunny.

No one laughed. I realized the kid was more like me than Moira realized. Smarting off to impress her. I let it pass.

"Moira tells me the Spanish Cobras have been leaning on Jack for a piece of the Heights. Has anybody heard anything?"

The crew exchanged glances.

"I've heard rumors about the Cobras," Gimp admitted. "Nothing solid."

"If they weren't pushing before, they will be now," Bobby Zee said. "Jack was the muscle of this outfit, the one with the reputation."

"Hey, I got a rep too," Beef said.

"For getting locked up," Benny said. "What should we do, Doc?"

"Whoa up," Beef protested. "Who elected him boss? Did we take a vote I didn't hear about?"

"Beef has a point," Bobby Zee said.

"We don't need a vote," Moira said. "Doc would have been Jack's choice."

"Says who?" Beef demanded.

"I do," she said. "Does anybody have a problem with that?"

"Not me, lady," Bobby grinned, raising both hands in mock surrender. "If Doc's got a move in mind, let's hear it."

"No moves," I said. "The opposite. Everybody goes back to the streets, no muss, no fuss, no explanations. Show the Heights it's business as usual."

"But if the Cobras push in, we can't stand against 'em, Doc," Benny said. "We're gofers, not gunmen."

"According to him, we're dogs," Beef griped.

"Not just dogs," I said. "Hitler's dogs. Somebody forgot that when he killed our friend."

Gimp glanced up sharply, reading my eyes.

"Oh man," he said. "You're goin' after them, aren't you, Doc?"

"That depends on what happened," I said. "Nobody's safe until we know. If the Cobras greased Jack for his territory, we need to show them it didn't work. Maybe they'll reach out, offer a deal."

"Or maybe they'll cap somebody else," Bobby offered.

"I don't think so. Whoever did this doesn't figure we count for much. Show them they're wrong. We take care of business, the same as we did for Jack."

"And while we're walking around with targets on our backs, where will you be?" Beef asked. "Hidin' behind Jack's desk?"

"Nope. That'll be Bobby's job."

"Mine?" the kid echoed, surprised.

"The campus can slide, sport. We need somebody here to look out for Moira. There's a shotgun behind the door. No strangers get in, understand?"

"They shall not pass," the kid said, grinning like a putz. God. Was I ever that young?

"What should I do, Doc?" Moira asked.

"Keep your phone turned on. If the Cobras are on the make, they'll call to ask for a meet. Whatever they ask, agree to it. I'll take it from there."

"This ain't right," Beef said, glowering at me. "You can't show up after all this time and take over. It should be me."

"You asked Jack about that a few weeks ago," Moira said. "He laughed."

"He ain't laughin' now, is he?" Beef said. He stormed out, slamming the door behind him.

"What's with him?" Bobby Zee asked.

"He seems normal to me," I said. "But I'd hate to be the first slow pay he tracks down."

"Still, it was a fair question," Bobby said, facing me. "If I'm holding the fort, where will you be?"

"Time traveling," I said.

* * *

Warsaw Heights is a hardcore Slavic enclave a few miles up I-75 from the dark heart of inner city Detroit. Locals call it White Harlem.

The Heights is my home town, I suppose. I don't know where I was born or who my parents were, but White Harlem is definitely where I grew up. Fast.

In the years I'd been away, a lot had changed. Arab immigrants were supplanting the Serbs and Poles of the old days. Most shop signs had Arabic subtitles, and the cathedral bells of St. Stanislaus had to compete with tinny loudspeakers calling the faithful to prayer.

I strolled the main drag, Kosciusko Avenue, like I owned it. But I barely recognized it. A dry goods store with Muslim headscarves on display, a shoe shop, boarded up now, a new dollar store gaily decorated for Christmas.

Finally, a familiar place. La Texana Bodega, a party store with eleven brands of tequila in the front window. A heavyset Mexican woman, her bountiful bosoms draped in cheap jewelry, was parked on a stool behind the counter. A brass bell tinkled as I stepped in.

"*Hola*, Mama Ruiz," I said. "Do you remember me?"

"No," she said automatically, without glancing up.

I took a newspaper from the rack and carefully placed it on the counter. This time she did look up. Her mouth narrowed a bit at the corners, but beyond that, her face showed nothing.

"I don't know you, mister."

"You should, Mama. I used to be your paperboy. I delivered the *Free Press*, and picked up numbers and betting slips for Fat Jack."

"I don't know nothing about that."

"I'm still in the same business, Mama. But instead of delivering news, I'm buying it." I counted out five twenties, placed them beside the newspaper.

"Maybe I do remember you," she said, deadpan. "What do you want, Paperboy?"

"Street buzz," I said simply. "Did you hear about Fat Jack?"

"Got runt over," she nodded. "Seen about it on the TV."

"Has anyone been around, asking about Jack's business?"

"No. Not lately."

"But someone came before?"

She considered that a moment. Her eyes strayed to the bills. I pushed them toward her.

"Maybe a month ago," she said quickly. "Some street boys came around. Wanted me to pay so my windows don't get broke. I say I pay Mr. Jack for insurance."

"Did you know these boys?"

"They wasn't from this neighborhood. From Eastpointe, I think." She said something in machine-gun Spanish.

"I'm sorry," I said, "I don't—"

"Spanish Cobras," she said. "I know their gang tats. My cousin's son is—anyway. I tell that Bobby Zee to tell Mr. Jack about it, he say he'd see to it."

"Did he?"

"I guess," she said, frowning. "Them boys never come back."

"How many were there?"

"Three come inside. Two more on the street to watch."

"What were they driving?"

"Didn't see no car, but they must've had one. They sure didn't walk here from Eastpointe. With they pants down around they ass, don't see how them boys can walk no place."

"Did you catch any names?"

"They didn't say. I didn't ask."

"*Gracias*, Mama," I said, folding the bills into her palm. "Good to see you."

"Hey, paperboy," she called after me. "With Mr. Jack gone, who do I pay the insurance to? You?"

"No, I just came for Jack's funeral, Mama. I won't be staying."

"Good," she nodded. "One funeral is enough."

As the door closed behind me, I noticed she crossed herself, murmuring something under her breath. I hoped it wasn't a curse.

Two more quick stops got me nothing. Had better luck at a newsstand run by a legless black vet. Sarge. The old guy remembered me vaguely. He was all smiles. At first.

"Always good to see someone from the old days," he said.

But his gap-toothed grin faded as he gradually remembered exactly who I was, back in those old days. Sarge was vague about a few things, but he damn sure remembered Fat Jack's star pupil. He avoided my eyes, answering my questions in monosyllables. It was depressing to see his fear. I kept our chat short.

His story was much like Mama's. A month back, a crew of gang bangers tried muscling the neighborhood. Spanish dudes, he thought. Not local. He got word to Fat Jack, and the thugs never came back. He assumed Jack warned them off.

"The Heights is a rough neighborhood," he said. "Nobody minds payin' Mr. Jack his tax to keep the riffraff out. Tell him Ol' Sarge said so, when you see him."

"I'll tell him, Sarge. When I see him."

My last stop was at Sweeney Todd's, an Irish bar. It was Beef Malenfont's favorite hangout and it suited him. Plank floors, a long, scarred counter, pool tables against the wall. Beef was in a dark corner, hunched over a draft. He saw me coming, scowled and shook his head.

"Go away, Doc," he said, as I slid into the seat facing him across the battered oak table, "I ain't feelin' social."

Up close, I could read Beef's mug like a history book. His temper's gotten him into a hundred fights and his face carries marks from most of them.

"I don't care if the others go along with you takin' over, Doc. I ain't takin' no orders from you."

"Just answer one question, Beef, then I'm gone. Or you are."

His eyes lit up at that. He slid his beer mug aside. Clearing for action.

"You think you can handle me, Doc?"

"Maybe we'll find out. It depends."

"On what?"

"On whether you've got the balls to give me a straight answer."

"I wouldn't bother lyin' to you. I always figured you were lucky once and built a reputation off it. Ask me anything you want, Paperboy."

"Moira said you haven't been around, Beef. Where were you?"

"I got busted for a bar fight. Got locked up at county."

"You got out two weeks ago. You didn't check in. Why not?"

He looked away, considering his answer. It was almost painful to watch the big man think.

"Okay, straight up," he said, meeting my eyes. "Jack's been terrible sick. You could smell the death on him. I couldn't stand seein' him like that. Dying an inch at a time."

"That's all it was?"

"Not quite. My parole officer's a prick and Jack's a known associate. If I got spotted with him, they'd throw me back inside. I hate bein' caged up, Doc. Maybe I really am one of them dogs you was talkin' about."

"Maybe we both are."

"Why don't you say what's really on your mind, Doc? Ask me if I done Jack. Give me an excuse to break your back."

"Maybe later," I said. "We've got troubles enough."

"The Spanish Cobras." It wasn't a question.

"What have you heard, Beef?"

"Ain't heard nothin'. But when I was locked up? A couple of Cobras came at me in the yard. Bad mistake on their part."

"Why didn't you mention this before?"

"At the time, I figured it was jailhouse games. Now I wonder if it was their first move."

"It's been tried before,"

"Last time, it was them Jamaicans from Ecorse," he agreed. "They grabbed you up for a first move. Too bad they didn't keep you." He rose slowly, glaring down at me. "Pay for my beer, hotshot. I'm fussy about who I drink with."

After Beef stalked out, I tried to chat up the bartender. A waste of time. He was Lebanese, new to the neighborhood.

"I got cold Coors on tap, corned beef and Lay's chips, mister. Buy something or go peddle your papers." His surly crack won a grin from me. He had no idea why.

I ordered a corned beef on rye and a Virgin Mary, carried them back to Beef's table, then ripped into the sandwich like a starving shark. Hadn't eaten since yesterday. Took my time sipping my tomato juice, though, stirring it with the celery stick. Thinking.

According to Mama Ruiz and Sarge, Spanish Cobras from Eastpointe tried to muscle into the Heights a month or so ago. Then they backed off. Why?

Streetwise and violent, with cartel connections, the Cobras were a crew on the rise. Sick as he was, Jack couldn't have scared off the Girl Scouts, let alone the Cobras. And with Beef locked up—

Was that a coincidence? Or had they reached out to Beef in the slam? Angry at Jack for brushing him off, he could have agreed to stand aside, give the Cobras a free shot at Jack.

Moira had misgivings about Beef. So did I. He'd always resented my rapid rise in the crew. Maybe that's not all he resented.

* * *

Dusk was settling on the Heights when I left Sweeney's, street lights flickering on, Christmas decorations winking cheerfully in the shop windows.

I paused in the pub's shadowed doorway, automatically scanning the street for danger, an old habit.

That saved my life.

Down the block, a Cadillac Escalade was idling at the curb on the far side of the street. White exhaust rising in the chill December air.

Black car, blacked out windows. I couldn't see inside—a rear window was rolling down. I caught a glint of metal coming up. Gun? Couldn't tell, didn't wait to find out!

Diving head first, I rolled behind a parked pickup truck as silent slugs punched into the wall where I'd been standing an instant before. No roar of gunfire, only muzzle flashes from the Cadillac's rear window and the thump of lead hammering into the pickup truck, blowing out its windows, shattering the pub's glass door into a thousand pieces. But the only sound was the breaking glass. The gunman was firing suppressed rounds.

For a silencer to work, the slug's velocity has to stay below the speed of sound, which limits their penetration. It'll zip through a man or even a door, but they won't punch through a pickup truck. I was safe as long as I stayed down.

But I'd just buried a friend, and I was in no mood to hide.

Crouching below the window level of the cars along the curb, I duck-walked along the sidewalk toward the Cadillac. I was carrying a .38 revolver, but didn't draw it. All I wanted was a plate number—the windshield of the Buick beside me blew out, triggering its alarm system.

The beeping car horn would scarcely raise an eyebrow in the Heights, but it was too much noise for the gunmen.

The Escalade peeled out, tires howling as it vanished around the corner. I dashed into the street, hoping for a glimpse—but I was too late. By the time I rounded the corner, the Caddy was a memory.

I kept running anyway.

Even in White Harlem, a shootout will generate 911 calls. I didn't want to spend the rest of the night cuffed in a squad car, answering questions.

I had questions of my own.

* * *

Warsaw Heights police headquarters is a six-story concrete tenement built back in the Great Depression. It looks every grim day of it.

I asked for Detective Bernie Czecho at the information desk. A bored patrolman said he was on his dinner break. Try the Verdict's Inn, down the block.

The Inn hadn't changed a bit. It's a tavern hangout for cops, lawyers and newsmen. You can order a burger and a beer, cut a plea deal or make a payoff without leaving your barstool.

The joint was jammed, the jukebox thumping out Motown oldies while cops swapped lies and lawyers dealt their clients' lives away like penny ante poker. Your criminal justice system at work.

I spotted Czecho in a corner booth, slurping a bowl of road-house chili. Not a pretty sight. Slope shouldered in a cheap suit, he looked like a Neanderthal trying to pass for a sapiens. I slid into the empty seat facing him.

Czecho barely glanced up. "I'm off duty…" He began, then hesitated. Cocking his head, he scanned my face. "I'll be damned," he said, grinning, leaning back in his seat. "Paperboy. Fat Jack's favorite punk. What was your name again?"

"Bannan. People call me Doc."

"I ain't people, sport, I'm the law. I should bust you right now. You gotta be guilty of something."

"You'd better call downtown first, Detective. Ask Tony Zeman if he wants me busted."

"You're not with Zeman, Doc. I'd know if you were."

"Which means you must still be on Zeman's pad."

"Keep your damn voice down," Czecho said, glancing around quickly to be sure we hadn't been overheard. "Why would you think I'm hooked up with Zeman?"

"Because you know I'm not."

Czecho leaned back in his chair, eyeing me with open contempt. "Fat Jack always claimed you were smart, Doc. But you walk into a cop bar, and get in my face? I could raise a finger and—"

"You'd lose money," I interrupted.

"What money?" I had his attention now.

"The best kind, Detective. Money for nothing. I'm not looking for trouble, Czecho, I only came back to bury Fat Jack. And to tie up some loose ends. I could use some help."

"Why on earth would I help you?"

"How about cash? Ten cee notes in your hand, right now. I just need a few answers." I slid a folded square of bills across the table. Czecho reached for it, but I quickly covered it with my palm. "Cash on delivery."

"What do you want, Doc?"

"For openers, who killed Jack?"

"Some drunk, probably. It was a hit and run. We get three a week in this town."

"Don't jerk me around, Czecho," I said, leaning in, my face only an inch from his. "Guys in the life don't die by accident. If he got struck by lightning, you'd be suspicious. Zeman wouldn't pay you if you weren't good at your job, so let's have it. Who did Jack?"

"We don't know," Czecho said, meeting my hard stare straight on.

"And you don't care?"

"Not much."

I leaned back in my chair, considering that answer.

"If you don't care, then Tony Zeman isn't worried. Has skimming the unions made him too soft to control the street? Or is he waiting to see who comes out on top?"

"I don't know what Mr. Zeman thinks, Doc. And if I did, I sure as hell wouldn't discuss it with you."

"If Zeman's not concerned, then it can't be an out-of-town crew muscling in. He'd worry about that."

"If you say so." Czecho slurped another mouthful of chili.

"Earn your money, Detective. Tell me something I can't read in the papers."

He considered that a moment. "Jack's death wasn't *exactly* a hit and run," he offered.

"How do you mean?"

"He got hit, all right, and the driver ran. But first he backed up over Jack's body. Twice. He made damn sure Jack was dead before he split."

"So it was definitely a hit, probably a pro. That explains Sweeney's. Somebody took a shot at me there. A crew in a black Escalade."

"Why do you think it was a crew? We don't have gangs in the Heights, Doc, mostly because of what happened to those Jamaicans a few years ago."

"The shooter used a silenced AK. Only a pro can afford a gun like that. Or know where to get one."

"A pro like Fat Jack, maybe?"

That stopped me. "What did that mean?"

"A few months ago, I got a tip that one of Jack's crew was smuggling silenced AK-47s in from Canada. ATF had a tail on him but he lost them in the Heights. They picked him up later, but he'd already delivered the guns or stashed them. Without the weapons they couldn't make a case."

"Who was the guy?" I asked, leaning in.

He told me. And everything changed.

He must have read it in my face.

"I guess I just earned my money," he said, raking in the cash. "You didn't know about that, did you?"

I shook my head.

"Some poet said you can never go home, Doc. It was good advice."

"It was Thomas Wolfe," I said absently. "But while I'm in town? Why don't you do what you do best, Czecho. Nothing. I'll see to this. Tell Mr. Zeman everything's under control."

"I'll tell him I saw a goddamn ghost," Czecho chuckled. "I take back what I said about how smart you are, Paperboy. See ya around."

He turned back to his chili. I headed for the door.

Outside, I breathed in the cold December air. Exhaust fumes, stale beer. Eau de White Harlem. As familiar as my face in the morning mirror. But Wolfe was right. You can't go home again. It isn't the same.

Neither are you.

'Paperboy.' I ditched that nickname when I left the Heights. But some things can't be undone. Like a missing finger.

People in White Harlem still remembered my name. And how I got it.

Like most things in my life, it came from Fat Jack.

* * *

I arrived in Warsaw Heights as a ward of the state. The foster care system dumped me into St. Stanislaus' Home for Wayward Boys, a massive old gothic cathedral with castellated revetments that make it look like a medieval prison.

Which it was, in effect.

Back in the eighties, the diocese converted the rectory into a halfway house for juvenile offenders. Home sweet home for me and a hundred more young toughs. The dank stone walls and open barracks were better than the steel cages in juvie hall, but not by much.

My first day in the Heights, I got caught shoplifting in a bodega. I punched the clerk in the face and ran like a scalded cat. Laughing all the way. Thought I'd gotten away clean.

I was wrong.

The next day I got called into Father Proctor's office. I had a visitor. Fat Jack Cassidy. The priest left us alone together.

Jack didn't waste words. He explained that merchants in Warsaw Heights paid him to keep punks like me from stealing them blind. If I did it again, he'd find me and break both of my arms. He meant it, too. I told him to screw himself.

I expected a beating. He offered me a job instead. He needed a paperboy, a kid to deliver the *Free Press* and pick up betting slips for his sports book. I started that afternoon.

The job was a major jump in status at St. Stan's. Fat Jack was a local legend, and a great teacher. I picked up the finer points of felony, arson, burglary, extortion. Street Crime 101. For a foster kid whose only family memories were beatings and blood, life in White Harlem was Sugartown.

Unfortunately, a Jamaican crew from Ecorse noticed how sweet it was, and tried to muscle into Jack's action.

For openers, they grabbed a hostage. Me. Snatched me up as I was leaving Mama Ruiz's bodega with the daily numbers take.

Their first mistake was holding me for ransom. They told Jack to fork over five grand or they'd send him my head in a hatbox. Jack told them to tie a ribbon on it. He could find ten punks like me at St. Stan's any day of the week.

No surprise. I knew Jack wouldn't pay a dime to get me back.

To prove they were serious, the Jamaicans cut a finger off my left hand. With a box knife. They said if I yelled, they'd cut my throat too. I believed them. I didn't yell.

Their second mistake was giving my finger to some Rasta stoner to drop off at Jack's office. Before he vanished into a landfill, the stoner told Jack everything he knew.

But the Jamaicans' worst mistake was locking me in a closet. Like the kid I appeared to be.

I'm claustrophobic. Locked in that coffin with my throbbing hand wrapped in a bloody rag, I was terrified out of my mind.

I knew their pal wouldn't be coming back. When he didn't show, they'd realize I was useless, slit my throat, and toss me in a dumpster. I was fifteen. I knew I'd be dead before dark.

A jam like that tends to focus your thoughts. I was too small to fight them. I needed a weapon, but there was nothing in the closet but a ratty bathrobe and a few coat hangers... One was the wooden kind. With a metal hook.

Straightening out that hook with my maimed hand was savagely painful, but I managed it, without making a sound. When I was finished, I had a workable jailhouse shiv, a wooden handle with a seven-inch steel tine that protruded from my fist. Straight as an ice pick.

Then I crouched down in the dark. Waiting.

Around six, the Jamaicans went out for food, leaving one guy to watch me.

When I was sure they were gone, I started bawling, wailing at the top of my lungs. When the guard yanked open the closet door to shut me up, I exploded up from the floor like a coiled spring, driving the coat hanger into his throat.

He went down, gagging, choking on his own blood. But as I raced for the door, I heard footsteps thundering down the hall. His friends were coming back! I was frantically frisking the guard for a weapon when someone kicked in the apartment door.

But it wasn't the Jamaicans.

It was Fat Jack. He'd come for me.

As it happened, he came late. I'd already saved myself. Still, it meant a lot. That he cared enough to come. No one ever had. Ever.

When the Jamaicans came back, they found me gone and their guy hanging from the clothes pole in the closet, like a trout on a fish stringer. Killed by a kid? Impossible.

And yet, there he was. And the story grew wilder with every telling.

Within days, two more of the Jamaican crew were dead. The two who'd grabbed me off the street. The cops found them in their car, both shot in the head at close range with a twenty-two caliber Saturday Night Special. A woman's gun, they thought.

But they were wrong. It was a kid's gun.

Jack made a counteroffer to the Jamaicans. They'd lopped off my little finger and had three corpses for their trouble. He figured things were about square. If they returned the money they took, *plus* ten grand, they could go home to Ecorse and he'd keep me in the Heights.

If not, he'd turn me loose on them.

Even coked-up psychos like the Jamaicans could do the math.

They took the deal and went home. No hard feelings. Another day in the Life. Everything was as it had been before.

Everything but me.

Some things can't be undone. A missing finger can't grow back. And I was not the same boy the Jamaicans locked in that closet.

Huddled in the dark, more terrified than I'd ever been in my life, my options were to die on my knees, begging for my life. Or to go down fighting, though I knew it was hopeless.

I chose to fight, and I survived. And received an amazing revelation.

Human life is incredibly fragile. A grown man can be killed by a boy armed with nothing but a coat hanger. Or a twenty-two pistol so small it looks like a kid's toy.

In a moment of murderous fury, I felt my first hunter's rush, a feral buzz more potent than dope. Stronger than hate, stronger than love. Stronger than death.

Jack recognized it, of course. When he found me crouching over the corpse of the Jamaican gangster, he knew exactly how I felt.

And that kill changed everything. At fifteen, I graduated to full membership in Jack's crew. I continued my regular route, delivering the Free Press, picking up numbers receipts and betting slips.

But when trouble came up, Fat Jack kept me in the room, like I belonged there. And I did.

I had a gift for battle tactics. I could analyze a situation, grasp the elements, and come up with a plan. I was an honest to God prodigy, like Mozart or Stevie Wonder. A towheaded kid with a loopy grin, born with a flair for violence.

I barely tipped a hundred pounds soaking wet. With my paper bag slung over my shoulder or schoolbooks under my arm, I could wander into almost any setup without raising suspicions. An obvious innocent.

Harmless.

"Beat it, kid, go peddle your papers," the mark would say. Sometimes it was the last thing he ever said.

But soon, people started making the connection between the clueless kid and the homicide rate. Rumors began circulating, whispers on the wind at first. But in time my reputation grew out of control. If a body turned up, the cops came looking for me first.

Which was just as well. The rage that had seized me during the Jamaican kidnapping had long since worn off. I recognized the battle madness for what it was. And realized where it would lead me.

So when Fat Jack told me Detroit was getting too hot, that I needed to disappear for awhile, I didn't argue. He gave me an envelope with a year's pay, paperwork for a new identity, and an address in Chicago where I'd be welcome.

And I went.

But not to Chicago.

I never used the alias Jack gave me. I drifted across America instead, working at odd jobs, then moving on. Until I hit New Mexico.

Arty, upscale and bathed in sunshine most of the year, Taos was as far from White Harlem as I could get. I took an entry level gig selling used cars. It was easy work and I was good at it. So I stayed on.

But soon I was restless again. And in the clear desert air, I faced a hard truth about myself.

I needed the action. It was part of my nature now. And it paid better than selling cars or anything else I could do.

So I analyzed the problem, and came up with a solution. I contacted Chicago, and contracted for the tricky, dangerous, free-lance jobs. Hits no one else wanted. Professionals only. No women, no kids, no civilians. Only thugs no one would miss.

Contracts that pay top dollar.

I stayed on in Taos. I hide in plain sight, working as a used car salesman on a lot I secretly own. Occasionally, I get a call from Chicago, and I drive to Vegas, or L.A., or Jersey in an unregistered car from the lot. No airport security, no baggage checks. No record that I've ever been there. Or anywhere.

If I do a job properly, the vics just disappear. No one's certain there's actually been a crime, let alone who did it.

Until now.

I've been successful because I've been objective. Cool. Analytical. Uninvolved.

But not this time. This time wouldn't be business. It would be personal.

I came back to Warsaw Heights for Fat Jack.

The same way he came for me.

* * *

I did a lot of thinking on the walk back to Jack's office. The lights were still on, so I rapped twice, waited a minute, then stepped in. Very slowly. Bobby Zee kept the shotgun centered on my chest, making sure I was alone. Benny the Banker was at Jack's desk, sorting through the day's betting slips. So far, Jack's death hadn't affected business. The only funeral that keeps a gambler from betting is his own.

Moira was pacing. And steaming.

"Where the hell have you been?" she snapped. "There was a shooting at Sweeney's—"

"I'm in one piece," I interrupted, waving her off. "What's the problem?"

"Your plan worked," Bobby Zee said. "You said we'd get a call and we did."

"But not from the Cobras," Moira said. "From Tony Zeman."

"No kidding? The Man himself? What did he want?"

"A meet," Moira said. "Oakland Avenue, at the tracks near the Chrysler Freeway. Seven o'clock."

"I'd better move," I said, checking my watch. "We don't have much time."

"You can't go alone, Doc," Moira said. "I don't trust Zeman."

"Neither do I," I agreed. "But we don't really have a choice. The Zemans have been a power in Detroit since Prohibition. Jack ran the Heights with their permission and paid a tax for it. If they want a meet, I have to go."

"Then I'm going too," Bobby Zee said. "You'll need backup on this."

"There could be trouble."

"You're not the only one here who owes Fat Jack," Bobby said. "I want in, Doc."

"Then leave the shotgun and take my piece," I said, pulling my Smith Airweight out of my waistband. "You can't handle a long gun in a car and they'll pat me down anyway."

Bobby hefted the small weapon doubtfully. "A revolver?"

"They never jam," I said. "But let's hope you don't need it. If they start shooting, you take off, understand? I'll already be gone."

"Works for me," Bobby said dryly, sliding the Smith into his jacket.

* * *

We took my car, an anonymous three-year-old Buick that looked like every other family sedan in Detroit. Which was the point.

Bobby drove, I rode shotgun. He kept glancing over at me as he wheeled expertly through traffic.

"What?" I asked.

"Nothing. From all the stories about you, I guess I thought you'd be bigger. And older."

"If you're as old as you feel, I'm a thousand and two," I said. "Where did Jack find you?"

"At St. Stan's," Bobby said. "I was peddling phony Ecstasy around the U of Detroit, dodging campus security and former customers. One day Jack was waiting on my corner. Told me I wouldn't live through the week, but he liked my style. Gave me your slot. Want it back?"

"No. I've got a new life now. Good luck with my old one."

"Actually, I'm not sure how lucky I was, hiring onto a crew of losers with a sick boss. You were smart to get out when you did."

"I didn't get out. Jack sent me away."

"Why? You were the best man he had."

"No, I was just one of the crew. He had no trouble filling my slot. He always did have an eye for talent."

"Some eye," Bobby snorted. "I could pick a tougher posse out of a rest home. He should have ditched those losers years ago. He was getting soft, near the end."

"No way. Jack was the coldest sonofabitch I've ever met. Everybody on his crew earns their keep. He took care of them, and they took care of him. You're a smart kid. I'm surprised you didn't pick up on that."

"Maybe you're right," Bobby shrugged, unconvinced. "We're here."

He eased the Buick to the curb at the end of the last block on Oakdale, a dead end street, facing the D and R tracks. Deserted as the back of the moon. Eyeless, abandoned buildings. A stray dog skulking up an alley, hunting rats. No other cars in sight.

"We must be early," Bobby said, glancing around nervously.

"Or it's a setup," I said.

"What do you mean?" he said, startled.

"Relax, kid. If it was an ambush, we'd be dead already. When you set up a mark, you should take him out right away, before he gets suspicious. Like now. Zeman's not coming, is he?"

He was quicker than I'd expected. In a heartbeat I was staring down the barrel of my own .38. It was quivering. His knuckles were white around the grip. He was nervous. And excited. But at this range, he couldn't miss.

"Damn it, Doc, I didn't want it to come to this. This isn't really my thing, you know."

"What is your thing Bobby? Using a car to run down a dying man? Or blasting away with a silenced AK?"

"You don't get it, do you?"

"I understand more than you think. This is all Moira, isn't it? Fat Jack was sick and the Cobras were pushing in. She cut a deal with them. You two would run things for them, but Jack had to go. And now it's my turn."

He didn't answer. Which was an answer, of sorts. He'd been honest about one thing, though. He definitely wasn't a gunman or he would have capped me the moment we stopped. The only thing I had going was his inexperience. Killing a man up close, looking him in the eye, is a big step. He wasn't quite ready for it.

Yet.

"Moira planned it," he admitted. "She's got more guts than—"

"One of Hitler's dogs?"

"Something like that," he nodded grimly. "I got nothing against you, Doc, but Moira said you wouldn't let it go. You'd figure it out."

"I'm sorry I did," I said, turning to face him. Knowing we were finally down to it. He'd never done this before, but I had. I knew he was ready now. Even so, his speed surprised me.

Raising the revolver, he pulled the trigger. Its muffled pop was no louder than a cap pistol.

Bobby froze in stunned surprise. I slid a twenty-two automatic from my sleeve into my palm. Jamming the tiny gun against his chest, I fired twice. A double tap that exploded his heart. He gaped at me in baffled amazement, wide-eyed, as if waiting for an explanation.

"Dud rounds," I said. "Did you think I'd let you kill me with my own gun?"

He didn't answer. Couldn't. His eyes were vacant, his jaw slackened. He was already gone.

I hauled his body out of the car and left him behind a dumpster. With luck, he wouldn't be found for days. Maybe weeks. One more crime statistic in a town famous for them.

By the time I fired up the Buick and pulled quietly away, I was already forgetting his face. I had things to settle up.

In one helluva hurry.

* * *

Moira was alone in Jack's office, working at his desk like I'd seen her a million times before. If I'd had any doubts about her involvement, they vanished the moment she saw me. Her face crumpled like a paper cup.

"I'm sorry," I said. It was all I could think of.

"Bobby...?"

I shook my head.

She buried her face in her hands. But only for a moment. Then she straightened up, and faced me.

"I swear to you, Doc, he didn't tell me about Jack until afterward. I wouldn't have agreed to it. You know that."

"Spare me the lies, love. I've known you since I was boy, Moira. Worshipped you, in fact. And the thing I always admired most about you was your intelligence. Even in this. Bottom line, taking Jack out was the smart thing to do."

"I don't understand," she said.

"His health was failing, his guys are worker bees, not fighters. Cutting a deal with the Cobras made perfect sense. You've got some flaws, lady, but stupidity isn't one of them."

"Doc, I swear—"

"Don't beg, Moira, it's insulting. You're like a sister to me. To all of us. I won't harm you. Jack wouldn't want that. But you don't get a pass for what you did. You're done in Detroit, Moira. Get out, tonight. For good. If I see you again, it'll be the last time anyone sees you. Do you understand?"

"Yes," she nodded, sniffling.

"I don't think you do, love," I said coldly. "Or you'd already be gone."

* * *

I didn't tell the others that Bobby ran Jack down, or why Moira was suddenly missing. I just said they were both done. For good. No one asked why. My tone was all the explanation they needed.

There was no formal election. I stepped into Jack's slot and the crew accepted it. Even Beef. Dogs intuitively recognize an alpha, a born leader. Jack had been the boss dog. Now it was me.

Benny the Banker took over Moira's job as our business manager. I recruited a teenager from St. Stan's to handle Benny's bookie action. The boy's in a wheelchair but he's terrific on the phone.

Beef found our new paperboy in the county lockup. A car thief, a roughneck punk with a bad attitude. He took Bobby's place. As Bobby once took mine.

Beef and I sat down with the Cobras, together. Nobody brought up the Jamaicans, but the Cobras knew who I was and they'd heard the stories. We all agreed to keep to our home ground. In peace.

Then I met with Tony Zeman, to explain the new setup. He had no complaints, as long as his checks cleared.

Before long, White Harlem was running as smoothly as before.

I had intended to move on as soon as things settled down, but I didn't. Instead, I rented a loft near Jack's office, then started looking around for a used car lot. A busy one. Where I can hide in plain sight.

Moira said people in our Life don't have families. She was wrong. Jack's crew may not be blood kin, but they're the only family I've ever known. I need them. And they need me.

The truth is, men and dogs come into this world poorly equipped to survive. We don't have turtle shells or a lion's strength. We compensate for our weakness by forming packs.

Gangs, tribes, nations, corporations. Call them whatever you like. At heart, they're all packs. And when men and dogs hunt together in packs, we're the most efficient predators on the planet.

Jack understood that. Every member of his pack was important to him. Even a fifteen-year-old boy.

I never kidded myself that Jack came for me out of love all those years ago. It doesn't matter *why* he came. It only matters that he did.

And there's only one way I can repay that debt.

I will stay on and look after his people, the way he did. And maybe one day I'll earn the same epitaph.

It was the only nice thing you could say about Jack.

Or Hitler.

Or me.

We took good care of our dogs.

When a magazine or anthology shows up with a story by Steve Hockensmith, I always read that story first. The tone of his fiction varies from humorous to extremely dark, which I appreciate. And I'm a big fan of his Holmes on the Range mystery series. The first book, appropriately titled Holmes on the Range, *was a finalist for the Edgar, Shamus, Anthony, and Dilys awards.*

Lately, he's been collaborating, first with "Science Bob" Pflugfelder on Nick and Tesla's High-Voltage Danger Lab, *and then with Lisa Falco on* The White Magic Five & Dime.

"Wheel of Fortune" is a standalone chapter from that book. He writes, "I ended up writing a flashback that explores our heroine's strange, sordid childhood. Not only did it turn out to be one of my favorite chapters, I thought it could stand alone as a short story. Fortunately, I wasn't the only one who thought that!"

Wheel of Fortune

Steve Hockensmith

It was morning in America, and the girl was in either a small city or a large town in the Midwest. She didn't know the name. What did it matter?

They'd just come from another small city/large town a week before. And another a week before that and another a week before that. In a few days, they'd be someplace else.

It was a slow-motion Cannonball Run, Biddle had joked when it began.

The girl knew the movies he was referring to. She'd seen both of them in the theater, the second one just a week before, though pre-teen girls were hardly the target audience. Over the course of one long, dark day, she'd sneaked into *Cannonball Run II, Star Trek III, The Natural, Bachelor Party* and *Friday the 13th: The Final Chapter.* She spent a lot of days like that. Abandoned in cineplexes, wandering from screen to screen, story to story, world to world.

But she didn't get the joke.

Biddle started to explain. Something about insurance policies they were taking out on cars that got stolen and wrecked and stolen and wrecked (and paid for and paid for and paid for) all across the country. But the girl's mother cut him off.

She'd been calling herself "Veronica" lately. She had brand new jet-black hair. In a few weeks, she'd have new hair again. And a new name.

"You know the rule," she'd told Biddle.

The girl knew the rule, too.

Some quick change raising or till dipping they could use her for. The precious pet scam or the Jamaican switch, too. She was an excellent roper, a competent cap. But there were plays they didn't need her for. A lot of them. And this was one.

So, the rule: Don't talk to her. Don't tell her anything she didn't need to know. Keep her in the dark. A prop in a closet, gathering dust.

"Right, right, O.K.," Biddle said to the girl's mother. And he turned back to the girl and winked.

Biddle knew the rule. He just chose to ignore it from time to time.

Now, weeks later, here they were in Genericsville USA, and the girl was watching yet another game show on yet another motel television.

Morning TV sucked. *The Price Is Right*, talk shows, detergent commercials, news. There weren't any *stories*, and it was stories the girl needed. Other people, other places, other lives. Anything other. Anything.

Veronica was getting ready to go to work—though her "work" wasn't anything like what the girl saw on TV. There would be no wacky officemates, no gruff but lovable boss, no laugh track.

The girl's mother was going to spend the day visiting every insurance agent in town. She was "dressed to impress," as she liked to call it. Biddle said it was more like "dressed to undress."

"Everywhere you go, you're gonna have guys trying to give you a piece of the rock," he said.

Veronica laughed.

Only Biddle could get her to do that.

Then she was gone. She didn't say goodbye. Why bother? She knew the girl would be there when she got back. Do you say goodbye to a chair, a lamp, the paper-thin towels hanging in the bathroom? Of course not. You use them when you use them and you don't when you don't.

Biddle would be leaving soon, too. He had mail drops to set up, mail drops to close down, connections to make, connections to break. But first he'd take the girl wherever she wanted to go. Almost.

One time she'd walked into a school and found a classroom of kids her age and tried to pass herself off as an exchange student from London. She did an excellent English accent courtesy of James Bond movies and PBS, but it hadn't mattered. Questions were asked, things got complicated, and she'd ended up running out of the place and laying low at their motel the rest of the week.

The girl never told her mother, but Biddle knew. And he didn't tell on her, though he never took her anywhere near a school again. Not the kind other kids went to, anyway.

"I think I can take the day off," he announced as a contestant on TV suddenly went bankrupt, lost it all, and had to do so smiling. "Wanna have some fun?"

"Sure."

Biddle's fun and other people's fun weren't quite the same. But the girl never said no.

First they went to a Bob Evans and stuffed themselves.

"Can't skip the most important meal of the day," Biddle said. "Those chocolate chip pancakes might feel heavy in your gut now, but before long they're going to be pure energy."

"For running?" the girl asked.

Biddle smiled. But there was no need to run. Not then.

They left without paying and did it so smoothly no one noticed for ten minutes, though half the eyes in the restaurant had been on them as they ate. "The Reverse Oreo Effect," Biddle called it. It sometimes complicated things, but he didn't seem to mind a little complication in his life.

He was black, the girl and her mother white.

After leaving the restaurant, they went to a party supply store and bought a roll of pink raffle tickets. Then they drove around while Biddle scanned storefronts and signs.

"Jackpot!" he eventually announced.

He pulled over in front of the Boys & Girls Club of Who-Cares? County. A few minutes later, he was walking out again with a stack of brochures and newsletters.

"People sure do love it when a man takes an interest in the youth of his community," he said.

"What's the pitch?"

"Fundraiser, of course. Raise five hundred dollars and your soccer team gets to go to Indianapolis for the state playoffs. It'd be a shame if you couldn't make it. Your coach was going to pay for the trip out of her own pocket, but after she came down with Legionnaire's Disease—"

"*Biddle.*"

"O.K., you're right. Too much gravy on the steak and you get no sizzle. Just stick with the trip to Indy. Now let's see those fishhooks."

The girl pouted and opened her eyes wide.

"Beautiful," Biddle said. "You'll be reeling 'em in non-stop."

They found the right neighborhood—middle class, quiet, white—and the girl worked a few blocks while Biddle went to get cigarettes and "call a guy about a thing with some people." When he came back, she was sitting on a curb waiting for him. Half her raffle tickets were gone, and she had almost a hundred dollars in her pocket.

"Are you going to stay now?" she said. "I don't want to be out here by myself anymore."

"Hey, it's the Boys & Girls Club, not the White Girls and Big Black Guys Club. I shouldn't even be sitting here talking to you. You just *know* the police are going to get a call about that."

"Then let's go do something else. Something we can do together."

"This isn't fun?"

"No. And I don't need the money anyway. I can't buy anything. My suitcase is too full as it is."

"You liked your Atari. Don't you want another?"

"So Mom can make me leave it behind like she did last time?"

"We have to travel light. You know that. And just look—you got the money for another like she said you would."

"Well, I don't want some dumb game I have to play back in our room. I want to do something out in the real world. With you. Can't we see if they have an amusement park or a waterslide or something around here?"

"An amusement park?"

Biddle looked thoughtful.

There are a lot of scams you can pull at an amusement park.

Movement caught his eye. A flutter of drapes in a picture window.

"Time to roll. I think someone's about to come rescue you from me."

"Let 'em try," the girl said, though she often fantasized about getting caught, arrested, even kidnapped. Just a few years before, she'd become obsessed with Sasquatch and the possibility that he'd come carry her off to his moss-covered cave. It would be scary, and she'd miss movies and TV and books and Biddle, but at least it wouldn't be another Holiday Inn. Then one day her mother walked in on her watching an *In Search of...* about Bigfoot, and the woman had laughed one of her rare laughs and said, "All this fuss over a guy in a gorilla suit? And I thought the biggest bullshitter on TV was Jim Bakker." And the girl had stopped waiting for the missing link to steal her away.

Biddle talked to a guy at a gas station. The nearest amusement park was three hours away, and it might not open till Memorial Day anyway. So Biddle bought ten scratch-off lottery tickets and gave half to the girl.

"What are these?" she said.

Official lotteries were something new. Most people weren't used to states running their own scams yet.

"Those raffle tickets gave me an idea," Biddle said. "Scratch off the gray stuff on these cards. Here, gently, like this. Just enough to see the numbers. No words. Just numbers. Then we'll have us some real fun together."

"You promise?"

"Scout's honor."

"Right. Like you were ever a Boy Scout."

Biddle pinched the girl's cheek.

"That's my girl," he said.

All the tickets were losers, but it didn't matter. They found two candidates. On one, a seven could become a nine after just a little careful work with a black Bic. On the other, a five could become a six.

Biddle did the seven, the girl the five. They agreed that hers looked better.

They had a winner.

"Now we just have to find the right neighborhood," Biddle said. "We may be in the Wonder Bread capital of the world, but they've gotta have a wrong side of the tracks around here somewhere."

It took them half an hour to find it.

Another half hour after that, the girl stepped up to a middle-aged man pushing a shopping cart out of a discount grocery store.

"Can you help me? I'm lost."

The man stopped.

"I can see that," he said.

He was black, and so was everyone in the store and the parking lot and the streets around them.

"I was on the bus and I must have gotten off at the wrong stop," the girl said. "But I didn't realize it at first and I started walking around and now I can't even find my way back to where I started from."

"Alright," the man sighed, "here's what you want to do."

He started giving directions. The girl nodded as if she cared. Then another man walked up.

"Excuse me, please," he said. He had a thick accent of indeterminate pan-Caribbean origin. "I need your help."

The older man rolled his eyes. "This is my lucky day."

"Maybe it is, sir," the other man said. He held up a scratch-off lottery ticket. "I think this is a winner, but I can't turn it in."

"Why not?" the girl asked.

"I'm not from here. I'm not supposed to be here. I don't have papers. I can't collect a hundred dollars from a state lottery."

"A hundred dollars? Let me see!" The girl grabbed the ticket. "Wow. You're right. It's a winner."

The older man peeked over her shoulder. He didn't get much time to look. Just enough to see that the right numbers seemed to match.

"Where'd you buy it?" the girl asked.

"Right here. In this store."

"And it can be turned in here, too?"

"Yes. You'd get the money immediately."

"And then I'm supposed to come out and just give it to you?"

"No. I'd give you...twenty dollars."

"Hey," the older man said. He had a "What am I—chopped liver?" look on his face.

"How do I know you wouldn't take it all?" the girl said.

The man from Trinijamahaiti looked offended.

"What a thing for an innocent little girl to say! How do I know *you* wouldn't try to keep it all? Maybe you would accuse me of being a thief when I tried to collect my money!" He snatched his ticket back and turned away. "I'll find someone else to help me."

"Hey," the older man said again.

"Wait! I know how we can do this!" the girl cried out.

She jammed a hand into her Jordache jeans and pulled out a wad of crumpled bills. She counted quickly.

"I'll give you twenty eight dollars right now. Then you just give me the ticket, and we can be done."

"Twenty eight dollars? I don't know...."

The older man whipped out his wallet.

"I can give you thirty nine! No! Forty! That's practically fifty percent, cash on the barrelhead."

He thrust the money at the other man.

The other man took it and handed over the ticket.

"No fair," the girl whined.

"The only fair's the one with farm animals and cotton candy," the older man said. He swung his cart around and headed back into the store. "Good luck catching that bus."

The other man and the girl stalked off in different directions.

They met again two blocks away, on the quiet side street where they'd left the car.

"Told you it'd work," Biddle said.

He unlocked the passenger door and let the girl in, then walked around and slipped behind the wheel.

"It's crude, though," Biddle went on. "There's gotta be a way to spin it into something more than a nickel-and-dime short con. The big lotto jackpots—that's the angle to play."

The girl was looking out the window. The houses lining the street were small and old. A few were boarded up. The rest looked like they should be.

"I don't like it when we take money from poor people."

"If it's good enough for McDonald's and Mogen David, it's good enough for me."

"I'm not joking."

"Neither am I. Hey, I've got family in neighborhoods like this. Believe me—plenty of these people are just as greedy and stupid as the rich people up the road. So why discriminate?"

"But it just doesn't seem...."

The girl stopped herself. She wasn't even sure if she'd been about to say "fair" or "right" or something else. But she knew the look she'd get.

She got it anyway.

Biddle cocked his head and gazed at her with eyes filled with pity.

"Sometimes I forget you're not a midget," he said.

"Oh, blow it out your ass."

"My word!" Biddle gasped. "Wherever did you learn such nasty language?"

Then he smiled.

He knew.

"Look," he said, "are all rich people bad?"

"No."

"Are all poor people good?"

"No."

"So what makes them different?"

"Money."

Biddle shook his head. "Luck. Dumb luck. Some people are born Kennedys, and some people are born here. It has nothing to do with who deserves it. Hell, nobody *deserves* anything. We don't deserve a Russian bomb to fall on us, but it might any minute. So we may as well buy us some ice cream with the money we didn't deserve to get today."

"I don't know, Biddle."

"You don't know if you want to go to Baskin-Robbins?"

"No. I don't know if—"

There was a hard rapping sound. Metal tapped to glass three times.

The glass was the driver's-side window.

The metal was the barrel of a gun. Pointed at Biddle.

The girl made a sound that wasn't a word and wasn't quite a scream. She wasn't surprised, though. Not entirely. Some part of her had been expecting this for a long, long time.

How long could you do wrong and not be punished? Forever? No. There had to be a *sometime*. There had to be a *finally*.

And here it was.

"Gimme your money!" someone said. He sounded young and angry. All the girl could see of him was his plain white T-shirt. It hung on him limply, like a toga. The body beneath was lean.

Biddle pulled out his wallet, then rolled down the window and handed it over. He was moving very, very slowly.

"Men with guns either want respect or to kill you," he'd told the girl once. "If they don't kill you right off, just give them the respect and you'll be fine."

"Hers, too," the boy or man outside the car demanded. He pressed the gun against the side of Biddle's head. "Come on, come on!"

Slowly, calmly, Biddle held a hand out to the girl. Her hands were shaking so badly the bills she pulled from her pockets rustled and fluttered like wings. But she managed to give Biddle every dollar she had, and he brought it all to the window, and then it was gone.

The gun and the T-shirt disappeared, too. The girl could hear footsteps slapping on asphalt hard and fast.

"Don't look back," Biddle said.

He was staring straight ahead. After a long, silent moment, he started the car and put it in gear. He was still moving slowly, slowly, slowly. He drove away slowly, too.

The girl felt light-headed. Her scalp and feet tingled. There was a low buzzing in her ears that sounded like the static between TV channels. Her hands were still shaking. A sob was welling up in her chest.

Biddle burst out laughing. He laughed and laughed and laughed. More than a block went by before he could even speak.

"Round and round she goes!" he said. "Where she stops, nobody knows!"

"It's not funny, Biddle! It's not funny!"

Biddle stopped laughing. But he couldn't keep the grin off his face even as he looked over at the girl and saw that she was crying.

"Oh, don't be upset, sweetie. Everything's fine. The universe just has to mess with you every once in a while, that's all. It's over now. Before you know it, you'll be eating rocky road on a sugar cone."

"What are we gonna do—steal it? That asshole took all our money!"

And the girl began crying even harder, though it wasn't the money she was crying about at all.

Biddle let her cry for a while. Then he pulled something small and stiff from his shirt pocket and put it on the girl's lap.

"Now, now," he said. "See there?"

The girl looked over at him, sniffling.

Biddle was still smiling.

"We've got another lottery ticket," he said. His smile grew wider. "People like us always do."

Right now, the current crop of mystery short story writers is among the best the field has ever seen. The superlatives I've piled on Doug Allyn and Steve Hockensmith could easily be placed on Brendan DuBois as well. His short work repeatedly appears in Ellery Queen Mystery Magazine, Alfred Hitchcock Mystery Magazine, *and many anthologies. He's won the Shamus Award from the Private Eye Writers of American twice, and is a three-time Edgar nominee. His short fiction has also appeared in* The Best American Noir of the Century *and* The Best American Mystery Stories of the Century. *Plus, he knows things. He's one of those illusive characters—a* Jeopardy! *game show champion.*

About "The Good Brother," he writes, "I've always been fascinated about the 'good brother' and the 'bad brother.' Born and raised in the same way, for some reason each will make different choices. Think of Jimmy Carter and his ne'er-do-well brother Billy or the brothers Bulger in Massachusetts: one becoming a State Senate president and the other becoming a convicted murderer."

Of course, Brendan puts his own spin on this topic, with chilling results.

———

The Good Brother

Brendan DuBois

That night I was working at home on a speechwriting project that was going about as well as the Hindenburg's final trip, so I decided to step outside to clear my mind. It had been a long time since I'd tried to come up with a speech of my own, and it was turning into a hell of a challenge. But instead of clearing anything, I nearly had a coronary when someone whispered from the shrubbery, "Hey, John, is that you?"

I froze. "Luke?"

A nervous laugh. "Yeah."

I came closer to my house, near a large stand of juniper bushes. In the dim light from the living room's windows, I made out my older brother, sitting with his back against the concrete foundation. It had been a while since I had last seen him. He was wearing dirty, torn blue jeans, work boots and a plain gray hoodie sweatshirt. His hands were in the front pockets of the hoodie.

"Luke, what's going on? How the hell did you get in here?"

He laughed. "What, you think a gated community like this can keep me out? Hah."

Lots of thoughts were tumbling through my mind, none of them particularly good. "So you're here. Do you want to come in?"

"Ah, well, is your wife home?"

"Terry? Of course. And the kids."

He hunched over. "I don't want to come in. I'll just mess things up."

It was a warm night but my feet and hands were getting cold. "Luke, what's going on? What did you do?"

"Ah, shit, bro, I'm in trouble. Lots of trouble."

It felt even colder. "What did you do? Does your parole officer know?"

"Of course he doesn't know! Christ…"

"Luke…."

"There was this guy. We were at a bar. He was dissing me… and I had to knife him."

"You *had* to knife him?"

"Yeah."

"You *had* to knife him?"

"John, heard you twice the first time. Look, you don't understand, you'll never understand, let's leave it at that. Your life, my life, it's all different, I know."

Out in the woods I could hear some birds calling around. Such a sign of peace and tranquility. Or so someone once said.

"So what now?" I asked.

"John, you gotta help me…"

"Luke…"

He pulled out an arm, checked his watch. "There you go. I'm already overdue at the halfway house. Pretty soon my P.O. will get the word that I've missed bed check, and then every cop in the state will be looking for me." He paused. "Not only because of me, you know... but because of—"

"Yeah, I know," I said, cutting him off. "So how can I help?"

A short laugh. "You're the one with the smarts, the money, the connections, the big house, wife and kids. Can't you figure something out?"

More thoughts bouncing around in my brain, including the deadline I was trying to meet.

But I had no choice.

I had to take care of my brother.

* * *

I took a breath. "You found your way in, you think you can find your way back out?"

"Sure."

"You know Toland Road?"

"Yeah."

"There's a Seven-Eleven at the intersection of Toland and Spring. I'll see you there in about fifteen minutes."

He sounded suspicious. "Why not put me in your car now?"

"You really have to ask me that?"

"Hah." Luke shifted some on the ground. "All right, I'll do it. But John..."

"Yes?"

"Don't get any ideas about calling the cops to pick me at that Seven-Eleven. You won't like what happens next."

"Never entered my mind," I lied.

* * *

After my older brother slipped into the shadow of the woods, I took another deep breath. What a night. What a mess. I walked around to the other side of the house, went into the large and shiny kitchen. Sounds of a television came from the adjacent living room. On a pegboard were two sets of car keys. I grabbed the ones belonging to my wife Terry and called out, "Honey, going for a little ride to clear my head! Be back as soon as I can!"

"Hey!" came a voice from the living room. "Shouldn't you wait…"

I ducked out through the door leading to the garage, went to Terry's black Lexus. Got in, started the car, toggled a switch that smoothly opened the door behind me. I backed out and went down the wide and empty streets with the big homes.

* * *

There were two main entries to our little neighborhood, but there was also a little-known access gate that was used for landscapers and deliveries, and which didn't have much in the way of prying eyes. I went down a narrow side road, went up to the gate, lowered the window. There was a keypad on a post, I punched in the code, and in a few minutes, I was on Toland Road, a residential street with a couple of convenience stores and gas stations. I slowed down, and from the shadows at the rear of the 7-Eleven, Luke came out, and got in.

"Thanks, bro."

"It's what I do," I said, as we sped off into the night.

* * *

From the illumination of the dashboard, I spared a glance at Luke. His brown hair was stringy and tied at the back in a ponytail. His face was gaunt, with a wispy beard. His eyes flicked around. His hands were moving in his lap. I looked again.

"That blood on your hands?"

"What do you think?"

I slowed down, reached over, popped open the glovebox. Thanks to Terry and our kids, there were a collection of napkins and Handi-Wipes. I pulled a handful out and tossed them into his lap.

"Clean up if you can."

"Thanks."

His hands shook as he wiped himself, best as he could. I kept on driving. He looked around and said, "What should I do now?"

"Dump them on the floor."

"You sure?"

"Yeah, I'll clean it up later." I couldn't help myself. I added, "That's what I've always done for you, isn't it."

* * *

By the dashboard clock, Luke stayed quiet for five minutes, and then spoke up. "That was a cheap shot."

"It was a true shot."

"So say you."

"Oh, come on, Luke. How many times did I cover for you when you were out late at night, telling Mom and Dad you made it back before curfew? How many times did I slip a few bucks to you for beer and smokes, when I was working after school and you just dicked around with your friends? How many times did—"

"Oh come on, give me a break. You're still pissed at all that school stuff?"

"I have a long memory."

"A pissy memory, I'd say."

* * *

There were exits up ahead for the nearest Interstate, which I passed. Luke turned his head as I drove past the green-and-white highway signs.

"Where are you going?"

"Why are you asking?"

"Hunh?"

"You wanted me to help you out, so I'm helping you out. Why the questions?"

He sunk some into his seat. "I just want to know. Don't I deserve that?"

"Maybe. Let me think about it."

* * *

I drove north, best as I could, by taking back roads and tiny state roads. Luke put his hands back into his hoodie pocket, sighed.

"So what happened?"

He shrugged. "You want to really know, or are you just going to give me some shit?"

"I really want to know."

"All right. Went to a bar in Porter, and—"

"Hold on. I thought you're not supposed to drink, part of your parole."

"You giving me shit?"

"No, I really want to know," I said.

Another sigh. "I didn't drink, honest. I just went in for a ginger ale. That's all. I swear. Check with the bartender if you don't believe me."

"Even if I didn't believe you, I don't think I'll make the call. Go on."

"So I was just having a drink or two, watching the ball game, just chilling. Okay? You know the job I got, part of my release? I bag groceries. That's what I do. A bag boy!"

"Maybe if you had stayed in school, you... sorry, that wasn't fair. Go on."

"A bag boy. So I wanted to go someplace where I could just relax, pretend I was a man, and do something normal. Okay? But I made a mistake, so sue me."

"What mistake?"

"It was warm in the bar, so I had my sleeves rolled up. Showing off my tats. My biker tats."

We came to an intersection, marked by a flashing yellow light. I went through, my heart thumping right along. "Your biker gang tats, you mean."

"Whatever. So I was minding my own business, and a couple of big guys, they belonged to the Mountain Men, and they started ragging on me. About my guys, about the Tacnic Brothers, about who I was... called me a pussy, called me a fag."

"That all?"

"You don't understand, they were dissing me!"

"So why not walk away?"

"Walk away? Let those guys push me out like a pussy?" my brother asked.

"Why not? Walk away, go back to your halfway house, things are cool, you do your thing, I do my thing…"

"I don't run away."

"You're here. Doesn't that mean you ran away?"

"No. It means I don't want to go back to prison. Different thing."

My turn to sigh. "Okay. Guys are dissing you. What happened?"

"Had to take a leak. Went to the rear of the bar. One of the guys followed me. Kept on ragging on me. Asked me if I wanted to take it outside. I said, sure. There was a service door. Went out back by the dumpsters. He came at me, I went back at him… he pulled a knife, so did I, and—

"Not giving you shit, just verifying, you're not supposed to be carrying weapons as part of your parole. Right?"

"Yeah, but if I didn't have weapons, I'd be dead, right?"

Another mile passed. I said, "So what happened."

"I was better than him. I got inside of him, turned him, and I was able to slip it into his ribs a couple of times."

"A couple of times?"

"Maybe four, five. Really wasn't keeping track."

My hands tightened on the steering wheel. "Luke, how bad did you hurt this guy?"

"Pretty bad, I guess."

"Well guess some more."

A shrug. "He wasn't moving when I ran out of there…"

"Was he breathing? Talking? Anything?"

"I didn't stick around to find out."

Had to ask it, although the words wanted to stick in my throat. "Luke, did you murder that guy?"

No answer.

"Luke?

He shifted in his seat. "Bro, you gotta help me."

* * *

A few more miles passed. "You know how many times Mom and Dad told me that you were the good son, that I should follow you? Me? Follow my younger brother?"

"Sure. About as many times as they ragged on me if I got a B on my report card. Told me if I didn't step up, I'd end up like a loser, like Luke."

"Guess we both served a family purpose, then, hunh?"

"Guess we did."

* * *

On a length of road we got stuck behind an old passenger van, going about ten miles below the speed limit. I had to slow down the Lexus real fast and for a couple of miles, passing through farmland and woods, we tagged along.

Luke spoke up. "Why don't you pass him?"

"We're in a no-passing zone. Don't you see? Double-yellow lines."

He laughed. "God, you're such a goody-goody, even now."

"Not as goody as you think," I shot back. "Not to be where I am now, that's for damn sure. Plus, what do you think would happen if I passed this clown and a cop pulled us over? You like that idea?"

"You see any cops?"

"They're out there."

"In this small town? Only one cruiser, if that, if they don't rely on the state police for coverage. Look, the road's straightening out, why don't you drive—"

"Hey."

"What? You want me to shut up or something?"

"No, just answer the question. Driving. Porter's about fifty miles away. How did you get to my house?"

"How do you think?"

"Stole a car?"

"Borrowed, that's what I did."

"Borrowed? Like, I got permission from a buddy of mine, I borrowed his car, he said bring it back, whenever you want. Or borrowed, I needed a ride, found a car, drove it out, left it on the street."

"The second one, I guess."

"So a stabbing and a car theft. Did you knock off a bank while you were coming out here?"

My brother folded his large arms. "Didn't have the time."

* * *

The van pulled to the side, to a dirt driveway, and I glanced down at the gas gauge for the Lexus, said, "Damn," and Luke countered with, "What's up?"

"Going to need to gas up in a few minutes."

"Oh. So we're driving for a while longer?"

"We are."

"May I most humbly ask, younger brother, where you're taking me?"

There was an edge to his voice but I couldn't blame him. We had been driving for nearly a half hour, and I was glad my cellphone was back at the house. No interruptions, plenty of time to think through things.

"Carver Lake," I said. "We have a house on the lake, and—"

"Oh, that's a great idea," he said, sarcasm oozing over his words. "By this time tomorrow, the cops will be hunting my ass, and the first place they'll go to is your house, and the next place will be your second home. Great idea. Makes me wonder how you've gotten so far in this world."

"You interrupted me, Luke. Care to hear the rest of what I have to say, or should I pull over now and let you fend for yourself?"

A grumpy sigh. "Yeah. Go on. One of my many faults. Always responding too quickly. You, though, you always seem to be the guy who thinks five or ten steps ahead. I'm always planning for tomorrow, or tomorrow night. You... I get the feeling you're planning months or years ahead. Like a lifetime, hunh?"

"Right now my planning is focused on Carver Lake. Like I said, we have a place there, and on the property, there's a small cabin, used to be used for a caretaker when the previous owners could afford it. Nothing fancy, but it'll hold you tight for a while. Has a good view of the main house. You stay inside, keep cool, you'd be able to see if there's any cops roaming around. I'll show you a hidden room in the cellar, where the caretaker used to stash deer carcasses when he shot them out of season. You see a cop or two poking around, you can get into that room, stay quiet until they leave."

"That... that sounds great. Then what?"

"Don't rush me," I said. "I'm working on it."

* * *

The country road we were on slid into a small town that had a couple of business buildings, and some service stations. I passed one brightly-lit station, and then another. Luke turned as I passed them both. "What, this Lexus takes special gas?"

"No," I said. "Didn't like the look of them."

"But you're running low on gas..."

"I know. I'm the driver. I got it covered. For once in your life, just shut up."

Luke settled back in his seat at that and I looked ahead through the windshield, relaxed when I finally came upon what I was looking for. A combination convenience store, breakfast grill, and bait shop, with two pumps out front. I turned in and pulled ahead as far as I could.

I switched off the engine. "Can I trust you now? Can I trust you to do one thing, and one thing only?"

"Cripes, yeah, of course."

"I'm sorry, I want to hear it. I want you to promise me right now that you'll do exactly what I say. And if you don't, we'll part ways, and when the crap hits the fan, I'll just muddle through, as painful as it'll be."

"John, no fooling, I promise, I'll do whatever you tell me."

I took my wallet out, passed over a twenty-dollar bill. "Go inside and pay for twenty dollars worth of gas, for pump two. Okay? That's it. Twenty dollars for pump two. Don't get a craving for beef jerky, or cigarettes, or Yoo-Hoo. Don't steal anything, don't bump into anything, don't do anything that makes you stand out. Don't flirt with the cashier if she's a woman, don't argue with the cashier if he's a guy. If the guy's wearing a Hells Angel T-shirt and tells you that you have carnal knowledge of your sister, you'll just nod politely and get the hell out. All I want you to do is to go in and pay for twenty dollars worth of gas, and then come back here. Have I made myself clear?"

"Yeah."

"Do you have any questions?"

"No."

"Is there anything you don't understand?"

"No, no," he said, taking the twenty-dollar bill from my hand. "I'm not one of your damn clients from back then."

"If you had been, you'd be in a better place."

* * *

When I was done pumping gas and stood by the Lexus, Luke came over, gave me a sloppy salute. "Mission accomplished, sir. Dropped off payment, ignored everyone and everything, and got back, safe and sound."

"Wonderful." We both got in and I started up the car.

"Hey, why did you choose this place instead of the other ones? The gas price is about ten cents a gallon more."

"It's run-down, a local place. Less chance of surveillance cameras keeping a view on the pumps."

"Oh." He put his hands back into his hoodie pocket. "So that's why you sent me in to pay, right?"

"Right."

* * *

After we left the small town and resumed driving north, Luke said, "You know, you keep on saying what a loser brother I am. Okay, I've made some bad choices. But I tried to stick up for you, you know? Help you out when I could."

"Name one time," I said.

"Back in high school. I was a junior. You were a freshman. You were getting the snot kicked out of you, as usual."

My hands tensed some on the steering wheel. For that and a host of other reasons, I've never, ever, attended a high school reunion of my class, as profitable as that might have been for me.

"Whatever."

"You remember how you were treated?"

"Yeah."

"Don't want to share anything more?"

"No." Funny how going back to that time made my chest and stomach all queasy, like I was thirteen years old again.

"Let me remind you, because I remember. You walking down the hallway at school, guys knocking books out of your arm. Stealing stuff out of your locker. Putting duct tape around your arms and legs, tossing you into the girls' shower room. Remember that? Girls laughing at you? All those girls?"

I checked the odometer. Getting closer. Luke said, "What I never understood is why you put up with it. Eh? Why did you let everyone do stuff to you, day after day?"

"Because I had more important things to do!" I snapped. "Getting into fights, getting into trouble, what would that prove?"

"It'd prove that you had a set, that's what. Instead of proving you could be a stand-up guy, what, you got debating team trophies, had internships at law firms, crap like that. But I took care of business, didn't I."

"If that's what you like to think, go ahead."

Luke laughed. "You don't want to remember this, but after a month or so, I went on a hunt. Knocked some heads together, put the fear of God into people. Told 'em to leave you alone. And they did, didn't they."

"To a point."

"What the hell does that mean?"

I flashed a look at him. "You left something out, brother of mine. I didn't ask for your help! Not at all! You did it on your own… and you told those creeps to leave me alone at school.

Which is what they did. So they started beating me up on the way home from school, on my debate field trips, and anyplace else they could. You couldn't stand the thought of your younger brother being teased at your high school, so you made it stop. For you. Not for me. Outside of school, I was still fair game. So everything got worse. Not better. And for that, you expect me to thank you? The hell with that."

I turned back to my driving. "The hell with that."

* * *

We entered another small town as the night went on. The usual bandstand, white churches, little shops, and a service station. As I drove by the last service station, which was closed, headlights from a partially-hidden vehicle flashed on, and the car pulled in right behind us.

"Cop," Luke announced.

"Okay."

"How fast were you going?"

"Around the speed limit."

"Around? What do you mean, around?"

"Not sure," I said, hating to be put on the spot by my older brother. "Might have been over. Might have been under."

He turned his head once, twice. "He's still behind us."

"Then for Christ's sake, stop looking back there! He'll get suspicious, and that might make him stop us."

"Your speeding will make him stop us."

"You don't know if I was speeding!"

"Yeah," Luke shot back. "And neither do you."

I kept my eyes focused on the night landscape ahead of me, the spread of my headlights, and the speedometer. I resisted the urge, over and over again, to glance at the rearview mirror. I sensed a motion. Luke had his right hand down by his boot. He noticed me looking at him. "I'm not going back," he said. "Don't care about you, don't care about that cop, all I care is, I'm not going back."

A sudden flare of blue and red lights illuminated the interior of the Lexus, as the cop behind us switched on his lights. Luke moved again. I said something foul. I started pulling over and Luke said, "What the hell are you doing?"

"You think I'm going to outrun him?"

"You could try! Sweet Jesus, there you are, wimping out, giving up without a fight, and you call me a loser..."

I was thinking of what to say to him when I pulled over, the police cruiser sped up and passed us by, roaring ahead, its blue and red lights flashing in a rhythm over the country landscape.

After waiting a few long seconds, I pulled back out.

Luke tried to make light of it. "Boy, that was close, hunh?"

I didn't say anything else.

* * *

Three miles later Luke announced he had to take a bathroom break, and on a long and empty stretch of pavement with pastureland extending on both sides, I pulled over and he did his business. I waited in the expensive and paid-for car, well-crafted and tuned engine murmuring, and my sweaty, dirty and tattooed criminal brother piled himself back into the front seat, loudly passing gas in the process.

"Thanks for not driving off and leaving me behind," he said.

"You're welcome."

Another laugh. "Of course, what choice do you have? Hunh? No choice, am I right?"

I didn't want to answer him, so I didn't.

* * *

We were approaching the lakes district when something came to me. "You know, I tried to help you out, too, Luke. You seem to forget that."

"Hunh? In what universe?"

"The universe where I was a sophomore and you were a senior. You had this military history class, a real gut course if I remember, but it was still too hard for you, Luke. Remember? You had a term paper due at the end of the year, you had goofed off like you always did, and then it was crunch time. Either the paper got done, or you'd flunk and not get your diploma. So I wrote the paper, remember? Wrote a nice paper, with footnotes and sources, and you passed your class."

Luke chuckled, but the sound had no humor. "Yeah, I remember that. It was a good paper, wasn't it? About the Greeks fighting the Persians, something like that. Sparta, if I remember right. The teacher, Mister Allard, he gave me an 'A' for that paper. Was so impressed he had me stand up in front of the class, read it to them."

"Good for you."

"The hell it was!" Luke suddenly shot back. "You could have written about the Civil War or World War Two, something easy to remember, but no, you had to choose something thousands of years old. Everyone in class was laughing at me, I was stumbling and bumbling through it, and then Mister Allard took the paper away, scratched out the 'A', gave me a 'D'. Thanks to you."

"Oh, I should have asked you before I wrote your paper if you knew how to pronounce Leonidas and Xerxes, right?"

"You knew I couldn't do that! You did that to set me up, didn't you, John. I know you did. Wanted to show off, once again, how damn smart you are, and how dumb I was. That's what it was all about."

I turned away again, not wanting to answer him.

* * *

I made a few turns, and we were really in the backwoods. We hadn't seen a house or a streetlight in nearly twenty minutes. Luke was quiet, moody, and said, "Christ, how much longer, hunh? How much longer?"

"Soon enough," I said, spotting a familiar stretch of road coming up ahead. "Hold on, I need to stretch my legs for a moment."

There was a narrow bridge with low guardrails on either side, spanning a wide stream that emptied into a nearby pond. I pulled over into the middle of the bridge, put the Lexus in park, and switched off the headlights, leaving the parking lights on. I got out and said, "C'mon, Luke, get some fresh air, why don't you."

The engine noise was soft and murmuring as I walked on the cracked concrete. It was an old bridge. I could see all right with the half-moon light and the illumination from the parking lights. Luke came around and stood next to me. He grunted. "Damn sure quiet."

"And empty."

We stood there in long empty and sad silence, two brothers who were really never ever friends. Luke said, "Everybody thinks you're the good brother, and that's a load of crap, isn't it. I've read about you, seen enough about you, to know what you really are."

"Pretty bold talk for a guy with another guy's blood on his hands."

"Don't worry about me," he said. "Just worry about yourself, and how you're gonna get me out of that cabin, someplace really safe."

"Canada," I said. "I've got contacts. People who owe me favors. We'll keep you up here for a week or two, until things quiet down some. Then we'll get you across the border, put you up someplace safe, go on from there."

"All right, then."

A loon cried out somewhere there on the dark waters. I turned to him "Luke... why didn't you just leave me alone, hunh? That's all I ever wanted. I didn't want a big brother to be my best friend, or a mentor, or somebody who'd look out for me. I just wanted you to leave me alone. Stop picking on me, short sheeting my bed, breaking my toys, ripping up my books, stuff like that. Why couldn't you just leave me alone? Even now, years later... why can't you just stop?"

Luke said, "Why didn't you just stop being a crybaby for Christ's sake? Whine, whine, whine... it's a miracle you've gotten this far in your life. And without me, you're not going any further, and you know it. Shit, thirty years after high school and you still haven't grown a pair."

I grasped the low railing. Cold, cracked concrete. "We're almost to the cabin. Hand it over, please."

"Hand over what?"

"The gun you have in your boot. Earlier you said you had weapons, plural. Which means more than the knife. And when that cop was behind us, I saw you reaching down to your boot. So hand it over."

"Like hell I will."

"Like hell I'll let you stay in my property, an armed fugitive. Not going to happen, Luke, and that's not goddamn negotiable. So give it to me now, I drop it in the stream, it disappears, and we go on our way."

Luke stared at me, and I stared at him, and for the first time in a very long time, I felt like I was his equal. I was not backing down. I was not shaking with fear. I was not cold with anxiety.

It went on and on.

"Ah, the hell with it," Luke said. He raised up his right foot, planted it on the low railing, reached down and pulled out a small revolver.

"Here," I said. "I want to look at it."

Luke passed it over. A small, evil looking thing. I hefted it in my hand.

"Pretty light," I said. "What is it, a .22?"

"No," he said. "Christ, don't you know anything? It's a .32."

I pulled the hammer back on the revolver, placed it against the side of his head, and I shot him.

* * *

The bark of the report shattered the quiet, there was a bright flare of light like a flashbulb going off, and Luke grunted, stumbled, and fell. He started choking, gasping, on his knees. Both hands were on the guardrail. Blood was streaming down the side of his head. His feet quivered. I walked around and got behind him, put the revolver at the base of his skull, through the long ponytail, and I shot him again.

It was easier the second time.

He slumped forward.

I waited. Trying to ease my breathing.

Nothing moved or quivered in front of me.

I reached down, grabbed his lower legs, pushed and lifted. His body balanced for a moment or two on the guardrail, and then he was over, splashing in the water. I looked down. His body bobbed up, and then the slow-moving current took him away. I put the revolver down on the guardrail, went back to the car. With additional Handi-wipes and napkins, I cleaned off the revolver, and tossed it into the water as well, and then tossed in the cleaning stuff Luke had used earlier.

Then it was done.

I stood there alone in the night air, breathing regular, breathing deep, and then I went into my wife's Lexus, made a careful three-point turn, and drove home.

* * *

As I crawled into bed with Terry, she murmured. "Long night?"

"Yeah, but I got everything done. The drive did me good."

She snuggled up against me. "So glad. So proud of you."

"Thanks." I kissed her forehead and said, "Oh, one thing. I got a milkshake while I was out driving around, managed to dump half of it on the floor. We're going to need the Lexus cleaned and detailed tomorrow."

I kissed her again. "Sorry."

She snuggled closer. "Clumsy man."

"I do all right."

* * *

Some days later, I sat alone, in a room far from home, feeling pretty nervous. Luke's body had been found, questions had been raised, and stories had been written.

The single door to the room was unlocked, and a police officer looked in.

"Sir? If you'll come with me, please?"

I got up wordlessly and followed him. In the tile and concrete corridor, a number of police officers swung in behind us, and I was in the middle of their somber group. We approached another door. It too was unlocked.

I was nearly propelled forward by myself.

Emerged alone on a narrow stage with a lectern in the center. Mind clear, breathing well, I stepped behind the lectern, looked out at the very bright lights, cameras, and expectant men and women.

"Good morning," I said. "Thanks for coming here today. Before I start with my prepared remarks, I'd like to extend my thanks to those in law enforcement who are currently investigating the recent murder of my brother. I have full confidence that those who were involved in this heinous crime will be arrested. I'd also like to extend my warmest thanks as well, to the residents of my state and those other citizens who have extended their prayers and good wishes to my family during this difficult time."

Paused, choked up some, looked out at the people. A question. "Sir, do you know any more about the circumstances of the crime?"

"Only that which has already been reported. My brother… who's had a very difficult life… was involved in a fight at a bar in Porter, where a man was subsequently killed." I took a deep breath for the benefit of everyone out there. "The police believe my brother's murder may have been in retaliation to this attack. But the fact that my brother had a rough life in no way excuses what he did at that bar. It was his decision to make."

I waited for another question. It finally came. "Sir, if I may… do you have any thoughts of how the two of you differed in your outcomes? I mean, it's almost a cliché, of the good brother versus the bad brother. You were both raised by the same parents. Both went to the same schools, had the same opportunities. But how did the two of you turn out so very, very different?"

I gripped the side of the lectern, looked down for a moment. Then raised my head. "A very good question, for which I have no answer. Who really knows what's inside of people, what drives

them, what makes them make decisions that have so many con-
sequences… I think that's a struggle we all face, in our day-to-day
lives, in the way we choose to lead our life, in the way we choose
between good and bad."

That seemed to quiet things down. I looked around. "Any
more questions about my brother before I proceed?"

A voice from the rear. "No, Governor, I think we're fine for
right now."

I smiled. "Thank you, Kate. Again, thank you all for coming today." I relaxed as I eased into the speech I'd just finished. "I
would like to begin by saying how honored I am that the President today has placed my name in nomination for Associate Justice of the United States Supreme Court."

I gotta admit: it's hard to write these introductions about myself. But I'd be slacking if I fail to note that I, too, am a multiple Edgar-nominee under both my Rusch name and as Kris Nelscott for my Smokey Dalton series. My Shamus nominations come in Rusch/Nelscott pairings as well. But only Rusch has been nominated for the Anthony Award and won the Ellery Queen *Readers Award twice. Of course, Nelscott received a Herodotus Award for the Best Historical Mystery Novel and lots of accolades from reviewers and libraries, so it sort of evens out.*

As you can tell, I write mystery under both names. Kris Nelscott usually writes about Smokey Dalton, a private detective in the turbulent 1960s. The long-awaited new novel in the Smokey Dalton series, Street Justice, *has just appeared from WMG Publishing. But I also publish crime novels as Rusch, including two last year, a noir called* Spree *and* Bleed Through.

"FoL" came from a challenge to write stories about rich protagonists. I don't believe the F. Scott Fitzgerald quote about the rich being different—except that they have funds to pay off people they've wronged. And that's how the story started for me...

FoL

Kristine Kathryn Rusch

Red lights churning against the black sky: fire engines, ambulances, cop cars—all red lights; flames flaring, then collapsing, sending red sparks into the darkness; faces red from the heat, black from the smoke. Nico stood on the other side of the driveway, facing the burning frat house. His back was cold, but his face, arms, and legs felt hot. If he took a step closer, he'd be enveloped by the heat radiating off the frat.

The sirens echoed. The noise level rose, low conversation, screams, shouts, the spray of the hoses, music from the nearby sorority, a car horn honking in the distance.

Nico's mouth tasted of smoke—the *air* tasted of smoke. Someone had wrapped him in a blanket, and he didn't remember who or how.

He stared at the frat. He hadn't even been there. He'd been in the history library, doing the damn primary research for Professor Chadwick's all-or-nothing, 30-page paper. Nico hated the dumb library card catalog stored in those bulky alphabetized drawers, the even dumber microfiche machines, the dorky gloves he had to wear before anyone would let him touch old newspapers.

Do not leave this for the last minute, Old Chad had said. *You won't be able to get it done.*

Well, Nico'd had no choice. The stupid idiot he'd hired to write the paper—an overpaid intellectual snob who'd come highly recommended—bailed two days ago, actually handing the money back and stammering something about seeing the light. The other dweebs who wrote term papers for money wouldn't take the assignment—*No time to do a new one, man. Old Chad's seen all my papers on this one. Sorry.*

Nico couldn't fail, not Old Chad's class. Not if he wanted to get into a good law school. He'd been thinking of calling one of his dad's fixers when someone he didn't really know—one of the real dorks, floppy hair, cheap clothes, clearly on scholarship—ran into the second floor room and yelled that Nico's frat was burning.

Nico ran here, got here ahead of the trucks, and tried to run in, only to get pushed back by flames. The frat had gone up like a pile of matches, and the alarms hadn't gone off. But none of the guys had been inside. Someone said—jeez, who? Everything was blurring—they'd heard Nico's voice through a bullhorn, telling them to get out.

It hadn't been him. He'd been in the history library or running, but he kinda liked that they saw him as a hero. As the voice that'd saved them. He was the de facto leader of the house, even if he didn't hold the official position. Some men didn't need titles to show power.

Not that there was any power left.

The firefighters had given up. They were hosing down nearby buildings, the grass, cars, to keep the fire from spreading. Voices—loud, authoritative—said the fire was abnormally hot, very strong. Clearly arson. Probably started in the upper west corner of the building.

His room.

His stuff. Jesus. Everything he'd brought—clothes, shoes, the twenty grand he kept in a lockbox under his bed (*pin money,* his mom called it), the dope he'd bought just two days ago, not that no one'd ever see it. Papers, books, a few trophies—and pictures.

Christ on a crutch. His pictures—three and a half years of frat life, pictures he'd never take to his folks' house. Gone. Everything. Gone.

He tried to wrap his mind around it, couldn't stop staring at the bits of ash floating in the air, tiny bats against the burning sky.

"Awww. Lookie little Nico. Gonna have to call Daddy for some fresh underwear."

A girl's voice.

He turned, saw Valda, fucking feminist lesbian bitch, wrapped in a shapeless coat, leg warmers over her fat unshaved thighs, hair in its usual messy knot. She looked uncommonly pleased—and she didn't even have her usual "Take Back The Night" entourage.

"You do this?" he snapped.

"Wouldn't you like it if I did?" She tugged on her fingerless gloves, pretending nonchalance. "Wow, Nico. Now you'll get to see how the other half lives."

She smiled. He'd never seen her smile before. She almost looked like a real girl. Then she waved at him and wandered down the sidewalk, into the growing crowd.

He didn't give her a second thought until—

The cops woke him up. He was sleeping on the floor in Bruce's dorm room, showered, wearing borrowed jeans, and an old sweatshirt that smelled faintly of piss. Still couldn't get the stench of smoke out of his nose. Wasn't really sleeping either. Heard the cops below—they were investigating everywhere, barging in, taking control, scaring kids not used to authority.

Two cops came through Bruce's door, fat middle-aged guys with round bellies and dead eyes, followed by two in uniform, trim and in shape. With guns.

"Jonathan Alexander Nicholas Ashworth?" the fattest cop asked.

Nico got up, smoothed the smelly sweatshirt, drew himself to his full height, and said in his driest, most dismissive voice, "You need to be clearer, officer. I'm Jonathan Alexander Nicholas Ashworth *the Fourth*. The Third is at his bungalow in the Vineyard, the Second is in Palm Beach because the winters are getting too cold for his thin skin, and the First is in Sun Valley with the rest of the elite, plotting the end of the world."

"We're looking for the one called Nico," the cop said, clearly humor-impaired.

"Which is so much better than Kiddo or Junior or Sonny Boy, or Trey like they call my poor father," Nico said.

"You're Nico?" the cop said.

"Jesus, what do I have to do, spell it out for you?" This time, Nico had his mother's tone, the one she used with housekeepers on the verge of instant and involuntary retirement.

"Perhaps I need to spell it out for you, son," the cop said. "You need to take us seriously. The fire started in your room, with a gasoline accelerant. Your gas-covered clothes were found in a Dumpster not a block away. And two witnesses saw you light the match and place it on the gas trail, then watch it run from the street to your window, before you walked calmly away."

Nico's stomach clenched. He hadn't done that. He *wouldn't* do that. But he was his father's son, and he'd learned early how badly things went when he didn't let his father's people step in.

So he stopped talking, let the uniformed officers lead him out of the dorm, saying only, "There's no need to use the handcuffs," not because he was afraid of them, he was afraid of the photograph that someone might take, the photograph that would then go into the papers and the tabloids and follow him for the rest of his life.

He went quietly out the back, and said only one more thing—a request for a lawyer—and clammed up the rest of the way. Thinking about the fake witnesses, thinking about Valda and her snide *Now you'll get to see how the other half lives.*

He used that—or actually, his father's lawyers used that—and they used the strange letter he got two days later to his campus post office box. A charred photo of him and the rest of the frat—not his photo, but one half-burned, and a business card with an odd logo. *FoL.* And nothing else.

FoL. Fool. That's what the lawyers thought. That's what his dad's fixer thought too. The charges went away as if they had never been. The witnesses vanished. And the frat got rebuilt, bigger and better—not just with insurance money, but with a little of the Ashworth family fortune.

Not that Nico got to live in the new palatial digs. He'd moved on to the best law school in the country because his family insisted he learn a trade. *Trust me,* his grandfather said, *someday you'll need something to do with your time.*

But by the time his grandfather had given him that nugget of wisdom, Nico had already figured it out. He did a lot of thinking that night in the jail, wearing the borrowed clothes whose piss-smell didn't quite overwhelm the odor of sweat and fear that surrounded him. Not to mention the foul toilet at the far end of the room. Or the men who leered at him and called him Pretty Boy.

He would have wagered that even Valda didn't know how the other half lived—how this half lived. She just envied his money, even though she wasn't that poor herself. She wasn't a scholarship student. Her family just didn't have as much money as his.

Not many families did.

He'd always thought his dad a sanctimonious asshole for talking about the obligation of the haves to the have-nots. And the have-nots in the jail didn't exactly inspire him. But that moment, standing outside in the strange ash-covered hot-cold night as he watched a world disappear in flames, that moment had.

He couldn't do anything much about the have-nots. Trying to stop poverty was like putting your finger in a river, in an attempt to create a dam. His mother's paraphrase of Matthew 26:11, the one she used when his father got too preachy, stuck in his mind: *The poor shall always be with us.* No matter what we do.

He didn't want to use a finger to dam the river. But he needed a purpose, and law was as good as any.

He even thought of criminal law, but decided he didn't want to set foot into too many more piss-scented jails, and you had to do that, no matter what side you took. So he followed most of his classmates toward corporate—not for the money (Lord knew, he didn't need money) but so he could understand what he and his siblings would inherit one day.

It all went swimmingly until his third and final interview with the most prestigious law firm in New York—the most prestigious law firm in the country, really. What should've been a hale-fellow-and-well-met moment felt furtive, Daniel Jorgensen, the partner pushing his candidacy, closing the door to the plush office, frowning, and saying, "I don't appreciate being lied to."

Nico hadn't even sat down in his usual chair, the thick leather one to the left of the desk. Instead he stood in the middle of the room, uncertain what to do with his hands. Through the glass window beside the door, he saw associates peering at him, one of them giggling behind her hand before someone hurried her down the hall.

"I haven't lied to anyone," Nico said, and he hadn't. He even told them about the arson arrest, although he didn't have to, since the charges vanished, and the entire incident got dropped.

"Sixteen letters say otherwise." Jorgensen was a friend of Nico's father from some charity board or another. Nico's grandfather had wanted Nico at an old D.C. firm, the one the family had used since the first million accumulated, back in the Depression.

"Letters about what?" Nico asked.

"Your character," Jorgensen said. "Considering one of them is from a major client in this firm, our interest in you is officially terminated."

"Terminated?" Nico asked, feeling slow. "But I haven't lied about anything."

"Sorry," Jorgensen said, without a trace of sympathy. "My hands are tied."

"Shouldn't I know what people are saying? Shouldn't I know who is making the accusations?" Nico's palms were damp. He resisted the urge to wipe them on the front of his suit.

"If it were just one person, we'd consider telling you. But sixteen, from various parts of the country...." Jorgensen shook his head. "We can't take the risk. Clearly, there's a lot more to you than your family, your excellent grades, and your seat on the Law Review. You're not the right material for this firm."

"But—"

"I'm sure you know the way out." Jorgensen sat heavily behind his desk, and stared at Nico.

Nico stood for just a moment, unable to move. He hadn't done anything. Unlike some of the other guys he knew, guys whose families were as rich and influential as his, he actually worked hard in law school. He didn't end up in the middle of his class. He had good grades and a brain and a stellar record. He'd even given up drinking—to excess anyway. No more parties. A beer now and then. Some good wine from the family cellar over the holidays. Nothing more.

He had no skeletons—

"Do I have to call security?" Jorgensen asked.

"No, sir. Sorry, sir." And Nico let himself out.

He walked through the wide, carpeted corridor, toward the elevator, conscious of the associates still watching him, smiling at his defeat.

He wasn't sure why he wanted law anyway, or why he needed a place like this. He had money. He even had influence if he wanted it. He could get the power, reflected glory off his family.

He'd just wanted to do it himself.

He got in the elevator, with its rich wood paneling and gold trim. There were other options. Maybe the D.C. firm wouldn't be so bad. Maybe.

He turned over possibilities in his mind as he made his way back to the apartment his family kept near Central Park. And as he walked in, the doorman handed him a letter, addressed to him. Plain white envelope, just his name in gorgeous calligraphy.

Nico turned it over in his hands. "Who left it?" he asked.

"Bike messenger," the doorman said. "I was to give it to you as soon as you came in."

Nico nodded, and opened the envelope.

Inside, a business card embossed with three letters.

FoL.

* * *

His father agreed: whoever had sent the business card had sabotaged Nico's chances at the New York law firm. And the entire family did damage control with their D.C. firm, the kind of damage control Nico hated: the threats of lost business, the demands that Nico join or else.

Nico didn't want that. He didn't need that. His dad's fixer had found the sixteen letter writers—none of whom had ever met Nico. They'd all been paid a fee to tell a variation of the same story, a story of sticky fingers and cheating on exams, a story of other iffy evenings that ended in gasoline-induced fires.

The fixer couldn't find who had paid the letter writers. Nico's father hired several private detectives and they couldn't track the funds either.

Nico couldn't think of anyone who would go after him like this. He figured—and his family figured—that a nutcase was harassing him because he was wealthy. *Eventually, we'll catch him,* the fixer said, and Nico believed him.

Maybe if Nico cared more about the New York job, he would have fought for another interview. Instead, he felt a bit relieved. He understood why they hadn't hired him.

Nico wouldn't have hired himself either, if any of the charges were true, which they weren't. And as his father said all the firm had had to do was investigate; they'd've realized these were lies.

But his grandfather pointed out there was no reason to investigate. The lies were enough. There were always a lot of sons of privilege looking for a sinecure at a prestigious law firm. They didn't need to take Nico, not without the family tie. So they didn't.

But the D.C. firm did.

And Nico settled into the expected role as the son of privilege whose ambition took a back seat to the silver spoon dangling ostentatiously from his mouth.

* * *

Not that it made him happy. None of it made him happy—the same old people, the same old clubs, the summers in the Hamptons or the Cape, the winters in Palm Beach or Malibu or Aruba. He'd done all of this since he could remember, and his work at the firm was to keep people like him and his father and his grandfather happy, which he was unbelievably good at, because—after all—he'd been doing it since birth.

The only bright spot was Molly. Molly, whose real name was Caroline Modestina Havier, who hated the family pressures as much as he did, who called herself Molly because it irritated her mother. The family called her Caro, her enemies—and she had a few—called her Modesty, and those who loved her, truly loved her like Nico did, called her Molly.

She'd had an actual debut in Washington society. She'd had another in Paris, because of all the family ties. Her gowns were written up in *Vogue*, her Paris debut became the subject of a column on the children of the rich and powerful in *Vanity Fair*, her good works made her the darling of the society page of *The New York Times*.

She was, as his father said, a catch.

But Nico cared less about who she was and more about how she made him feel. He'd finally found a kindred spirit, one as lost in this world as he was, doing the expected thing, but rebelling in tiny ways.

She had a loft in Soho—all hers, hip and beautiful, inspiring him to find a place in D.C. instead of the family manse. She insisted on vacationing in Madera and St. Petersburg, none of the usual places. She hated dressage, and loved Las Vegas. Her only real nod to the privilege she'd grown up in—the only place among the rich and powerful (or the R&P, as she called them) that she truly loved—were the fashion shows. She took time away from her job at an upscale New York P.R. firm, a job as much of a joke as his, to go to Milan and Paris for each fashion season.

That spring, he didn't go along—he saw no need to. She didn't really want him there. Besides, they'd already had their big moment in a cheesy diner outside Saratoga Springs where they'd gone because she wanted to see "the ponies."

The ring he gave her probably cost more than the diner itself. But the patrons had waited breathlessly when he got on one knee on the filthy linoleum floor, and proposed, and applauded when she accepted.

They had to have a big society wedding because, after all, It Was Expected. She had debuted, and he was the eldest in his family, and their union was to Society as important as a corporate merger.

They picked a date one year away. They wanted to marry in three months, but his mother had a fit. They tried to find something within six, but her mother caught them, and straightened them out. No one should expect their friends to clear their calendars for a marriage, unless, of course, there was a reason for the haste…?

It took him a while to realize she thought her daughter might be pregnant. But he couldn't understand why, in that case, she'd want to wait even six months.

Even though he'd been born to this world, he didn't always understand it.

They booked a date at all the proper venues. A famous fashion photographer, a friend of Molly's, took their engagement photo—or, more accurately, photos, so that a different one could go to the *Times*, *Le Monde*, and the *Post*. Molly wore a specially designed dress, which got them in *Vogue*, and his family threw a special party for the elite, which got them into *Town and Country*.

It was a Big Deal, perhaps the largest thing he'd ever been involved in, and required more troops than the Invasion of Normandy, or so it felt to him. Even though no one insisted he pick his grooms-men with care, they did insist that his friends (some of whom were societally challenged) go through an extensive three-week evening course on the social graces.

The courses were underway, the hall paid for, the chamber or-chestra booked, when he went to Molly's Soho apartment to pick her up for their first quiet evening out in nearly a month.

He knocked, the sound echoing on the empty floor. The only thing he didn't like about her loft was that it was on the top floor of a warehouse in a neighborhood that could be dodgy at night.

When she didn't answer, he knocked again, feeling his heart pound.

Finally, the door banged open. Molly was barefoot, wearing her oversized U-Conn sweatshirt and a pair of briefs with *sweetie* written in hearts across her delectable ass. Only he didn't dare say anything, since her face was blotchy with tears. She held a Big Gulp cup in her left hand, and judging from the smell, that cup was filled with beer.

"What the hell do you want?" she asked.

He frowned. "I thought we had a date."

Her mouth curled upward and she mimicked his tone. "I thought we had a date. Moron. Why the hell would I date you?"

He was beginning to recognize this feeling, this the-world-has-shifted-on-me feeling. "We, um, planned the date yesterday...?"

She snorted. "Yesterday. Yesterday's gone, asshole. Didn't you get my message?"

"I haven't been home," he said.

"Home," she sneered. "You don't check voice mail?"

"I came straight here."

"Of course you did," she said in a tone that meant she didn't be-lieve him. "Well, go home, asshole. You'll know what happened then."

He put a hand against the door, meaning to slip into the loft, but she blocked him. "Tell me what happened now."

"I sent your fucking ring back, that's what happened," she said. "It's off. You're a damn pig, and I can't believe I fell in love with you. Piggy."

He hadn't seen her. He hadn't sent a message. He hadn't told anyone to talk with her. He hadn't done anything.

"What went wrong, Molly?" he asked.

"You." She shoved him away from the door, but he didn't budge. "Get out of here."

"Not until you tell me what's going on," he said.

"What's going on?" Her eyes narrowed. "You're harassing me, that's what's going on. Get. Out."

She shoved him again, and when he held his ground, she brought her knee up sharply and hit him full force in the balls. Pain radiated through him. He bent in half, and she slammed the door. For a moment, he thought he was going to puke. He clutched the wall, unable to catch his breath. When he did—when he finally did—he turned toward the door.

The deadbolts clicked shut, one after another, until all three were engaged. She'd been watching him, and had done that deliberately, just so that he would know that he wasn't welcome.

"Molly!" he shouted.

"Calling 911," she shouted back. "You wanna be in the news? I'm calling the tabloids first. Your daddy would love to see you on the front page of the *Enquirer*."

She knew how much both families would hate that.

He stood for a minute, uncertain what to do.

"I'm dialing," she shouted.

He raised his hands in supplication, but knew it would do no good. So he turned his back and headed for the stairs. He'd call her in the morning when she sobered up. He'd apologize for whatever the hell she imagined that he had done, and he'd make it up to her with an even nicer ring and maybe a matching necklace. Something custom-made, specially designed just for Molly.

He limped down the stairs and took a cab back to the family place, where the doorman—a different one—handed him an envelope.

Nico looked down, expecting calligraphy. Instead, he saw a font used in 1970s rock posters. He held the envelope between his thumb and forefinger, and asked the doorman for a letter opener. The doorman had one and watched with great interest as Nico slit the envelope open.

A business card fell out. Embossed in gold in the same font as the envelope, the card said simply: *FoL*.

* * *

This time, he got mad. Not why-me self-pitying mad, but full-blown anger, powerful enough to scare the doorman. An anger that Nico hadn't indulged in since he stopped drinking. It took all of his strength to maintain control.

Nico used the phone in the lobby to call his father, who called in all the fixers, who were going to solve this.

And so was Nico.

Nico hadn't really cared about the NY job. The loss had been a blow to his pride, and it had angered him that someone had messed with him and his life.

But he loved Molly, and he wasn't going to let go without a fight. He called her, and left messages, which she didn't answer. He didn't go to her loft—she had made that clear, and his father reiterated it (*the last thing you want the press to call you is a stalker, boy*), but he sent her mail and he called and he sent a few friends over, all to no avail.

Soon he found out why.

His father's best fixer, a burly man named Stansbury who had rumored CIA connections, came over with copies of "the evidence."

He poured photo after photo on the dining room table, and within minutes, Nico was glad he was the only family member in attendance at the family apartment.

Photos—graphic photos—of every sexual encounter he'd had since college. The girls, sometimes unrecognizable, always looked pained, or drugged, even though they weren't. He'd stopped combining sex and drinking after the fire, and he'd made damn sure that every girl he'd been with since then had given sober and aware consent.

Some of the articles about the fire had postulated that a group of girls, angry at the way the frat boys took advantage at drunken parties, had gotten their revenge. He never thought so because if that were the case, the girls would've gone after one other frat, the one that prided itself on screwing the most unscrewable girls. Someone there even claimed that a member had gotten Valda into bed.

Nico hadn't believed that either.

But these photos—jeez, they did make him look like a pig. Especially so many of them, especially with the women's eyes closed or their faces in a pre-orgasmic grimace.

Molly had known he wasn't a virgin. She'd even known he wasn't a saint. But she hadn't known how many women there had been. Even if these women had all been smiling, she would've been angry.

The fact that they weren't—

Well, that wasn't the worst part. The worst part were the letters. Dozens of them, supposedly from the girls, saying that he'd paid them and they hadn't enjoyed it.

The letters were fakes. They didn't have the right names, not that it mattered. The girls in the photos were mostly unrecognizable.

And Nico had never paid for it in his life, not that that was a defense.

"Did my dad see these?" he asked Stansbury who gave him a whadda-you-think-kid look.

Nico nodded, and sighed. Then he handed Stansbury the envelope with the FoL business card.

"We have to find these people," he said. "They're ruining my life."

* * *

Stansbury did a tremendous job. He tracked down the girls—the real ones—and they were all willing to defend Nico (after Stansbury explained that Nico hadn't taken the pictures, someone else had without Nico's permission). Stansbury tracked down the fake girls too, and found they'd been paid just like the letter writers from the NY case. He even found the photographers—some human and some operating remote cameras planted in Nico's various bedrooms.

Lawsuits, harassment suits, criminal investigations, all of them public at Nico's insistence, didn't sway Molly.

She talked to him, though, long enough to say, through tears, that she'd never ever ever get those pictures of him out of her mind. She was sorry, but the wedding was off. The relationship was off. She'd never been so humiliated in her entire life.

You? he wanted to shout. *What about me? I just found out that I've been watched at the most intimate moments of my life. I'm humiliated.*

And violated. And shaken.

But he didn't pursue her any longer. Although his father talked to hers, gently letting the man know that whoever had photographed Nico had also photographed Molly. They'd gotten those pictures from the various photographers with more finesse than they'd used on the others, just to protect her privacy.

Not that it did much good.

The flunkies all went to jail. But no one could trace the perpetrator of these crimes.

"It's gotta be personal," Stansbury said. "It's gone on too long to be otherwise. Know anyone who hates you with a passion, kid?"

Nico didn't. But he'd never paid attention to the haters. The only one he remembered was Valda and that was because of her comments on that fiery night all those years before.

His father put the full resources of two upscale private detection firms on the problem. They found nothing. But they did do a profile for the family, a profile that Nico could've done for free.

In fact, Nico had already figured out most of it. The perpetrator, whom they were calling by the letters of that business card—F. O. L.—for lack of a better name, seemed provoked by the press. The law school had published an interview schedule for its best candidates, including Nico, and of course, his engagement to Molly had made societal news worldwide. The only attack that couldn't be explained was the frat fire, and there was no real proof that it was aimed at Nico. None of the other frat members remembered getting a letter with a business card stashed inside, but that didn't mean they hadn't.

Still, the detectives figured there was a campus connection.

They just couldn't find out what it was.

Nico let them look. He already had his solution.

He was leaving the East Coast, leaving his prominent position in the family, stepping out of the limelight and into obscurity.

He went to California and didn't move into any of the family houses. He bought a modest house in Santa Cruz because he liked the hippie vibe. He didn't even buy anything with a view of the ocean. And he drove a VW Bug.

He started going by Jan Ashworth (which he pronounced Yahn)—J.A.N. being his first three initials—and he quietly invested in some interesting companies, all start-ups, all worth his time, all either at the cutting edge of technology or with some admirable social goals.

He became, as his great-grandfather sneered, a hippy-dippy California type, completely unrecognizable from the frat boy who went into the family law firm and nearly married the most eligible deb in all of society. His great-grandfather might sneer, but Nico was finally happy.

And he finally felt free.

* * *

Eventually, he married, and made his own fortune, based on his own business savvy and his ability to manage the tech bubble. His wife, also Caroline, only this one adored her name, knew his entire past from the boy he'd been to the dark frat years to the strange FoL incidents.

She saw the pictures before he'd let her say yes to the engagement, and she'd laughed, saying that if someone took a picture at the wrong moment during sex, everyone would look unhappy. She read the detective reports, listened to the stories, and declared herself unconcerned.

She lived up to that, too, bearing him two daughters and raising them with a firm hand. Supporting him in his unwillingness to go to the family haunts, instead insisting on meeting his family off-the-beaten path, or at least, off the R&P path. He never went to Aspen or Vail or Palm Beach or the Hamptons or the Cape. He didn't use the family apartment on the few visits he made to New York. He bought his own condo in D.C. for the necessary business trips.

And for twenty years, he didn't hear from FoL. In fact, entire years went by without anyone giving a thought to those business cards. The incidents were, he assumed, long in his past.

They didn't come up when he moved to San Francisco and got elected to the City Council. They didn't come up when he took his place in the California legislature.

He wasn't private any longer. He'd become a political animal with Caroline's enthusiastic support. And he was good at politics—that natural charm combined with the deference he'd learned at his father's knee. He knew how to get the most intransigent people to compromise by appealing to their better selves and their own best interest.

He was, according to the *San Francisco Chronicle* and the *LA Times*, a Politician To Watch.

He got his own fixers—not at the level of his dad's—but just in case. He'd learned that lesson long ago. And a group of backers approached him, convinced him that—at fifty—he had the chops to follow the Golden California Path. Legislature to Governor, Governor to Senator, Senator to President. Or maybe he could skip the Senator to President step. Reagan had.

Nico was good: he gave the handlers all of the information, had them search for FoL, gave them the photos and the history which his handlers slowly leaked to the press, putting his spin on everything.

It wasn't smooth sailing, but the bumps weren't extreme. He came off as human, a man who had lived and had shed the burdens of his heritage. Eventually, it looked like he might be a shoo-in for his party's nomination, depending on the debate.

The debate. No one watched debates, particularly primary debates between candidates vying for their party's nomination. No one, except the party faithful and the press, who would use the occasion to eviscerate anyone who made a gaffe.

Nico was usually gaffe-proof. Not because he was robotic, but because he was good at debate. He'd excelled in it at law school, which was one of the reasons he'd nearly decided to go into criminal law. He didn't skip the prep then, and he didn't skip the prep now. In fact he over prepared, particularly when it became clear that his opponent was the formidable Tinsley Monroe.

Tinsley Monroe, a tall striking blonde with a history amazingly similar to his. An Ivy League education, a top sorority, a top law school, and a refusal to debut. She had moved to California to pursue her own dreams regardless of the family demands. She hadn't married money, and she'd come up through the ranks just like he had. Unlike his, her daughters had returned to the Ivy, and were already making names for themselves. His daughters had gone into the UC system and kept a low profile, which he applauded.

He'd run into Tinsley a hundred times since he'd started his political career. She'd been helpful, even contributing to his campaign for City Council. Her help stopped, understandably, when she entered politics herself. Her agenda was proto-feminist, although she didn't use the words: programs for women and children, better work laws, more shelters. He'd supported those initiatives as well, and still tried to have a pro-business attitude. He figured the pro-business side would help him in the larger campaign, but he never counted Tinsley out.

If anyone could best him in a verbal contest, it was Tinsley Monroe.

So when he met her backstage at the largest auditorium on the UCLA campus, television cameras set up, podiums on their marks, he silently congratulated himself for his tendency to over prepare. Not because he thought he'd win, but because he would at least have a fighting chance.

She looked stunning—a mane of golden hair around her well-made up face, glasses that caught the highlights of her dress and made her look like a particularly intelligent CEO. She wore a simple black dress, which slimmed her, and heels that showed off her tremendous legs.

He didn't have the flash—what man could in a simple suit?—but he knew he looked as serious and intelligent as she did.

He extended his hand, and she smiled a moment before she took it looking, he thought, like a particularly well satisfied cat.

She slipped paper into his palm. He looked.

A business card that read *FoL*.

His heart lurched. "Who gave this to you?"

She tilted her head, more catlike than ever—a lioness with her prey. "No one, Nico," she said. She called him Nico. Before, she had always called him Jan. "I'm a member of FoL."

"A member of…?"

"Friends of Liz. You remember Liz Bodey, right?"

For a moment he didn't. For a moment, the name was just a name, and then he did remember.

"You knew Liz Bodey?" he asked.

"Still do," she said, and headed toward the stage.

His handler pushed him forward. Nico had missed the bell, warning him that he was about to go on. He knew he looked ashen, knew he was shaken. For a half second, he debated walking out, then decided that no one would chase him away.

The lights glared; it was already hot. They had practiced the on-stage handshake, only this time, she pulled him close and whispered:

"I'm not going to mention Liz in the debate. I don't see any need to invade her privacy."

Instead of reassuring him, the sentence shook him worse. He found his podium, listened to the introduction and damn near forgot his opening speech.

Liz Bodey. He could still see her face, swollen so badly on one side that she looked deformed. She'd been a virgin—he hadn't known that—she'd been sober and unwilling and terrified, and he hadn't been any of those things. She had been tiny and he could hold her down so easily. It wasn't until the end that he realized his slap to her face had actually broken her jaw, the twist he'd given her wrist had snapped it.

He'd been drunk, but not that drunk. He'd known he fucked up. Literally. The hospital report disappeared, the police case vanished—if one had ever started. His final indiscretion—that was what his father called it, an indiscretion, just like all the others— that *final* indiscretion had cost a quarter of a million dollars plus legal fees for the confidentiality agreement. That was just for Liz Bodey. He had no idea who else had gotten paid.

Nico stammered his way through the debate's first few questions, tried to shake it off, couldn't, not quite. The answers to his entire past were right beside him. Tinsley answered debate questions smoothly, sweetly, even offering to give him a moment to gather himself.

He looked at her, saw the glint in her eyes. Friends of Liz. FoL. God, no wonder they couldn't track anyone down. There wasn't one person to track.

The debate went on forever. He got belligerent when it came to the women's issues questions. He'd done enough, more than enough, he had daughters for heaven's sake, he understood what women went through. Every guy is insensitive young, some worse than others, but men—the best men—learned, improved, helped, grew.

Tinsley let the statements stand, didn't argue, didn't walk through that open door. She was professional, competent, and she won on points. He could tell that, with fifteen minutes to go.

Off stage, finally, he pushed past his handler, headed toward the men's room. Tinsley found him, stopped him.

"There was a bunch of you, wasn't there?" he asked.

She nodded. "We all saw her that night, took her to the hospital, helped her. We knew you'd pay people off. We knew there'd be no case. We all come from money too. We know how it's done."

The room spun. He felt ill. He put a hand on the wall. "You could've brought it up years ago. I'd've owned up to it. I'd've apologized and helped her more if she needed help."

"Ah," she said, "but that's what people like you miss. What happened to Liz wasn't a one-time event. People like Liz live with the trauma—the memory—every day of their lives. She has post-traumatic stress. Attacks show up at the strangest times. She'll pay forever for what you did."

"So I have to too?" he asked.

"Shouldn't you?" Tinsley asked.

He didn't answer that. He knew what answer she wanted, and he wasn't going to give it.

"What do you want?" he asked. "Me to leave the campaign?"

She smiled. She looked so sweet when she smiled. "You will, but not because I want it. Wait until your backers see that performance."

"You're not going to leave me alone, are you?" he asked.

"I probably will," she said. "But I don't know if Liz's other friends will."

"You committed arson," he said.

"When?" she asked. "Your frat fire? I was in an entirely different town, taking an exam. With a hundred other witnesses. Really, Nico. You're paranoid."

"I can tie you to this now," he said, feeling desperate, feeling angry. "I have the card. With your fingerprints."

He held it up, expecting her to grab it.

"That business card?" she asked. "The one you dropped before the event? The one I picked up for you?"

His breath caught.

She patted his shoulder, the perfect example of a graceful winner to anyone watching from a distance. "Think it through, Nico. Who has the most resources here? And who is the most determined?"

He couldn't think it through. Not even after she walked away, not after he stumbled into the men's room and lost the steak dinner he'd consumed with his best backers before his woeful performance.

He'd reformed. Dammit. He'd been respectful and nice from that night on. He stopped drinking. He changed his attitude. He donated time and money to women's causes, shelters, rape crisis centers.

He had daughters, for god's sake.

He paid. He was paying.

And he paid some more.

Cold hard cash, to his fixers, his father's fixers, detectives. Once Tinsley told him who FoL was, it was easy to find the other members. Only nothing tied them to any attacks. No money trail, no leaks on the arson, alibis everywhere.

Ten women, all with the same resources he had. With fixers of their own, people to hide the evidence, bury the past, sink anyone who got in their way.

Like he had.

He knew how the game was played.

From the other side.

Usually he stood with the winners.

Except when he faced off with the FoL.

I met Julie Hyzy before she became a bestselling, award-winning author. But her storytelling abilities were obvious even before her first publication. She's currently writing two amateur sleuth mystery series for Penguin/Berkley Prime Crime: The White House Chef Mysteries and the Manor House Mysteries. She's a New York Times *bestseller who has also won the Anthony, Barry, Lovey, and Derringer awards for her mystery fiction.*

Even though Julie is known for her cozies, the story she wrote for us here is anything but. She writes, "Mentors can make all the difference in an impressionable young person's life, as I well know. In 'These Boots Were Made for Murder,' Mallory and Carrie came alive to tell me their story of friendship, growth, and revenge. I simply wrote it down."

————

These Boots Were Made for Murder

Julie Hyzy

Mal was a tough chick. Told me so herself the first time we met. I remember thinking that anyone who used the word "chick" had to be older than dirt, and maybe Mallory Jenkins was. My mom's age, I guess, but stronger and tight all over with clingy clothes and sassy red leather boots. In the right light she was still pretty, with the kind of body that made the men in town stop and give her a second look.

She came pounding at the front door last night, less than a minute after Brody took off.

When I answered, she didn't even say, "Hey, Carrie, what's up?" or anything. First words out of her mouth: "What was he doing here?"

A thick evening wind whipped at Mal's red-brown hair making it twist up around the back of her head like a dark flame. Her cheeks were flushed. She was still kind of new to our little town, and the residents of Carnich, Texas hadn't exactly warmed up to her.

"Why is Brody coming to visit when your ma's not home?"

I shrugged. At eighteen years old, shrugging meant "yeah" and "no" and "what's it to you?" all in one easy move.

She pulled open the flimsy screen door and reached for my face. Grabbing my cheeks and chin with one hand, she turned me side to side, then stared hard until my face grew hot under her glare. "He's having his way with you, isn't he?" Her hand dropped in disgust. "The pig."

I still hadn't said a word.

"I've seen him sniffing around you ever since I moved here. It's wrong for a slimy middle-aged cop to be sullying someone so sweet and innocent."

"I wasn't supposed to tell anybody."

"How long has this been going on?"

I shrugged.

"Pig," she said again, getting a faraway look in her eyes. "Wonder what his wife'll have to say about it?"

"Don't tell her. She'll think it's my fault."

Mal looked at me again. "What do *you* have to say about it?"

I shifted my weight. "What do you mean?"

"How did this all start?" Her eyes narrowed. "Do you *like* it when Brody comes over?"

"He started checking on me when my mom took off this time. Said it was his civic duty to make sure I stayed safe."

Mal's boot tapped an angry rhythm on the scarred wood floor. "You tell him to leave you alone?"

This time when I shrugged, she shook me.

"Did you?"

"I don't remember. Maybe I did. Could we just stop talking about it?"

She studied me. "When will your ma be back?"

I didn't know. I never knew. "Soon."

"You come next door and stay at my house. Brody won't need to check on you there."

I felt my eyes go wide. "He won't like that."

"Will *you*?" She brought her face closer to mine. "I'm asking you straight up. Tell me and don't lie. You like what's going on here? Or do you just go along because you're scared to tell him no?"

I dropped my gaze to the floor. My bare toes came together, making it look like my feet were trying to shake hands.

"Carrie," Mal said. I flinched but didn't look up. "When he shows up here are you happy about it? Or do you wish he'd drop in a deep hole and never be seen again?"

My voice felt small and far off. "I wish he'd go away."

"Thought so. You're staying with me from now on. I'll square it with your ma." Under her breath, she said, "Whenever she gets back, that is." She made a shooing motion with both hands. "Go collect some of your stuff, now. Go on."

* * *

I was nearing the end of my shift cashiering at the grocery when Brody came in. Wearing his beige uniform shirt tight and his pants way too low, he sauntered like he always did, thumbs jammed into his holster belt. He nodded hello to people wheeling their food and kids out the front doors. He pretended not to be looking for me.

I slid a couple of green peppers onto the scale, and tapped in their code. Mrs. Bautista watched me like a hawk, hoping I'd make a mistake. I pulled a wrapped pork roast past the scanner. "I want that in its own plastic bag," she said. "Don't be letting the meat touch my other groceries."

"Yes ma'am." Like I didn't do that for everyone.

Brody was still making off like he just happened by. "Hey, Carrie," he said, all nonchalant, "I forgot you're working here now. How's it going?" To Mrs. Bautista, he tipped his hat. "Afternoon, ma'am."

Mrs. Bautista, older than my mom by at least twenty years, fatter by at least forty pounds, went all giggly and soft. She stopped watching my every move to bat her lashes at Brody. "Nice to see you, Sheriff. Keeping our town safe?"

"It's my solemn duty," he said.

I rolled my eyes and turned to weigh a bag of grapes, pressing my thumb down on the scale, hard. It probably wouldn't cost the old lady more than a buck, but it sure felt good to screw someone else for a change.

There was no one else in line after Mrs. Bautista. I finished bagging her food while she flirted with Brody one last time.

"Bye-bye, Sheriff," she said, like she was thirteen.

The minute she was gone, Brody rested an elbow on the check-pay stand and leaned forward, talking soft. "Where were you last night?" He worked to make his brows come together like he was worried, but the spark in his eyes was pure anger.

I sprayed Windex on the conveyor belt and ran a paper towel along it as it hummed, giving me something to do, something to look at besides those mean eyes.

My hand shook so I sprayed again. "I'm staying with Mal."

He didn't say a word.

"For a while," I added, cleaning furiously. The conveyor belt went completely around once. I kept scrubbing. "Until my mom gets back."

Brody had brought the warm in with him from outside. Sweat, and his particular b.o. poured off of him in waves. "How'm I going to be able to take care of you while you're staying there?" When he was silent too long, I looked up. "I take good care of you while your mom's away, don't I?"

I stared down at the paper towel in my fist. My heart was racing, faster than it ever had. I'd never stood up to him before and my legs started to tremble. Mouth dry, I said the first thing that came to mind. "Mal made dinner last night. Chicken and rice."

He leaned closer, making his voice rumble. I knew he thought that made him sound sexy, but it came across stupid and whiny. "Don't you miss me? You like it when I stay with you. Admit it."

I started to shake my head.

"Sheriff!" Dave, the manager, called to Brody from two aisles over. He wanted to talk about the vandals who'd been knocking over the Dumpsters out back recently. Relief made my knees go weak.

I shut off the light above my line. "Taking my break now," I said to no one in particular.

"Hold up a minute, Carrie," Brody said, a bit too loud. As my manager joined us, Brody leaned on the check-writing stand again, as casual as anything. "What do *you* think, Dave? About that new woman who moved in. Mallory Jenkins?"

Dave's mouth turned down. "Can't say I have any opinion. Why? Did she do something we should know about?"

"Nah," Brody said, waving a thick hand as though it was of no concern. "You've seen her, though. Struts around town like she's got something to sell." He lowered his chin and sent Dave a meaningful stare. "You know what I'm talking about."

Dave laughed. Uncomfortably, it seemed to me.

Brody leaned across the conveyor to pat my arm. "I worry about her influence on little Carrie here." With that, he winked at me. "Don't want to see our young people going down a dark path."

Dave frowned. "Mallory is eccentric—"

"Good word, there. Eccentric. She's surely that. Makes me think it wouldn't hurt to do a little background check. You know, just to be safe."

Safe. He threw that word around a lot.

"I gotta go," I said, and ducked away.

* * *

After I got off work, I stopped back at home just long enough to make sure Mom hadn't got back yet. I picked up more clothes and stuff to bring over to Mal's. My room there was small, but she'd given me a dresser and my own set of towels. I felt warm and safe in the twin bed that she'd made up with pink sheets.

That night, I told Mal about Brody's visit while I was cashiering. I warned her that Brody was mad and told her how he said he was going to look into her background. That bothered her, I could tell. She called him a dirty name under her breath, then said, "I thought I was done with that," so soft I almost couldn't hear.

"Done with what?" I asked.

"You just be careful," she said. "Don't answer the door for anybody. Not until I get home every night. You understand?"

Home, she said. Like this was my home, too. I hoped Mom would stay away for a long time.

* * *

"You got a teenager's appetite, that's for sure," Mal said with a laugh the next night. "What did you take for lunch today?"

I lifted a shoulder. "Peanut butter sandwich."

"Your ma taught you to cook for yourself, didn't she?"

I would have laughed but it really wasn't funny. "My mom doesn't know how. She never makes anything except sandwiches, or whatever frozen packet you can heat in the microwave."

Mal got that sad look in her eyes again. My insides squirmed, knowing she felt sorry for me. "Maybe I should teach you to cook so that you wouldn't have to wait so late for me to get home every night."

The way she said it made it sound like I'd be staying here forever. "I wouldn't mind learning. Then maybe you could have dinner right away when you get home, too."

She smiled, making the faint lines in her face crinkle up. Mal had the look that said she'd lived a lot of her life outside. "I learned to make do with whatever schedule I have at the moment," she said, "but teaching you how to cook will be fun. We'll go shopping together this weekend."

"I get a discount at the grocery," I said.

"Even better."

* * *

On Saturday, as promised, Mal took me shopping, teaching me how to pick out fresh fruits and vegetables, and then when we got home, how to prepare them. Before long, there was steam, and smells that made my stomach growl.

She asked me about future plans and I told her I thought I might make manager at the grocery some day. She asked me about boys. "How many boyfriends have you had?" She fixed me with one of her tough looks. "I mean guys you slept with."

"Just one. And then Brody." It should have felt weird to be telling her stuff like that, but it was okay. Like we were girlfriends. "Guys around here don't ask me out. Not since…"

"Not since he scared them off, huh?" She shoved a little garlic clove into a press and squeezed so that bits came flying out. She showed me how to sauté them. "You should be going out with boys your age." Handing me the press and a fresh clove of garlic, she pointed to the frying pan simmering on the stove top. "Your turn."

I squeezed, but the gadget didn't budge. "How did you get so strong?" The metal legs of the press were harder to pull together than I thought. I needed to use both hands.

"Practice. You'll get it."

She waited and watched without rushing. When garlic shreds finally hit the sizzling oil, it made me jump. I used a wooden spoon to push the bits around. "You're not afraid of anything, are you?" I asked.

When she smiled, she looked sad. "I used to be scared all the time. Didn't care for that much." She handed me another clove, then went on, "I know you don't like being scared either. So here's my advice. Don't be."

More shreds of garlic landed in the fragrant pan. The kitchen smelled like the best meal I'd ever eaten, and I hadn't even tasted it yet. I shook my head. "That's a whole lot easier to say than it is to do."

"I know." She nudged me with her elbow. I looked up. "You gotta stop being afraid. You just need a little kick in the pants."

"From you?"

"Yeah, from me."

We were bantering. Like girlfriends do in movies and on TV.

She lifted one foot in the air. "You see these boots? You think I wear them all the time because I can't afford new shoes?" She waited, but I knew she didn't expect me to answer. "Uh-uh. These boots saved my life."

"How'd they do that?"

Pulling up two chicken breasts that had been waiting nearby, she laid them side by side in the pan. "Another day," she said. "One lesson at a time."

* * *

Brody jogged to catch up with me. "Where you going so fast?"

I'd seen him hanging across the street like he'd been waiting for me to get off work. It was like one of those stalker movies, except without the scary warning music. "Don't you have some crimes to investigate or something?" I asked.

He grabbed my arm, stopping me in my tracks. Nobody paid any attention. A cop stopping a kid on the street wasn't exactly news. "Sassing me back now, are you?" he asked. "Didn't your mother teach you to respect authority?"

My mother hadn't even taught me to respect myself. But I knew Mal thought I had it in me to stand up to him. I looked him straight in the eye, and even though my voice jiggled, I said, "You don't have no say over me."

His eyes went hard, his grip tightened. "You watch yourself, little girl. This Mallory Jenkins is trouble. You'd be smart to steer clear."

I tried wrenching my arm away, but he held on.

Bringing his puffy lips close, he whispered. "She killed a man. In cold blood."

I stiffened.

"Didn't tell you, did she? Got off on a technicality."

The eager glint in his eye made me believe he wasn't lying. "How…?"

"Cops have friends everywhere. Don't you forget that." His words flew out fast and hot against my ear. "I'm going to keep a close eye on her. Don't want anything bad to happen to my little Carrie, do I?"

With that, he let go, propelling me forward. I stumbled.

"You have yourself a good evening," he said, nice and loud.

* * *

When Mal walked in that night, she'd barely said two words when I blurted, "Brody says you murdered somebody but you got off on a technicality."

Mal dropped her bag on the closest kitchen chair. She worked on the highway, repairing roads, and she always came home sweaty and worn. I should have let her take her shower first, but I couldn't stop my mouth from running off on me.

For the first time since I'd met her, Mal looked her age. She studied me for a minute, shut off the stove burners and pointed to the nearest empty chair. "Sit," she said.

I sat.

She pushed her bag off the other chair then dragged it forward and sat so we were almost knee to knee. It looked like she was fighting a war inside herself. "I'm going to tell you the truth." Her eyes were wide, focused, bright. "But it's up to you to decide what you believe."

My heart was shooting fireworks in my chest. I almost couldn't breathe. "What happened?"

Her jaw was tight, her eyelids low. I wished I'd kept my mouth shut. "My ex was a lot like our Sheriff Brody."

I didn't say a word. Didn't move.

"Randy wasn't a cop, mind you, but he was mean and strong. Worse, he was afraid."

"Of you?"

She laughed. "I wish. No. He was afraid of somebody screwing him. Or making him feel stupid. A small man in a big body. I didn't see it before I married him." She shook her head. "What can I tell you? I was young and stupid. It took me a couple of years…" She stared at me. "…Years of bruises and broken bones and telling the cops that everything was just fine and to go away, before I knew I had to get out before Randy took *me* out. Permanently."

"I can't believe anybody would mess with you."

She held up a finger. "That was before I learned how to be strong. I used to be scared."

I made a face.

"I was. Scared for my life. I wasn't strong at all. I should have faced him but I ran."

"Where did you go?"

She shrugged. "Away. Fast as I could. But I knew he had ways of finding me. Knew it was just a matter of time."

I shook my head, not understanding.

"Found a job working for a crusty old broad who owned an auto repair shop." Mal shook her head, remembering. "Dawn saw I was in trouble and took me in. Taught me a lot."

Mal didn't say it, but I couldn't help thinking it was just like she'd done for me. "Yeah?" I prompted.

"Dawn bought me these boots, out of her own money. Told me that when Randy came for me, like we both knew he would, I needed to be ready. Needed to remember I was strong." She ran a hand lovingly down the side of one of her red boots. "Made me believe that as long as I was wearing these, nobody could touch me."

Mesmerized, I waited for what she'd say next.

"He showed up at my apartment one night. I let him in because I knew we had to end this once and for all. He sat on the couch and told me I had to go back with him. Calm as anything, he sat there talking, thinking I was gonna drop my head and follow him out. But I had these boots on. I said 'no.' He gets this look in his eye, then. He could tell something changed." She hit her fist against her chest. "Changed inside me."

"What did he do?"

"Grabbed me by the throat," she said, her hands coming up to rest against her neck as though reliving it. "Lifted me onto my toes and told me I was either coming back with him or I was going to die. Told me it was my choice. 'What'll it be?' he asked. I could barely get the words out, but I played along like I was meek and scared again. He put me down. I walked over to the sink like I was going to be sick and he laughed. Laughed so hard he didn't see me pick up the knife. I turned around and pointed it at him. For a couple of seconds I thought maybe I could just scare him off, but I took another look at that face and I knew there was only one way to get rid of him for good." She shrugged. "He came at me. I stabbed him. Fourteen times."

"Oh," I said.

"If that makes me a murderer, so be it." She glanced down at her boots and wiped the top of one with her hand. "Blood got everywhere. All over these. I got arrested, but they let me go. He had tracked me down, and I had bruises on my neck from where he'd grabbed me." She gave me a look. "There's your technicality."

"Then Brody can't come after you," I said. "You didn't do anything wrong."

"Men like Brody and Randy don't care what's right. That's why I never take chances anymore. I got myself a gun…" She led me to her room where she opened the top drawer of her nightstand. A silver revolver winked in the light from the lamp above. She shut the drawer and grinned. "The thing is," she went on, "you never know exactly when idiots will come for you. I don't take chances anymore." Wiggling her fingers to have me follow, she made for the kitchen. "Right here." She reached up into the cabinet above the microwave, feeling around until her hand rested on what looked like a rolled dishtowel. She pulled the bundle down, unrolled it in front of me and said, "I keep the semi-automatic up here. Hope I never need to use either one."

Terrified and a little bit thrilled, I reached out a finger, running it along the side of the black metal weapon. Mal pressed a release button and the magazine dropped out. She emptied the chamber and handed the gun to me. "See how it feels."

I raised it, two-handed and pointed it out the back window, closing one eye as I aimed at a fat tree.

"You ever shoot?" she asked.

"Couple of times. With my dad. He taught me some."

"You got a gun in the house?"

"My mom used it to chase my dad off, then sold it when she figured he was gone for good. Needed the money, I guess."

She eased the weapon out of my hands, snapped the magazine back into place, and chambered a round with clacking metallic ease. She gestured toward the bedroom with her chin. "That one's registered. This one's not." With a shrug she returned it to its hiding space. "I keep it hidden, just in case."

* * *

Halfway up the steps to Mal's house with my key ready and a bag of groceries in my hand, I heard the shrill voice calling to me from across the front yard.

"Where you think you're going?" my mother shouted. "You forget where your own house is, girl?"

I felt sudden pain. From nowhere, from everywhere. It got dark in my eyes—the kind of tunnel-dark that lets you see only one thing, but see it so clearly it hurts. I was seeing my mom like that right now. Dishwater blonde hair straggled down to her skinny shoulders. She was wearing the same dress she'd been in when she'd left, and from its ragged, dirty look I wondered if she'd changed out of it, even once.

In a rush of anger that shocked me so hard I had to suck in a breath, I wished she'd go back where she'd come from. Disappear and never come back.

"Get over here." Her words were a fist, slamming straight into my chest. "You hear me? You look like you seen a ghost."

I hadn't moved, but my fingers tightened around the grocery bag.

"Carrie Ann, you get your skinny backside over to this house right now. What is wrong with you?"

It was like watching myself in a movie. I crossed the yards to my house, stopping when I got close my mother and could smell the stink on her. This had been a bad trip.

"Come here," she said, still snapping at me. I took a step closer and she reached up and ran a hand along my cheek, eyeing me critically. "That's better. I missed my girl. What have you been up to?"

I stared down at the bag of groceries. "I was going to make dinner," I said, "for Mal and me."

"Make dinner?" she said, as though she'd never heard of such a thing. "How about you make your fancy dinner for me instead? A nice welcome home for your poor traveling mom."

I hefted the bag. "But Mal paid for all this."

"What's going on here?" Her eyes narrowed. "I been gone, trying to make us some money and I come home to find my house empty and my kid living with a stranger?"

"Mal's not a stranger."

She slapped my face. "Don't talk back to me."

I blinked back the sting behind my eyes. Stared at my shoes. "Wasn't talking back. Just saying."

"Don't you lie to me. I left you here with a job to do. And what happens? You take off, leaving the house empty."

"Nothing went wrong," I said, inching backward in case she thought that was more backtalk. "I checked the house. Couple times a week."

"Your job," she said through gritted teeth, "was to stay *in* the house. That too hard for you to understand?"

"No ma'am."

She pushed my shoulder. "Get inside."

As I crossed the threshold, I smelled how different it was in here. Mal's place was always cool and smelled like fresh linen. My house was stale, hot. Made me think of wet boards left to warp in the sun. As I got into the kitchen I detected a faint sweetness. Mom was drinking again, too. The bottle on the counter and the half-empty glass next to it confirmed it.

I cleaned a space on the kitchen table and started digging out the groceries, placing them next to her piles of trash. "You win anything this time?" I asked.

She lit a cigarette. "Of course I won."

I knew the answer, but I asked anyway. "How much did you bring home?"

She came around the side of the table, studying the groceries, not looking at me. One hand bracing the elbow of the other, cigarette tight between two fingers, she said, "You know it ain't like that. You have to put it back if you expect to win big."

"And did you?" I asked, "win big?" My words came out sharp like little knives. I was desperate to cut into that "so what?" attitude of hers. "Or did you put it all back like you usually do?"

She took a deep drag of her cigarette. "When did you get so sassy? What's that woman been teaching you? You haven't gone lesbian with her, have you?"

I threw the food onto the table and spun, heading out.

"What do you think you're doing?" she asked, cutting me off at the front door. "You're not going anywhere."

"What difference does it make where I go?" I asked. "All you want is to get back out there, gamble more, then come home and sit and cry when you lose. You don't need me."

Her eyes were bloodshot. Her cheek twitched. "I need money."

"I don't have any."

"Liar."

"I don't have any to give you, then," I said. "That's no lie."

"You owe me, kid and best you don't forget that." Her breath stunk and I turned my face away from it.

"Sell the house then," I said. "Get what you can and go. Go away."

"You never talked back to me before." She took a step back, regarding me. "What else that woman teach you?"

I didn't answer.

She took another deep drag of the cigarette. "Can't sell the house. Mortgage is higher than it's worth."

My heart dropped. I'd suspected as much, but had held out hope. There was nothing left. Nothing at all.

"Seems you like living off the kindness of others," she said with a smile I didn't understand. "Ain't so bad is it?"

"I gotta tell Mal that you're back. She'll be expecting me."

"I'll take care of her. She cost me some good luck that was headed my way."

"What are you talking about?"

"Just make your dinner food and keep your mouth shut. I like you better when you're quiet."

* * *

I watched and listened to my mom yelling at Mal outside that night. Staring out the front windows, I could barely hear Mal's replies, but I knew she was just as mad as my mom was. Mal said that I was eighteen and could make my own decisions. My mom told her to stay out of our business. They kept at it until one of the other neighbors threatened to call the cops.

My mom stormed in and slammed the door behind her. "That woman don't know what's good for her," she said. I heard her go into the kitchen and pick up the phone. I didn't care. I just wanted out.

Mal had originally told me that I could stay until my mom came back. But now, it seemed like she wouldn't mind if I stayed with her for good. I ran to my room and started stuffing the rest of my clothes into a plastic grocery bag. Mom was throwing back a shot of whisky when I came to tell her I was leaving.

"I don't want to stay here," I said. "Mal's right. I'm an adult. I can decide things for myself."

Just like in the grocery store when I stood up to Brody, my legs started shaking. I knew my pronouncement had come out too soft, too weak. I held up the plastic bag. "I got everything I need. I won't bother you any more."

I started for the door but my mom stopped me, her eyes searching, her voice wheedling. "You can't leave your poor mom," she said. "What would I do without you?"

"All you care about is chasing that next win," I said, my voice getting stronger. "You don't really care about me. Why not go back on the road? Just forget that I'm here. That'll make us both happy."

It was like I'd slapped her. "No, honey," she said. "That ain't going to make me happy a'tall. The only thing that's going to make me happy is you carrying your fair share."

I rolled my eyes. She pushed me back, deeper into the kitchen. My plastic bag fell to the floor. "Get into your room, girl. Quit acting like an imbecile."

From the front of the house I heard a door open. A familiar voice. "What's the trouble here, ladies?"

All my blood rushed down to the floor. My throat went hoarse. "What's he doing here?"

My mom looked at me like I was stupid. "We're in the kitchen, Sheriff," she called. "Carrie here was just telling me how much she missed your visits."

"I didn't," I said, backing away. "I don't."

He loomed in the doorway, blocking my path to the living room. My mother stood in front of the back door, smug. "I asked the good sheriff to keep an eye on you while I was gone. Imagine how upset I was when he got hold of me to say you weren't holding up your part of the bargain."

"My part of the bargain? What—?" Then reality hit, taking my breath away.

She locked the back door, pulled the key out, and jammed it into the top of her bra. "I'm going back on the road, darling," she said to me. "You be a good girl and mind whatever Sheriff Brody tells you."

My words came out strangled. "You can't. This is wrong. I'll report you. Both."

Mom looked sad for a second, maybe two. "Nobody's going to believe you." To Brody, she said, "We okay now?"

He tipped his hat. When she left, he took it off, and began unbuttoning his uniform shirt. "Carrie, little darlin'. We got off to a bad start. Let me explain things to you."

"Get away from me."

"Your friend Mal?" he said, eyes bright, "I got more on her. Plenty more. I can take her down and you'll never see her again. Or you can be nice to me and I'll forget all the background that turned up. Bet you didn't know she's a cold-blooded killer," he said. "Four men, four states. Never enough evidence to convict."

My breath caught. It couldn't be true. Mal would have told me.

"If she so much as jaywalks in Carnich, I'm going to haul her in." His face was hateful when he smiled. "But I'm willing to be lenient," he said. "You get my drift?"

* * *

Brody was on top, grunting, eyes shut, sweating. A shadow crossed behind him. Two heartbeats later came a sound that split my ears. Gunshot. Loud, so close. Too close. Brody roared, gurgling a noise so feral and deep I heard myself scream along with it. His chin came up. His body bucked. He dropped on top of me, huge, sticky, hot. I pushed him, pushed hard until he rolled to the side, Blood was everywhere.

Mal was there, tugging my arm. "Get some clothes on. Get out of here."

"What did you do?" I asked.

Brody's face contorted, his hands reaching. Futilely grasping at the blood leaking out of him. "Get dressed," she said again, pushing me. "We gotta run."

"You shot him."

She looked at me with a mixture of pity and impatience. "He deserved it. He deserves worse. Now come on."

I pulled on my jeans, grabbed on my shirt, all the while trying not to look at Brody who wailed and begged for help.

Breathless, I asked, "Where are we going?"

She held both my shoulders, and stared me straight in the eye. "I didn't tell you everything about me. Just part of it. You gotta trust me now, okay? I know how to get away. I know how to hide. Can you do that? Can you trust me?"

I nodded, numb with fear.

"Come on then," she said. Grabbing my arm, she pulled me toward the door.

"Is he going to die?" I asked.

She glanced back. "Pretty sure."

We didn't make it past the front door. Neighbors had heard the shot and called police. Two deputies threw us to the ground. A minute later we heard more sirens, saw more flashing lights.

"Mal," I called as they dragged us apart.

* * *

Months later, I was home by myself cooking up chicken breasts in garlic. Thinking about Mal. Wishing I could visit her at the prison. It was far away, though, and I had no way to get there and back.

Brody was leaving me alone these days. He'd vouched for me. Said that Mal had exercised "undue influence" and I wasn't at all to blame. I never even got charged. But nobody believed a word I said when I told them what really happened. Nobody wanted to hear the truth.

Brody knew better than to pay me any attention until things settled down again. But I had no doubt that the time would come and he'd be back. I needed Mal. I needed her to tell me what to do.

The doorbell rang, pulling me out of my thoughts. I shut off the stove and found a lady at my front door. She was about thirty years old, holding a box. The box wasn't pretty like a present, more like the kind that people use when they move. "Carrie Mooreland?" she asked. I'd met court-appointed advocates before. She looked like she might be one.

"Yeah?"

"May I come in?" she asked.

"What do you want?"

"I have some bad news for you," she said. And before the words came out, I knew what she was going to say.

"Your friend Mallory Jenkins."

No. No. No. Don't say it. Don't say it.

"She's dead."

Pain screamed in my brain, hot and angry. I grabbed the door jamb. Pressed my head against it.

"I came from the prison," she said. "I work with some of the women there." She hesitated, inching closer. "It's been a long ride. If I could just—"

"How?" I asked. "How did she die?"

The woman hoisted the box to her hip and used the fingers of her free hand to wipe at her brow. "Suicide," she said. "In her cell."

"Not Mal," I said. "Mal wouldn't do that."

"I'm afraid she did." She shrugged like it was no big deal. Then catching herself, she added, "I'm sorry."

Brody once told me cops had friends everywhere. He wasn't kidding.

I stared at the blue sky. I blinked into the sun. I missed Mal. I missed her so bad my heart hurt.

"For you," the woman was saying. "Ms. Jenkins told me that if anything happened to her, she wanted me to get this to you." She practically shoved the big box into my hands. "She gave me very specific instructions about how she wanted things handled."

"She knew she was gonna die," I said.

The woman shrugged again. "Suicidal people do."

"Yeah," I said. "Right."

* * *

Inside the house, I lifted the lid of the cardboard box. There was another box inside it, a letter taped to its top.

Dear Carrie,

If you're reading this, then things haven't gone so well for me. But I wouldn't change how I got here. You understand? None of this was your fault. You understand that? Now listen to me. Three things I want from you. You got to do all of them. All.

First, you sell that house of mine. Take the money and start somewhere new. Find a place that makes you feel good.

Second: Get an education. You're smart and it's about time you get recognized for it.

Third: Everything in the house is yours now. Everything. Including what I showed you, remember?

I swallowed. The semi-automatic. The cops had made a big deal out of the revolver she'd used, but they'd never mentioned finding the other gun. I nodded, almost as though I was talking to Mal right here, right now.

Listen, honey, always remember that I needed you as much as you needed me.

I wrinkled my nose to fight the heat in my throat.

Last thing: You're a strong woman, Carrie. Don't ever forget that. Don't be afraid. You got strength in you, I've seen it. You just need to tug it out of hiding. Give it some sunlight. It'll grow.

Now, honey, open the box. You'll understand.

I peeled back the lid, but I knew what I'd find.

The red boots.

I sucked in a burning breath, blinking hard. As I lifted them out and placed them on the floor, I caught a whiff of Mal. Her scent engulfed me like a warm embrace.

"Oh, Mal," I said. I ran my fingers along the carved leather designs. I pulled the boots on, slowly, reverently. I stood up and walked around some. They were a little big. I looked in the tall mirror in my mom's bedroom. "I'm strong," I said to my reflection. "Mal says so." With a lump in my throat, I crouched and hugged them close to my knees. In this way, at least, Mal would always be with me now.

* * *

I sold her house, left no forwarding, and found a new, bigger town where nobody paid me any attention. I got a job waiting tables at night and took college classes during the day.

One hot, sunny afternoon, I sat down to get some studying done in the local coffee shop. Somebody had left yesterday's newspaper on the seat. I'd seen it already, but there are stories worth reading more than once. Like the tragedy back in Carnich, Texas. Seems the little town's sheriff was found shot and killed at a fleabag motel just outside of town.

I found it interesting that the newspaper account left out the part about him being sprawled on the bed, wearing nothing but an unused condom. But then again, the good folks running the paper in Carnich wouldn't want Brody's reputation sullied, would they?

Smiling, I looked up.

Two tables away, a teenage girl stared out the dusty windows. Seeing nothing, I could tell. She had red eyes, a bruised lip, and wore fear like a tattoo on her forehead.

One of the shop clerks rapped his knuckles on her tabletop. "These spots are for paying customers."

The girl blinked up at him, nodded, and made ready to leave.

"I've got it," I said, standing. To the girl, I asked, "What do you want?"

She said, "Oh, no, I couldn't—" but her eyes went wide with hope.

I ordered her a sandwich and grabbed two bottles of water. Sat down across from her.

"What's your name?"

She stopped chewing her thumbnail long enough to answer. "Sandy."

I crossed my legs. "I'm Carrie."

"Nice boots," she said.

"Thanks." I ran my hand along the cool leather. Maybe someday I'd tell her how they saved my life.

Emergency room physician Melissa Yi writes medical mysteries about Hope Sze. The latest in that series, called Terminally Ill, *just appeared. She lives with her young family outside of Montreal, Canada.*

About "Because," Melissa writes, "At the Oregon Coast mystery workshop [in June of 2013], Kris Rusch asked us to write a short story based on our areas of expertise. I wrote [a story] about yoga, and then I had just enough time to squeeze out this story about motherhood.... 'Because' was the first thing I wrote at the workshop that felt exactly right."

It is right. The story's short, but it's powerful. And if you want to read Melissa's yoga story, it'll appear in an upcoming issue of Ellery Queen Mystery Magazine.

———

Because

Melissa Yi

Because you were so fat that I could count the rolls through your T-shirt, and know that they'd build across my belly and back in the exact same way.

Because you spent the check every month, and you never gave me a penny, not even if I needed a new eraser for school. "You just ask your fancy teacher for one. Go on, ask."

Because I had to ask, and their eyes would burn me with their pity.

Because you'd spend hours painting your nails, but never let me touch any of the bottles, just because I broke one when I was two.

Because I hated the sound of your crinkling chip bags.

Because when Daddy said he was leaving, you said, "Go, then," and let him walk out the door, even though I screamed and cried.

Because when they put an eviction notice on our door, you just smoked a joint.

Because you made us move to Butthole Town, U.S.A.

Because I have to get out of this place, away from the fucking cows and the falling-down barns.

Because there aren't any jobs here unless you want to shovel shit or ask, "Would you like fries with that?"

Because the other kids are always in my face, saying who's having sex with who and who got so shit-faced drunk that he banged his head on the bathtub and didn't wake up for six hours.

Because of every single "uncle" you put me through.

Because I thought I'd kill myself until I met him.

Because he laughed when he saw you for the first time. Just a little snort, but I heard it, and it made me want to cry.

Because when you met him, you giggled and said, "He'll never stay."

Because the clouds have wiped out the sun, and all I see and smell and hear is rain.

Because our apartment roof drips, drips, drips, and I'm the one who has to wake up in the middle of the night and dump the water out of the coffee can while you keep snoring away.

Because the snow has melted, and it's easier to hitchhike in the rain.

Because you wouldn't let me call him.

Because you took my cellphone away and used up all the minutes.

Because last week, you slapped me across the face in Walmart, in front of the photo counter, when I dropped your coffee.

Because he's the one person who's never raised a hand to me. Not once. Not even as a joke.

Because he thinks I'm beautiful.

Because I knew you hid your money in the freezer.

Because he had a gun.

Because he said he would do it, and I didn't have to look.

Because he loves me.

One of four pseudonymous writing Crowes, Dæmon resides in Nobtucket—a quintessential, if mythical, Cape Cod town. Crowe stories have appeared under various guises in both Daw Books and Level Best Books' Best New England Crime anthologies.

Dæmon spent a tumultuous junior year in Paris, living through les événements of May 1968. "City of Light and Darkness" provides a noir take on the era—when political assassination, Vietnam War fallout, and civil unrest reached a worldwide crescendo.

—

City of Light and Darkness

Dæmon Crowe

April showers were supposed to bring May flowers, not more fucking rain—*la* fucking *pluie*.

Kevin Cooper turned up the collar of his freshman football warm-up jacket and wished he'd hocked it instead of the London Fog with the zip-out lining his mother had sent him for Christmas. Hugging the collar around his neck, he leaned against the soot-stained stone building and reread the letter addressed to him at *poste-restant*, c/o American Express, 11 *rue Scribe*, Paris 9e.

He'd felt like a bum walking into the place, his hair greased and matted, his fingernails black, his teeth covered in a fuzz fit for the Monday after a week-long frat bash. He'd headed straight for the restroom—a clean American oasis in a city of narrow, dark *toilettes* with porcelain feet set beside a hole in a crusty concrete floor and toilet paper—when there was any—coated in wax. He'd relied on COLUMBIA blazoned across his chest to ward off any question he still belonged, and, if necessary, his passport—soon to expire. He couldn't afford to be taken for a student protester left over from the riots the night before.

So far keeping his visits short and infrequent had worked. Another sleepless week or two huddled under a stone bridge arching over the Seine and nothing would disguise the metamorphosis. How long would it take to develop the *clochard's* deep gravelly voice soaked in wine and despair? He didn't want to find out.

Yet, there it was in his hand, the paper already sodden with rain. Sentences popped off the page. Burned the words in his soul.

> .... *Your father is furious!!!*
> *So am I. .... Come home at your peril.*
> *..............no more help from this end.*
> *Love,*
> *Mom*

Fuck you, too, Mom.

She'd enclosed his second draft notice. Greetings, your friends and neighbors have chosen you to go kill gooks in some Southeast Asian rice paddy for the greater glory of truth, justice and the fucking American way.

He wasn't a coward. It wasn't his war. Why wouldn't Dad understand?

He let the ink run away in the rain, his hopes dissolved down the drain.

He'd come to Paris to study the greats—Beaudelaire, Verlaine, Vian—and that was the best he could do?

His laughter—high-pitched, semi-hysteric—evoked a steady stream of eyebrow raises and slightly curled upper lips from the well-heeled Americans in their wingtip shoes and business suits or chino slacks scurrying like frightened lemmings in and out of the doors of the American Mecca in Paris, *face à l'Opéra*, the great grey wedding cake of a building looming across the street.

He reined himself in, pushed off the wall and began the long walk back down the *avenue de l'Opéra* to the *Quartier Latin*. His desert boots squished with each step, one crepe sole flapping, the other super-soaking his sock through a hole.

He still had an acquaintance or two among the students attending the *Sorbonne*, the *Beaux-Arts*, the *Polytechnique*. He could find someone whose friendship he hadn't already stretched beyond repair in the year and a half since he'd flunked out of the overseas program, in the year since he'd had a valid student *carte de séjour*—no gainful employment allowed—, in the six months since he'd had a room of his own, in the weeks since he'd found a niche among the winos and whores under the *Pont Neuf* along the left bank of the Seine. There had to be someone who would let him crash for a night on the floor of a one-room under the mansard eaves, let him wash in the bidet. Maybe loan him a few *sous* for a bath or a shower or a crust of bread.

The image of Jean Valjean loomed large.

He wore the only thing he had left worth a good flying fuck—a pair of genuine, made in the USA, well-worn-in, button-fly Levis. Dirty, sure—filthy more like it. A small rip at one knee—de rigueur. He could get at least a couple hundred francs, maybe more.

And leave his ass in the wind—not that it wasn't already hanging out there.

The rain had stopped, the sun broken through clouds as he passed under the arches at the *Louvre* and crossed over the *Pont du Carrousel* into the *6e arrondissement*—home territory. The sight of the wreckage from the night before on the *rue des Saints-Pères* stopped him cold.

A lingering scent of hot tar on a blistering August day hung in the air over a hint of spilled gasoline. His eyes began to sting, then to water. The burned out hulk of a *Citroën traction avant* blocked the way. Paving stones, dug out of the roadbed, littered the sidewalk and street.

At *Boulevard St. Germain* he turned left. He'd once had a comfortable room in a *pension de famille* on the sixth floor of a multiuse building on *rue du Four*. No doubt some starry-eyed co-ed occupied it now. Maybe she'd take in a fellow countryman. Maybe not. He thought of Marie-Claire, the one French girlfriend he'd had and lost when he landed on the street. She would run the other way if she saw him now.

He caught a glimpse of himself in the window of the *Café de Flore*. Drowned rat. He'd lost weight, down at least fifty pounds from his football days. Gone the straight blocky look of a tackle. His shoulders still filled his jacket, but his jeans hung low on his shrunken waist, his narrowed hips. He looked less and less American. Without the COLUMBIA across his chest, his six-foot-two height and the strawberry blonde hair hanging limp to his shoulders, he could pass for the kind of Frenchman he'd seen prancing around the *quartier* before the riots drove them to ground.

He hurried through surprisingly light traffic in the crossroads at *St. Germain des Près* and down the eerily quiet boulevard toward the *Boule Mich*. The closer he got to the student quarter, the more disorienting it became. He tripped and almost fell on a loose ironwork grille surrounding the base of one of the famous shade trees lining the boulevards. Baby leaves dotted their heavily pruned branches, sticking up grey and still skeletal into a now azure sky.

The *Boulevard St. Michel* in front of the Sorbonne resembled the *rue des Saints-Pères*—pavés everywhere, burned out cars, sidewalk grilles upended to pry out the paving stones. A phalanx of *CRS* riot police cordoned the ancient university buildings. The mere sight of them in their black helmets, black uniforms, shields and truncheons, sent shivers up and down Kevin's spine. He still had his passport. They'd send him home—into the arms of the Army or Fort Leavenworth, take his pick.

A group of young females—colorful scarves tied Apache style around their throats, mini-skirts revealing more *cuisse* than their mothers would approve—walked by carrying armloads of books. One fumbled in her purse for a key and opened the doorway two steps from where Kevin stood. He ducked in behind them.

Their hysterical cries drove him out, into the arms of Jean-Jacques Minaud.

"Keveen?"

"Jean-Jacques." Kevin put his arm around the slight Frenchman's shoulders. He hardly knew Jean-Jacques. He was always hanging around at the edges of the student life. Kevin extended a greeting. "*Ça va?*"

Jean-Jacques shrugged him off, held his nose. "*Tu pus.*"

Kevin explained his lamentable circumstances in his fluent, but badly accented, French. "So, as you can see," he raised his arms to let out a full blast of BO, "I could sure use a shower."

Two CRS officers standing at the side of the phalanx turned their attention toward them.

Kevin froze.

Jean-Jacques grabbed his elbow, escorted him, in the French manner that would get him clocked out in New York, across *Boulevard St. Germain* and into *rue Hautefeuille*. He talked a mile a minute as they walked at a brisk pace back toward *St. Germain des Près*.

"I have a friend. He will like you. Don't worry. He won't care that you stink. He has a very large apartment in a private house, many rooms, two showers and a bathtub as large as a swimming pool. You will see."

They arrived at a *hotêl particulier rue de Varennes*. Jean-Jacques had a key to the outer door and let them both in. They climbed the staircase winding round the walls of the central core of the building, foregoing the elevator with the *hors de service* sign on its wrought-iron cage, hitting the light switches on each landing to keep the bulb burning.

Jean-Jacques knocked at the set of double doors on the third floor. When no one answered, he used another key to let them inside.

The apartment, like so many in Paris, was a maze of rooms set around the central stairway. In some ancient time, before the house had been split into apartments, the staircase may have been open and the rooms visually connected across it. Not now.

Jean-Jacques led Kevin down a narrow, parquet-floored hallway. On the staircase side, bare plaster walls. On the other side, room after room behind curtained glass French doors—salon, dining room, den, sitting room, and bedroom after bedroom behind plush velvet draperies until they came to a solid oak door.

"*La salle de bains.*" Jean-Jacques knocked, listened, then swung the door open.

It was by far one of the largest bathrooms Kevin had ever seen. Jean-Jacques had not been kidding about the size of the tub. He could have swum laps.

"Get undressed," Jean-Jacques told him. "I'll take your clothes to the washing machine."

"You're kidding." Since when did anyone in Paris have their own washing machine?

Jean-Jacques shook his head. He held out his hand for the clothes. "Do you want a bath or not?"

Kevin didn't need to be asked twice. He peeled off his jeans, his COLUMBIA jacket, his button-down shirt, his skivvies, his socks encrusted with the filth of the streets and handed them all to Jean-Jacques.

"Take your time. You can soak while the washing is done. It will help get the grime out of your pores. There are shaving things in the cabinet, there." He pointed to a medicine cabinet over a bank of sinks. "And a toothbush."

Jean-Jacques turned the hot and cold faucets and let the water run until it steamed into the tub. He said, "Don't drown," and closed the bathroom door.

Kevin washed his hair three times and lounged in water as hot as his skin could bear until his nails were clean and his fingers had pruned and he thought he might well fall asleep and drown. He rinsed with the hand-held spray in exquisite lukewarm water, then shaved and brushed his teeth. God, he felt like a new man.

Jean-Jacques appeared just as he was splashing eau de cologne on his face. It smelled of exotic spice and stung like a thousand little Napoleonic bees. He sucked in his breath.

"A thousand apologies," Jean-Jacques said. "There seems to be a problem with the dryer." He held out a paisley dressing gown in gold and dark burgundy silk.

Kevin hesitated.

"Don't worry, my friend won't mind. I have done this many times. He is a great admirer of students. He would like you to have something to eat."

Kevin devoured everything Jean-Jacques placed on the small table in one of the richly furnished salons—bread, wine, cheese, a peasant pâté, roast potatoes, thin slices of cold roast beef, fresh tomatoes on a bed of Boston lettuce in a vinaigrette dressing. He ate so much he could barely keep his eyes open by the time Jean-Jacques' friend, Henri, arrived late that evening.

A short, but still good-looking, forty-something man with a slight accent Kevin couldn't place, Henri wore immaculate evening clothes complete with a fringed white silk scarf hung around his neck.

"I come," he said, "from the opera. They cut the performance short. More student riots. Can you believe? I was lucky to make it home in one piece."

Kevin was still barefoot in the paisley dressing gown. He felt Henri's eyes make a quick assessment.

"But you are tired. I can see it in your eyes. Come, I will show you to a room with the most spectacular view of *rue de Varennes*."

The view was spectacular all right. CRS indiscriminately bashing heads. Teargas rising like fog into the apartment.

"Don't rub your eyes," Henri warned, shutting the window and placing a warm hand up on Kevin's shoulder. "You will make it worse."

They stood at the closed window, tears streaming down their faces as the riot unfolded below in muffled shrieks, distant booms and muted sirens. When it ceased, Kevin crawled gratefully into a warm double bed beneath white silk sheets and slept the sleep of the dead.

Rose tinted sunshine streamed in the French window when Kevin opened his eyes the next day. He'd already missed the morning, the afternoon and the early evening. The street below, still littered with the detritus of last night's *manif*, echoed in stillness.

Jean-Jacques appeared in the doorway with a set of French clothes—pleated-front slacks, a fine-knit sweater in sky blue cashmere, a ribbed undershirt, skimpy French bikini underwear and thin silk stockings that matched the sweater. He held up a pair of highly polished, kid leather, oxford-style shoes in an oxblood color.

"A thousand pardons, the dryer seems to have a problem. We have called for repair, but...," he shrugged in that very French way, "with the manifestations and strikes there is not a repairman in all of Paris. Henri asks that you accept to wear these until your own clothes have dried. I am afraid it may take some time in this humid weather we are having." He turned to go, then turned back, speaking as though in afterthought. "Henri has guests for dinner. You will join us?"

Kevin could hardly refuse. His stomach still thought his throat had been slit. "I'd be honored."

A group of six exceedingly handsome—almost beautiful—young men sat with Henri and Jean-Jacques at the Louis XV dinner table in the intimate, formal dining room, when Kevin entered dressed in the clothes Henri had provided. They fit as though they had been tailor-made for him.

"Splendid." Henri rose and escorted Kevin to the last empty seat at the table. "The clothes, they make the man. Do you not agree?"

Seven well-coiffed heads nodded around the table. Kevin felt like some kind of dandy as all eyes fell upon him. His blood rose and he blushed like a schoolgirl.

"But come. We eat." Henri clapped his hands and a small man appeared carrying their first course.

Kevin plowed through seconds and thirds of a gourmet's delight—seven courses: leek soup, sole almondine, pâté, rack of lamb, medley of spring vegetables in a hollandaise sauce, salad greens tossed in *sauce vinagrette, tarte aux pommes* for dessert. Five of them moved to the salon for demitasse coffee. They talked of *les événements*, argued cause and effect, while the sounds of breaking glass and running feet wafted up from below and the orange glow of car fires reflected in the window panes. Well after midnight three of them, Kevin and Paul and Cristophe settled into plush fauteuils in the drawing room overlooking the *rue de Varennes*. They sipped 15-year-old Napolean brandy from two-handed crystal snifters until Kevin's head reeled with good luck and good cheer and good company.

Paul and Christophe helped him to bed.

For the first time in weeks, maybe months, Kevin dreamed. Or was it a nightmare?

His body, striped naked, floated in a sea of warm silk and soft caress. Smooth hands stroked him, fondled him, cradled him until he burst like a schoolboy in his first wet dream: surprised, frightened, and full of a pleasure he had not known existed.

He woke the next morning with a strange taste in his mouth and a stiffness in places he'd not felt before. He took a long, hot shower and swore off Cognac.

Henri and Jean-Jacques were already reading what passed for a morning paper in this strike-ridden land, sipping café au lait from large cups and eating croissants and jam, when Kevin staggered into the salon in a new pair of pleated trousers and a forest green sweater with matching stockings.

"*Café ou café au lait,*" Jean-Jacques asked as Kevin slumped into a chair.

"Coffee, black," he answered. He needed high-test, for sure.

Jean-Jacques left to fetch the coffee.

"You slept well?" Henri asked, his eyes watching Kevin over the rim of his *café au lait.*

Kevin shifted in his seat, unable to find a comfortable position. "Reasonably."

Henri nodded. "Paul and Cristophe were quite pleased. You were most responsive."

A lump formed in Kevin's stomach, panic shriveled his balls.

Henri finished his coffee and placed the cup in its saucer. He dabbed at his lips with the tip of a white linen napkin. "I'm sure Monsieur Dubois will find you most pleasant."

"Monsieur Dubois?"

"Oh, come now, my fine American friend. Do not pretend you thought I would provide this," his hand moved in a flutter from the room to Kevin to the food on the table, "from the goodness of my heart?"

Kevin's stomach clenched. His tongue tangled in his teeth. His words came out in a whisper. "I'm not your whore."

Henri laughed. "And you would rather return to your whores under the *Pont Neuf?*" He clicked his tongue against the roof of his mouth and shook his head in short rapid jerks from side to side. "It would be such a waste. But, if you must.... Your so-called clothes are clean and dry. My tailor has even repaired them. Shall I have Jean-Jacques bring them to your room?"

Jean-Jacques arrived with the coffee and a basket of warm-from-the-oven croissants. He placed them in front of Kevin. The buttery smell made his head spin.

"Perhaps," Henri continued, "since the métro is on strike, you would like a ride to your Embassy. I am sure they will provide transportation home before our *gendarmerie* finds you here without papers and provides an escort themselves. Your army awaits you, am I right?"

Henri smiled.

Jacques patted Kevin's hand.

"You will see. We choose well. You will have a good life."

* * *

The good life lasted through the strikes and the demonstrations and the national elections. By fall Kevin was working for Henri on the streets of *St. Germain*, dodging anyone he had known in his previous existence, learning to loathe himself more every day.

On a day in October, as the skies clouded over and the rains fell cold and drear, he was not quick enough to avoid Marie-Claire. One look at him and her eyes said she knew. Her face filled with disgust.

"Gay. Okay. No problem," she said. "But a whore, a *pute de pédé, jamais de ma vie!*" And she spit in his face.

He left the spittle and walked to the *Pont Neuf*. A single wino snored on the embankment under the bridge. The whores were out on the streets.

He climbed up the long stone stairs to the bridge, walked the sidewalk to the middle of the span and stared into the cold grey waters flowing in an endless, meandering stream toward the Atlantic—toward home.

They fished him out at Épinay-sur-Seine.

The American Embassy shipped his unadorned coffin home—C.O.D.

Libby Fischer Hellmann's tenth novel, a thriller called Havana Lost, *appeared last September. She's received fantastic reviews for her novels and the anthologies she's edited. She's also been shortlisted for the Anthony Award and* Foreword Magazine's Book of the Year Award. *She has a background in public relations and news, helping produce PBS's coverage of the Watergate hearings, among other things.*

About "No Good Deed," she writes, "The bare bones of this true story, set in the 1960s, came from TV newsman Steve Sanders of Chicago's WGN....I switched the story [from Alabama] to Indiana, where I learned what prison is like from Les Edgerton, a crime author and former inmate himself. Without his patience and generosity, 'No Good Deed' would not have been written."

———

No Good Deed

Libby Fischer Hellmann

Gertie Morton's baby kicked so much in the womb that she knew the kid was going to be a troublemaker. Luther didn't disappoint. Born in 1943, the colicky baby screamed so much that Gertie thanked the Lord their closest neighbor lived half a mile away. Once the colic was over, teething began, and Gertie gave Luther liberal amounts of whiskey that her husband cooked up in their still. She sometimes wondered if that was the root of Luther's problems.

Luther grew into a rowdy boy and even rowdier teen: stealing bikes, then cars, then whatever he could get his hands on. Which wasn't much—they lived in a dirt-poor area of Southern Indiana. Luther wasn't much of a student either, until a sheriff's deputy caught him smoking and drinking whiskey at the pool hall. Luther seemed to clean up after that, and Gertie was surprised when he came home with a decent report card in twelfth grade. She proudly proclaimed to everyone she knew how he was one of the best students in the school.

She learned the truth a few months later when Luther told her that his high school English teacher was a member of the Ku Klux Klan and had recruited him into the group. Gertie remembered the problems the Klan had caused in Indiana over the years, and while she didn't exactly disagree with them, she didn't think it would end well.

It didn't. A few weeks after Luther's twenty-first birthday, he was convicted of taking part in a lynching. Sentenced from fifteen to life, Luther was sent to the state prison at Pendleton near Indianapolis.

* * *

1967—THREE YEARS LATER

Luther was working in the Pendleton library when rookie inmate Wendell Washington got out of quarantine. Quarantine was the place where they checked you in, made you take a slew of IQ and personality tests, and indoctrinated you into the system. But the prison grapevine was way ahead of official pronouncements and everyone knew Washington, a colored boy, was in for raping a white woman. He'd claimed he was innocent, but the jury didn't believe him. He narrowly escaped the death penalty, but he would be inside for the rest of his life.

None of that mattered much to Luther. He was white and Washington was black, and in Pendleton the two didn't mix. Although they had to work together in the laundry or the kitchen or the barber's, you'd never hear "We shall overcome" at Pendleton, never see any marches or demonstrations. After work the whites had their own turf, the blacks theirs. It wasn't only the prisoners. The guards, or hacks as they were called, were often more bigoted than the inmates. In fact, Pendleton had been singled out on national TV by LBJ as the worst prison in the country. Luther chuckled, remembering how everyone cheered when they heard that, like they'd won the goddammed World Series.

So when Washington showed up at the library with a hack, Luther arched his eyebrows. No one ever came to the library. It was about the only place, besides a cell, where a man could get some peace and quiet.

"Well, well, what have we here?" Luther said. "This boy even know how to read?"

Branson, one of the nastiest hacks in the joint, sneered. "He ain't here for no book, Morton."

Luther nodded. "Prob'ly wants a magazine or comic book, right? With plenty of white girlie pictures. Well, tell 'im he come to the wrong place."

Branson sniggered. "Tell 'im yourself. He's your new helper."

Luther frowned. Was this Branson's idea of a joke? "The hell you talking about, Officer?"

Inmates always called hacks "officer" to their face, even though they barely made minimum wage and usually didn't deserve respect. Many supplemented their meager salary by smuggling stuff in and out for prisoners.

Branson gave Washington a shove, and the boy stumbled, lost his balance, and fell against Luther. Luther recoiled and stepped back. The boy dropped to the floor. He picked himself up but kept his eyes down.

"Sorry Luther," Branson shrugged. But the glint in his eye told Luther he wasn't sorry at all. "Was the dicks up in quarantine decided it."

"That's fucked! I hadda earn this job. Two years of hard labor. How does this 'coon get it for free?"

"Everyone's getting twitchy these days. All that Martin Luther King shit."

"So that means it's OK to give a nigger who raped a white woman one of the best jobs in the joint?"

Branson shrugged. "Some people don't have the brains they was born with. So lemme tell you the deal, Luther. You do what you gotta do, and I'll make sure you get extra time in the yard."

Luther knew what Branson meant. A fellow Klansman, he wanted Luther to mess the boy up. Teach him what happened to 'coons who thought they could go after white meat. Branson was like that, always stirring the pot. Bribes and threats. That's how it worked in the joint. He was supposed to do the bidding of this asshole if he wanted a break. He watched Branson walk out of the library, still grinning. Luther's only consolation was that he wouldn't last long. Pendleton saw a huge turnover of hacks.

He shifted his gaze to Washington who snapped to attention like a soldier.

"This ain't no army," Luther growled.

The boy didn't move.

"You unnerstand English, boy?"

The boy nodded. He couldn't have been more than nineteen, Luther thought. Not too tall, and didn't look strong. Wooly hair, dark brown skin, and jet black eyes that contrasted with the whites around 'em like one of those black and white Holsteins you saw in the fields.

"Then stop standing there and go make yourself useful."

Washington examined the room with a worried glance. "What'cha want me to do? I cain't read."

Shit. Luther let out a sigh. He should have known it'd be something like this. Wait 'til he told the others. Most of them would refuse to even touch a book if they knew a black man's paws had been all over them. And now he had one in the library who couldn't even read. What the hell were they thinking?

Luther dug out an Oreo cookie he'd hidden in a desk drawer, bit into it, and glanced around. You really couldn't call the place a library. Just a windowless room with cinderblock walls. A couple of shelves held a bunch of Zane Greys, a few paperbacks with the covers ripped off, and one or two hard covers. Luther sat in front at a battered desk with an index card box on top. He had devised a check-out system for the books. Nothing fancy, just alphabetized by title, but he was proud of it. He marked down when the book was due back, although some men would hoard them in their cells, especially if a woman on the cover managed to slip through the censors. Still, if this moron couldn't read...

"Well, you just go on and sweep the floor."

"Yes, suh."

"Broom's in the corner behind the Zane Grey books."

The kid looked puzzled.

"Back there." Luther yanked a thumb toward the rear of the room. He finished the cookie and brushed the crumbs off his hands. Sweets went a long way toward filling the bitterness inside.

* * *

That afternoon in the cellhouse—inmates alternated between the yard and the cellhouse where they played cards and watched a TV bolted to the wall—Luther told his crowd, a group of five other inmates, what'd happened.

"Holy shit," Decker said. "They can't expect you to work with a nigger."

Luther flipped up his hands. "Branson says the warden and all... they're cranked up over this civil rights shit."

"Yeah, well, Branson says a lot of shit that ain't true."

Luther nodded. "He wants me to take care of the boy."

"Why don't he do it himself?" Billy said. "You seen what they did to those coloreds last month. Hung 'em upside down over the steps till they screamed for mercy."

Another man cut in. "Branson could be fixing to set you up, Luther. Don't do it."

Luther shook his head. "'Course not. I'm aiming to make parole. But it don't mean I don't want to."

"You still got your shank? Billy asked. "Whatever happens, you best be prepared."

Even in the joint, there were ways to have a weapon, and most had a home-made shank of some kind. Weakness was never tolerated.

"What do you care?" Decker said to Billy. "He'll be somebody's doll in Little Africa before long anyway."

"I heard the kid's not the sharpest knife in the drawer," Decker said. "Maybe they'll ship him to Logansport."

"He's slow, but he seems all there to me," Luther said.

"Well, he won't be for long."

That night before he fell asleep, Luther heard a dog baying outside. Long soulful howls. He wondered what kind of dog would hang around Pendleton.

● ● ●

For the first week Luther had Washington stack books, dust, and sweep, tasks that took less than an hour. What was he going to do with him the rest of the time? He ran a hand over his head. This had been a lousy idea, that's for sure, no matter who thought it up.

Two days later, Washington walked in with a shiner. He was limping, too. Luther, at his desk, didn't say a word. He had an idea what'd happened. The boy didn't say anything and went to the back of the room. Luther thought he'd pulled out the broom, but when a minute passed without the swish of straw on the floor, Luther turned around.

Washington was hunched on the floor, arms hugging his knees. He rocked back and forth.

"What are you doing, boy?"

Washington didn't say anything, but he didn't stop rocking. At the same time, a distant expression came across his face, like he was someplace else altogether. Luther began to wonder if the boy *was* retarded.

"You hear me, boy?"

Washington gazed at Luther with a blank stare. Luther stood up, thinking it was time to call in a guard, when the kid's expression turned from blank to scared, and he ducked his head between his knees.

"What the fuck are you doing?"

His response was muffled. "I been saying my prayers, suh."

Luther was taken aback. "Ain't no God in here, don't you know that?"

Washington raised his head and looked at Luther. "My mama says God is everywhere."

"Your mama don't know shit."

Washington averted his gaze. A minute later, a slow tear trickled down his cheek.

"You stop that, boy," Luther said gruffly. "Go get that broom and start sweeping."

Washington didn't move.

Luther walked over. "You got any brains at all?"

Washington scrambled off the floor, and backed away from Luther, panic spreading across his face. "Please, suh, don't hurt me. I a good boy. My mama says so."

Luther scowled. "Yeah, sure you are. Good enough to fuck a white girl, ain't you?"

Washington raised his arms in front of his face as if to ward off a blow. "I didn't do it."

"Sure you didn't." Contrary to what people saw in the movies, most men in prison never claimed to be innocent. Why bother? In the three years Luther had been at Pendleton only one guy maintained he didn't do the crime. And now this nigger. Luther shook his head and went back to his desk.

A few minutes later, the boy tapped Luther on the shoulder. Luther spun around. "What the fuck is it now?"

"I gots to pee," Washington said.

Luther yanked a thumb toward the back of the room. "There's a toilet in the corner."

"But there ain't no door."

"You never peed in front of other people?"

"It ain't that. I gotta go but it don't come out right. And when it do, it got red in it. So, please. Don't look. That's all."

Luther scratched his cheek. Someone must have worked him over real good.

* * *

The second week started off much the same as the first. Washington came to the library after breakfast, his face purple and swollen and bruised. He was limping worse than before.

"What you do, boy?"

"Nothin'."

"So why they beat you this time?"

"That hack say I look at 'im funny."

"Branson?"

146

Washington nodded.

Luther let out a breath. "You can't do that inside. Don't ever look a hack in the eye. If you have to, you keep your gaze flat. Like you don't see nothing." Luther made his eyes go empty. "Like this."

Washington cocked his head.

"And when you smile, you make it real small. Like this." Luther gave him a short quick smile. It felt more like a grimace to him, but the boy smiled back. "And when you go into a room, you pick a spot near the wall and try to make yourself invisible."

"Invisible? Like a fairy?" Washington folded his arms across his chest. "I ain't no fairy."

"Is that what they call you?"

"No, suh. They says I be like Emmett Till."

"You know who he was?"

"Yes, suh. He a colored boy accused of messing with a white girl. He was killed."

Luther nodded, surprised the boy knew his history.

"But they wrong. About me. Least ways."

"Spare me the bullshit. We're all in here because of something."

"What you do?"

Luther didn't say anything for a minute. Then, "I lynched a nigger."

Washington gazed at him. "He dead?"

"Uh huh." Luther let it sink in. "So you listen up. You lie to me I'll make sure you never come back to this room. You'll get some job you ain't gonna like. See, you're on shaky ground. If the hacks don't get you, the inmates will." He paused. "And don't keep calling me 'sir,' you hear?"

Washington was quiet. Then he looked up at Luther. "She done lied. Up there on the stand."

"Who?"

"Miss Mary Jane Barber."

Something stirred in Luther. Maybe it was Washington's insistence that he was innocent. Or maybe it was the desperation in his eyes. Or maybe it was the fact that he didn't look strong enough to swat a fly, much less rape a woman.

"Man, I wish I had more Oreos." Luther sat back down at his desk.

"Oreos? Dem cookies you was eating?"

Luther nodded. Then he found himself saying, "Tell me what happened."

Washington's eyes widened, as if he hadn't expected Luther to ask. He came over and squatted by Luther's desk. "See, I had this job in a grocery store back home. I was a bagger," he said proudly. "Hadda take three buses to get there. Store's in the white part of town. But I never missed a day."

Luther grunted.

"Sometimes they let me do other stuff. I knows my numbers. I wanted to be on cash register one day. That was my dream." He shifted. "So one day I'm on parking lot duty, which means I load bags into cars. Miss Mary Jane Barber come out of the store with lots. I done help her load the car. She give me a whole dollar." He almost smiled.

"But when I get home that night, the police there, and they take me to jail. Say I followed her home, made her go into her house, and raped her. But it weren't me, Mr. Luther."

"You sayin' she made it up?"

"Yeah. But she got witnesses. They swear they see me there. I dunno who dey saw, but it weren't me. Then we goes to trial and I gets convicted."

* * *

At lunch in the chow hall later that day, Luther didn't say much. Inmates ate in shifts of five hundred. They could sit wherever they wanted, but whites and blacks never sat together. Didn't matter much, since they only got fifteen minutes to wolf down the greasy meat and crap they called vegetables. Luther listened to his pals guffawing, talking about the latest shanks they'd made, and what they were going to buy at the commissary when they got their paychecks, even though the checks never were more than a couple of bucks. After a while Decker, who was across the table, leaned forward.

"Why you so quiet, Luther?"

He waved a hand. "Just thinking." Luther knew better than to say anything in public, or what passed for public in pop. Most inmates put on a special kind of armor in the joint. If you were smart, you were always watching, alert to hacks, wheeler-dealers, or other inmates who wanted you to be worse off than them. Luther was always on guard. But Wendell Washington didn't have that armor. He was just a kid. Probably shouldn't even be in the population. He couldn't read and barely knew his numbers. The schemes of other men were beyond his grasp.

The conversation shifted to rumors about the hacks and Little Africa. Word was the guards had something planned. Something that would go down in a few days.

Luther looked up. "What is it?"

"Who cares?" Billy snorted.

* * *

Back in the library that afternoon, Luther asked, "So why did you never learn your letters?"

"It got too fast for me in school. My mama said the Lord'd look out for me. That He had a plan."

Luther harrumphed. "You ain't gonna be any help to me here unless you learn to read. You gotta file stuff and put books back on the shelves where they belong. You can't do that unless you know your letters." He hesitated. "You wanna learn?"

"You gonna learn me?" Luther could see the anticipation building in Washington's eyes.

"You gonna have to work real hard." Luther put on a stern face.

"I don't mind, suh. I mean, Mister Luther."

Luther swung his chair around. "Okay. The first thing you gotta learn is the alphabet. You know what that is?"

"Not really."

"You know how to count, though."

Washington nodded. "I uses my fingers. And toes."

"Well the alphabet is letters, and there's only twenty-six of 'em. But the way you put 'em together makes all the words in the world."

Washington grinned. "Just twenty-six?"

"That's right. Six more than your fingers and toes together. You think you can learn 'em?"

Washington furrowed his brow. "I surely thinks so."

Luther rubbed his forehead. What the hell was he doing? He cleared his throat. "Well I know a way for you to learn 'em, but you can't tell no one. It's a secret, unnerstand?"

Washington was all eager curiosity.

"There's this song they teach little kids in school..." Luther taught him the alphabet song and printed the letters on a sheet of paper.

By the end of the day, Washington knew the song by heart. But figuring out the letters was something else. It would take time, Luther knew. Before they closed up for the day, he warned him again.

"Now, you don't ever sing this out loud when you're not in here, you get it?"

"Why not?"

"The men—in pop—and the hacks... they won't get it."

Two weeks later Washington knew his letters and could pick them out of books. So Luther began to teach him the sounds letters made. He figured it was easier to start with consonants, but it was slow going. It took the better part of a month to get him to understand the connection, but once he did, the kid's comprehension zoomed up.

At one point Washington looked up from the Zane Grey he had been studying. "How come when you read, you don't make no sounds?"

"How do you know I don't?"

"I seen you read. You quiet. Not like me."

"I am making sounds. I just make them in my head."

Wendell frowned. "In your head?"

"I pretend the sounds. And when you know them well, the letters turns into words."

"How?"

"Here." Luther took the book from Wendell and pointed to the words on the page. As he did, he sounded them out slowly. "That's what I do in my head."

Wendell's eyes darted from the page to Luther's face, then back to the page. A moment later, those eyes grew as big as plates, and he smiled so wide that his teeth shone.

Luther smiled too. He couldn't help himself. The kid got it.

"Hey!" A voice barked from outside.

Luther, whose back was to the library door, turned around. His pulse started to race. No one came to the library in the middle of the day.

Branson leaned against the door jam, one hand on his hip, the other on his holster. His gaze, hard and flat, went from Luther to Washington. "The fuck you doing, Luther?"

"Nothing," Luther lied.

Washington looked confused.

"You making him your doll?"

"No sir," Luther said, making sure he emphasized the word "sir."

Branson shifted and rubbed his hand across his nose. "Uh-huh." He crossed his arms. "I guess we'll see." Then he turned and ambled away, as if he had all the time in the world.

Washington followed him with his eyes. "I don't like him much."

"Nobody does."

"Why you lie to him?"

"You wouldn't understand." Luther said. "Crap. I do want some Oreos. But I don't get paid for another three days."

* * *

Luther didn't see Washington over the next couple of days. He didn't know where he was, didn't know if he'd be back. But that's how it was at Pendleton. The first couple of days felt odd and empty, but then Luther adjusted. In fact, he had almost forgotten about him when Washington showed up.

He looked worse than before. One eye was swollen shut. His right arm was in a cast. There were bandages on his neck. He looked like he'd been hit with a tire iron.

"What happened?" Luther asked.

Washington shook his head.

He'd learned.

Then Washington reached into his pocket took out a package of Oreos, one of the four-packs. Luther's mouth fell open, and he jerked his head back. "What's this?"

"You the first white man ever hep me, Mister Luther. Maybe the first man ever. I wants to thank you."

Luther was quiet for a moment. Then, "Don't you go telling that to anyone. They hear you talk like that, they'll come after you again."

"Why?" Washington threw him a puzzled glance.

"It's just the way it is. Like I said before, don't give anyone a reason to pick on you."

Washington looked down, like a goddammed puppy hanging his head.

"What is it, boy?"

"I already done told."

"Who?"

"Guy who got me dose cookies. Told 'im I was learning to read. And a white man learning me."

"Shit."

"But dat make no sense, Mister Luther. God don't want it like that."

"Like I told you, there ain't no God in this place."

That night, Luther couldn't sleep. Strong gusts of wind grabbed the prison walls, carrying the howl of the dog in their wake. Damned hound must be tracking a possum, he thought. Or a skunk. Luther heaved a breath. Had he been playing God?

* * *

Next morning when Luther got to the library, the unopened package of Oreos lay on his desk. But Washington wasn't there. In fact, he never showed up. Luther learned why at lunch. Washington had tried to escape, the hacks said. It happened a lot more than people on the outside thought. The guards caught him, then penned him up like the animal he was, with a rope around his neck. How it got tangled up and choked him no one knew, but come morning Washington was dead.

"No big deal," Decker said. "Shit like that happens."

Billy laughed. "Especially in Little Africa."

Luther kept his mouth shut. He went back to the library and picked up the package of cookies. He'd never thanked Washington for them. He slid the cookies in a drawer, his throat thick, the back of his eyes hot. He couldn't open the package. He knew he never would.

Karen Fonville usually writes romance. She's ventured into mystery this time, with spectacular results.

About this story, she writes, "My research into rationing in WWII yielded some interesting facts, such as a black market in England strictly centered on rationed items. I played with that aspect for a while, but canning has fascinated me since I was a child watching my own mother sterilize mason jars before using them. In a way, this story is in memory of her efforts and in honor of her life."

———————

Rationing

Karen Fonville

1

The heat of the day wilted the starch right out of me. Bees buzzed outside in the meadow, and flies zoomed past through the open window. It was the dog days of summer and I couldn't hate it more.

Ma was still working, so the kids and I were taking up the slack. The stove bubbled with the peaches from the orchard. Ma and I had gotten this part ready last night. Today, we were supposed to finish the canning, boil the jars and seal them up. Mrs. Percy, the preacher's wife, was expecting 30 quarts before the weekend. Hopefully, that would give us enough money to buy our pound of meat for the family meals next week.

Jessie sat at the table shelling beans for our next project as Sally and Thomas came chasing through the kitchen screaming and giggling at full volume. "Stop, y'all. We don't need..."

Thomas hit the metal table the stack of jars was on, and they all went down, boy and jars. Glass flew everywhere. I felt a sting as a shard hit my knee.

With big eyes, Thomas looked at the mess around on the floor. When his eyes hit the blood on my leg, he shouted and took off out the window. I guess he figured he was in trouble.

Jessie screamed and jumped up, knocking the bowl of beans over on the floor, Sally started bawling, and I shouted.

"OUT! All of you, OUT!"

At thirteen, I was in charge. Now, we were all in trouble. I bit my lip, trying hard not to cry.

Jessie stopped screaming and grabbed the broom. She's a good girl, and usually pitches right in. I used a towel to stop the flow of bright red blood down my leg, while surveying the mess. The clink and tinkle of broken glass being swept up filled the room.

Once the blood stopped flowing, I knelt on the floor and helped her. We separated out the whole ones. Fully half of the jars were shattered. And the others might have cracks I couldn't see. We couldn't trust them to hold while boiling. We'd have to get new jars.

Just what we needed. Another expense.

Didn't look like we'd have meat this week, either.

* * *

I left Jessie in charge while I went to the store. She had Thomas and Sally singing while they helped clean up before I'd even gotten out the door. Eleven was a magical age.

The sun was half way through the afternoon sky, and Ma wouldn't be home for hours yet. I grabbed the ration books and headed into town. Maybe I could trade for some of the Bell jars we'd need. My mind shifted through the neighbors, trying to come up with options, thinking who'd need an extra pair of hands, who might have company coming and need more ration stamps. These days, trading was just about the only way to get anything.

The government was cracking down on black market activities, but here in the country, barter was how we'd gotten along during the depression. It served us in good stead now, too.

The General store is the gathering place in our town. Mayor Bentley would like to believe the gathering place was his new city building, but that's not so. People don't feel comfortable there. They look for a place to feel at home. The General Store has the lunch counter, and the barrels that everyone sits on. Some people talk about the Dewdrop Inn as a gathering place, and that's true if you like liquor. For the family, though, the General Store almost beats out the church.

The store was crowded when I got there, mostly men, which was strange this time of day. Mr. Crowder, old Mr. Smith, and Sheriff Baines were whispering around the pickle barrel. The checker game on the Pork Rinds barrel was forgotten as Mr. Barnes and Mr. Settles listened to Sheriff Baines, and four of the town's ladies were holding court by the cloth goods.

The doorbell jangled when I walked in, and a hush fell over them until they saw who I was. Then the whispering and talking started up again while I went to look at the canning stock.

"I tell you the Jerries did it." Old Mr. Smith's whisper nearly broke my eardrum. He took his purchases to the counter, followed by Mr. Crowder and Sheriff Baines.

"Hush, Wilbur, and you don't know that." Mr. Crowder tapped Mr. Smith on the arm. "The police will find it all out, and there won't be anyone we know that did it."

Sheriff Baines nodded. "When we get it all figured out, I'm sure we'll find that one of the tramps did it." He shifted the dead cigar in his mouth, and drew a match from the box on the counter. An odor of sulfur filled the air as he struck the match, and then lit his stogie. Clouds of blue smoke billowed around the sheriff as he puffed. The clerk and Mr. Smith haggled some, cause Mr. Smith's ration stamps weren't in his stamp book. At a nod from the Sheriff, the clerk finally took the loose coupons.

I wondered what they were talking about. Then, figuring I'd hear soon enough, I began calculating how many stamps and how much money I'd need to replace those jars. Fifteen cents a dozen and 41 points, so figure 45 cents and 123 points. No way did I have enough of either.

I looked at the crowd around me. Maybe Mrs. Lawson needed some help. I eased closer to the cloth goods.

"—head bashed in. George says it made the most horrible mess. I just can't imagine who'd do something like that, even to..." At that point, Mrs. Baines saw me coming. "Amanda Stevens, don't you know it's impolite to eavesdrop on your elders?" Mrs. Lawson and Mrs. Percy turned to watch me too. The frosty tone and blazing eyes Mrs. Baines aimed my way would be enough to embarrass someone who felt guilty, but since I wasn't trying to listen to their silly old conversation, I refused to let it embarrass me.

"Good afternoon, Mrs. Baines, Mrs. Lawson, Mrs. Percy. I was wondering if you had a need for an extra pair of hands, or two, that my sister and I might supply?" If I'd had a hat, I'd have held it in my hands.

Mrs. Percy had a tear in her eye, which she quickly wiped away. "What kind of help are you offering, dear?"

"Oh, any kind, ma'am. Cleaning, cooking, I'd offer to sew something, but I have to admit I can't sew straight to save my life."

The ladies laughed with me, a high pitched tittering that shook the rafters and caused the menfolk to stop talking themselves.

With a red face, Mrs. Lawson said, "Tomorrow I'll need some help with the laundry. I can pay ten cents if that will help."

"Thank you kindly, ma'am. I'll be much obliged for the work." With a promise to be there by eight o'clock in the morning, I placed an order with Mr. Johnson for the jars.

Then I left to find some more work. I headed back toward home, stopping at every house. Nothing. So, I went on down the lane past our house. Each house looked like ours, paint peeling, yards needing trimming, and broken things waiting for new parts. Waiting for men who had yet to come home from war. In some cases, they never would. Like my dad.

Five houses past the Mayor's house was the German house. That's what we called it, although Mrs. Schmidt called herself an American. She and her husband had moved here during the Depression, before Mr. Hitler tried to take over the world. To hear Ma tell it, Mr. and Mrs. Schmidt started a bakery and made lots of friends. Mr. Schmidt also made ale, but we didn't talk about that.

When the War broke out, some government men came and took Mr. Schmidt away. I guess they thought he'd learn a lot of government secrets here in Tennessee. At first, everyone here was real upset. Like the government didn't know what they was doing taking Mr. Schmidt off like that. But that changed after Pearl Harbor. People stopped going to the bakery, and Mrs. Schmidt had to close it. Then, things started happening.

Her car broke down, when it had been new just the year before. Her house got more damage on the sides of it than anyone else's when the spring storms hit. The gate to the chicken coop slid open, letting some wild dogs in. Lots of things that you couldn't point to meanness but were sure that was the root of it just the same.

I yanked up my courage and walked up to her door, painted a pretty blue color that was starting to fade. No one else had a blue door, and I liked it. I knocked, and it sounded as if it echoed, like the house was empty. No one answered, and I went around back, figuring she might be out back in the chicken coop.

The back yard was quiet, except for the buzz of some flies. I started to get spooked. Even if Mrs. Schmidt wasn't around, those chickens should be making noise. I didn't see any movement at all, and I had just started to turn around when the wind shifted.

An odor hit me so hard, it made my eyes water. It was the smell of death, and I coughed with it, trying hard not to gag. The only thing for it was to breathe through my mouth instead of my nose.

I gulped back the bile in my throat, and resolutely started forward. No way could I leave now. I had to know was it Mrs. Schmidt. Easing forward, I tested the coop door. It was still latched, so I opened it and slid inside. My heart pounded in my chest so hard I could feel my pulse in my fingertips. I wanted to be anywhere but there.

Around the edge of the door I peered, until I saw a black sturdy shoe attached to gray flesh lying on the floor of the chicken coop.

2

Finding Mrs. Schmidt and her hundred dead chickens didn't help me with our problem. It only made it worse.

Sheriff Baines and his men asked me questions at the Sheriff's office until it was eight o'clock and I was near starved. Ma stayed with me some of the time, they'd called her home from the factory. Then she had to go do the canning I was supposed to have done, and I was left with those hard-eyed men.

I could see that Sheriff Baines was getting very upset with my crying, but I couldn't help it. I kept seeing Mrs. Schmidt with the ax sticking out of her chest. I swallowed, determined not to lose my lunch. "That should not happen to anyone."

"No," he agreed. "It shouldn't. Tell me again, why you went to see Mrs. Schmidt today."

I took a deep breath. "Sometimes I get some work from her. I came to see if she had any for me today."

"And what did you do when you found her?"

"I came to get you as fast as I could."

"What did you find in the house?" His voice was silky, all of a sudden. He tried to look like he wasn't interested, like the answer wasn't important, but the vein in the side of his temple throbbed.

"I didn't go into the house. I don't go into ANYONE'S house without an invitation."

He was looking at me funny. I rubbed my hands on my pants and shifted in the hard chair. "Why? Did someone go into her house?"

Deputy Miller came in and whispered in the Sheriff's ear. We play with Deputy Miller's daughter, Tilda, sometimes. I've never seen him like this, his brown hair standing on end, and huge sweat stains under his armpits. His face was grey, too, like mine felt.

Sheriff Baines followed him out the door and closed it. Five minutes later, they still weren't back. I counted the broken tiles on the ceiling—fifteen. Then I counted the black tiles on the floor—twenty-three. I'd just started counting the white tiles—anything to keep from thinking about poor Mrs. Schmidt—when he came back in and perched on the edge of his huge wooden desk.

"How often did you get work with Mrs. Schmidt, Amanda?"

I gave it some careful thought. "Not often. Maybe once or twice a month. Mostly cleaning, although sometimes, when she went to the county seat, she'd have us take care of the chickens."

"Did she pay you well?"

I watched his eyes. They were calmer now, but still full of the sadness that spoke of death.

"Yes, sir, I guess she paid just about like everyone else. Sometimes in barter, sometimes with cash."

"Would you know enough about her house to know if something was missing?" Sheriff Baines leaned forward slightly.

"I don't know. Maybe. Depends on what it is." I swallowed hard, not sure if that was the answer he was looking for or not.

* * *

We went back out to Mrs. Schmidt's house the next morning. Sheriff Baines, Deputy Miller, Ma and me. The faded blue door stood open when we got there, and some of Sheriff's men were coming out. Pete Stalls had the camera and the burnt flash bulbs, stinking up the place as he walked by.

"Sheriff, it's all yours. Once I get these developed, I'll compare them to the others and let you know."

Sheriff Baines nodded and then led us inside. We stopped in the doorway and stared. Ma gasped.

Mrs. Schmidt kept a neat home, everything in its place. She even washed the front porch once a week. I always felt better when she invited me in.

She would not have gone to the store leaving the house the way it looked now.

I turned on Sheriff Baines. "WHAT DID YOU DO? Why did you tear her house up? I know you think her husband was a spy for the Jerries, but she wasn't and you had no right to do this to her house."

Ma put her hand on my shoulder, to comfort me, but I also felt her nodding.

"Sheriff, my daughter is right. Gertrude Schmidt would never have left her house this way." She straightened her shoulders as if to dare him to disagree.

"Ma'am, I believe you. We need to determine if there's anything missing. We don't think so, but we have never been in the house. Could you and your daughter see?"

Ma and I shared a glance and nodded. "But Sheriff, we'll have to put everything back in its place," I told him. "Would that be all right?"

Sheriff Baines slowly nodded. "That's why I had the pictures taken. So we can prove the extent of the disruption."

We worked painstakingly throughout the day. Ma worried at being off work, but Sheriff Baines promised to make it right with her bosses. By the end of the day, we had most everything back in place, or near as made no difference. But we couldn't figure it out. Not at all.

We went home, exhausted, and had a meager dinner of vegetables from our garden—lima beans and carrots and corn with some corn bread. We still couldn't afford the meat. Ma took the leftovers and put them away to add to the stew when we could get meat. I heard her muttering to herself about the hundred dead and rotten chickens at Mrs. Schmidt's house. I'm sure she wasn't the only mother thinking about that.

3

Over the next few days, I noticed that anytime I went to town, one of the deputies followed me around from place to place. They even tried to make it seem like they weren't interested in me or in what I was doing, but that didn't work.

"Ma, why do they follow me like that?" We were in the shade on the back porch, shelling peas from the Victory garden.

"I don't know, Amanda, but I wouldn't worry 'bout it so. More'n likely they're just spooked cause they didn't know Mrs. Schmidt was dead for three days." Ma's fingers flew through those pea pods like lightning. Most times, shelling took on the slow steady speed of the rocker in the evening, but tonight hers was on fire.

Snap, snap, snap.

All day long, I'd been thinking—about Mrs. Schmidt and about what I'd heard at the store before I found her. Jessie, Thomas and Sally were weeding in the garden and picking some of the beans, so now was a good time to ask. "Ma, did someone else die?"

The rocker stopped rocking as Ma looked at me, her eyes dark pools in the fading light. "What do you mean, die?"

I told her about hearing Mrs. Baines and the other ladies when I went to price the jars, and about old Mr. Smith's assertion that it was the Jerries that did it—whatever it was.

She flinched, and closed her eyes. With a deep breath, she started rocking again, slower this time, and her hands went back to breaking the beans. Crack, crack, crack.

"You hear too much, Amanda." She opened her eyes, with a small smile. "And you pay attention when it is MOST inconvenient. They found Mr. Tannenbaum the day before you found Mrs. Schmidt. He'd been dead for several days, too."

I put down the bowl of beans I was snapping and climbed on the porch railing in front of her. I wanted to see her eyes clear. "Ma, we ain't never had any murders here, have we? And now we got two in a week?"

Ma sighed. "Don't say 'ain't', Amanda. It's not proper. You're right, though. It's mighty peculiar. Now, let's go start these beans for supper."

* * *

We got the peaches finished finally. Thomas and I took the thirty quarts to Mrs. Percy on Monday. She paid us extra, even though she didn't have to, cause she'd heard we had to buy new Bell jars.

Mrs. Baines showed up as we left, all excited. "Mrs. Percy, did you hear? They've arrested Morris Smith, old Wilbur's son."

Mrs. Percy finished showing Thomas and me out the door before we could hear anymore. I figured she was watching, so we went on out the gate, and then circled back. Folks don't want us kids knowing what's what most of the time. But I needed to know. I had a funny feeling about Morris.

I got to the parlor window just as Mrs. Baines was finishing up. "They say he did it for the ration stamps. He'd wanted some new shoes, and Mr. Tannenbaum wouldn't give him a break on the ration stamps. I think he thought the blame would fall on someone like Mrs. Schmidt, since Mr. Tannenbaum was Jewish. And then, when he needed some more, he thought no one would care about Mrs. Schmidt, her being German and all. Can you believe it?" She waved her handkerchief in the air, and then dabbed her eyes. "That poor woman. Who'd really believe that she would or could do anything so heinous to Mr. Tannenbaum? Did they even know each other?"

"Land's sakes. What's this world coming to? And Morris is as American as anyone else." Mrs. Percy picked up a hand fan beside her, and swatted furiously at the air.

"Everyone knows that if he wasn't 4F, Morris would be out there fighting too. At least, he always spouted that he would!"

I thought about old Mr. Smith and wondered what he would do now that Morris was in jail.

Thomas tugged on my sleeve. "Can we go home now?" he whispered. "I'm hungry."

We finally had enough money to get the meat for dinner. Time to be on our way, for sure.

Karen L. Abrahamson writes marvelous fiction in every genre she tackles. So far, she's tackled romance, fantasy and mystery. Her fantastic Cartographer Universe has garnered praise for its uniqueness and depth. In addition, Karen's an adventure traveler who blogs about her solo visits to countries around the globe. You can read those blogs and more at karenlabrahamson.com.

Once upon a time, Karen worked as a Family Court Counselor in her native Canada. Those experiences inspired this story.

Neutrality

Karen L. Abrahamson

The word came just as I was going to court, in the form of a pink spiral of paper thrust into my hand by the sweet-young-thing court clerk. She then turned with a perky smile for the lawyer next to me and tottered away on her platform shoes back towards the main court office. The lawyer was young, tall, good looking and most of all, male. Me, I was a forty-something family court counselor. So not her type.

It was 9:30 and the lino-floored hallway loomed full of well-dressed lawyers in bad-news-hushed conversation with their Applicant and Respondent clients. The quiet voices seemed to rustle around the baseboards like frantic mice and the air carried the noxious odor of sweaty fear. Some of the clients wore an omnipresent defeat as if they'd subconsciously already conceded the battle that waited beyond the courtroom doors. And these were battles that went to the death—the no-holds-barred battles of custody and access. Me?

Think of me as a slightly overweight Solomon. I'm the neutral one who makes the courtroom recommendations.

I simply accepted the message and slipped inside the courtroom as the call to order occurred. I stood with the others at the back of the wood-paneled room, inhaling the poison and angry perfume off the heated bodies. Family Court. It sounds so pleasant. As if families could just sit themselves down and come to some pleasant agreement. But that wasn't the case. The cases in this room were the hardest, the roughest. The cases that tried every neutral bone in my body, for who do you recommend get care and custody of a child when neither parent is fit for the job and when children cared for by the state are passed from stranger to stranger as if they were homeless?

I knew. I'd done enough investigations into who should have custody of a child and who should visit.

Judge McHale swept his red and black robes behind him and seated himself on the walnut grained bench that loomed judgment. Of course the walnut wasn't any more real than the justice he had to give out. Family Court is like that, sort of a thin veneer of justice pasted on the jumbled plasterboard remains of a family. But McHale tried, unlike other Provincial Court judges sentenced to preside over family court. At least this one tried.

He was an older man, nearing retirement, his blonde hair faded grey and gone thin at the top. His body bulking out around the belly as if to make up for the hair loss. But the best thing about him was his eyes. They were kind and he looked like he cared. I even think it was mostly for the kids.

He nodded at the lawyers and at me and then the court clerk called the first case. I looked down at the message.

Casey Turner filled the 'to' slot. That was me.

Merissa Sandu, filled the 'from' slot. She was the lawyer for the Applicant in the case I was here on. Come to think of it, it wasn't like Merissa not to be here right on time. I craned my neck around looking for Rick Hunt, her client, and his unrepresented ex-wife respondent, Natalie Hunt, or as she was known on the street, *Mouse.* Neither was present and that didn't bode well, though perhaps wasn't unexpected. Neither of them was exactly reliable. Then I read on and got the gist of just how bad it was.

Rick in hospital—serious. Natalie in custody. Set case over for 48 hours to sort this out.

What the heck? A little bead of cold sweat ran down my back. I wasn't a lawyer. I didn't work for Merissa Sandhu's firm. I was just the government-employed Family Counselor who had done the custody and access study after mediation failed.

Judge McHale was referring the unhappy looking thirty-something couple before him to mediation, the lawyers thanked him, and I was pleased that I wasn't doing mediation anymore. This looked like a bad one, the two parties both with their heels dug into hating the other for whatever discord their family was in. She started for the rear of the courtroom first, then her husband went after her, hands clenched as if he'd held a dagger he would use it. Have fun with that one, I thought to the mediation staff. At least in my world I don't have to see them together.

But then Judge McHale looked in my direction. "Ms. Turner, I believe your case is next on the docket but we appear to be missing a lawyer and both our parties. Can you shed any light on the situation?"

I stepped forward to answer, carefully composing words for the courtroom.

"Your honor we're here, on behalf of our daughter. She's been detained elsewhere."

I spun around at the unexpected voices and recognized Natalie Hunt's parents, Quinn and Jeffrey McGuire, standing at the back of the room. They weren't supposed to be here, but I guess they couldn't help themselves.

I should have seen them when I first came in; they were hard to miss. Jeffrey McGuire had a buzz cut head, dark determined eyes, and stood about six foot six. He was an ex-cop from Vancouver City Police and still had the muscle across his shoulders, and the slow-hipped way of moving that went with years of walking the beat. Quinn, on the other hand, was physically an older version of her dark-haired daughter: just as slight of build at no more than five foot four, with the same overlong nose and darting eyes like a bird. There the similarity between mother and daughter ended. Where Natalie's body and face held the exhausted defeat of her lifestyle as a heroin addict and prostitute, Quinn showed the restless fire of the endlessly driven. I had to wonder what role Quinn had played in driving her daughter's collapse into the drug addict's oblivion. When I'd interviewed Quinn McGuire she'd been one of the most contrite mothers I'd ever known.

But the 'why' of how people get to where they do doesn't really matter in my line of work. My focus is reporting the facts of *what is.*

As I turned back to McHale I felt the weight of Quinn's stare on my back and a trickle of sweat run between my breasts. The woman was something and so was her husband. Formidable, sprang to mind.

"Your Honor, I've just received word from Council that the Applicant is in the hospital. I don't have the details, but I also understand that the Respondent, Ms. Hunt has, as Mr. McGuire put it, been detained. Council requests the matter be set over for 48 hours."

I left it there, but held my breath. McHale was an old pro. He could read between the lines, but he could also get pissed off enough to make an order *in absentia.*

A small flicker of a frown crossed McHale's face. He didn't like matters not to proceed as planned and he'd like it even less if a family court matter had led to violence.

"This is highly irregular, Ms. Turner. Please convey to Council that in future they should not expect a neutral Family Justice Counselor to do their job."

I nodded. My sentiment exactly. Neutrality's my reputation and they pay me well for it. I turned and left the court.

* * *

The case of Rick and Natalie Hunt was the usual sad tale of men and women trying to live together. My investigation and report to the court showed that Rick was a self-employed plumber. He worked hard for a living and had thrown himself into trying to get a business running after spending his twenties running wild on the bar scene in downtown Vancouver. He admitted chipping a little H and to experimenting with cocaine, but all of that, he claimed, was behind him and had been behind him since his marriage and the birth of his five-year-old daughter, Savanna. Too bad it wasn't all quite true because a little bird told me Rick was still using—sporadically, yes. But still.

Rick had met Natalie during his wild days. They'd both hung at the same grunge bars in the downtown eastside—Rick for relaxation and Natalie looking for the tricks she was pulling to pay for university tuition. At least that was the story she always told and that she told me when I interviewed her in her parent's upscale home. University is pricey these days. Apparently so pricey that Natalie has been saving up for at least ten years and still has taken no steps to enroll. At the time of the interview she'd said she'd been through addiction treatment and was clean.

Of course that was the fourth time she'd been through treatment and when we talked about her time on the street she got this faraway dreamy look in her eyes that most junkies-on-hiatus have. She'd be back on the streets soon enough if I was any judge of character. She just needed this custody and access thing to be done with first. Because the one thing I would say about Natalie, she did love her daughter.

She was a rotten mother most of the time, fixing while golden-haired Savanna was playing in the next room and going out to turn tricks and leaving Savanna alone, but her daughter meant something to her. She talked about times when things would be better and they'd have the white picket-fenced house and they'd laugh and play and sing together as if Savanna would be five years old forever. But she held on fierce to her dream whenever we talked of Savanna possibly going to live with her father. She wasn't prepared to give up her dream.

And so the couple failed at mediation. They wanted the court to make the decision for them and neither would back down in their dogged fight for their daughter. Like ships taking on water, there were always going to be times when Natalie or Rick were going to go under. That was the sad thing. Neither one was good for their daughter.

The question I had to answer was which would be better.

When I got back to my office I sank down in my desk chair and considered the three additional messages from Merissa updating me on Rick's condition. The chair shrilled each time I picked up the messages, each one more dire than the last. When I finally reached her by phone, Merissa, bless her heart, broke down crying. Not the hard fighting lawyer at all. This case had gotten to her, too. There was always one.

"He's gone, Casey. The bastards did him in good."

I knew what gone meant. To Rick. To the case. To the world. I inhaled the verbena potpourri I used to hide the omnipresent scent of sour breath and tears. "Hold on a minute. All I've got is a cryptic note that he's in the hospital and Natalie's been picked up. What the hell happened?"

There came a moment of choked-back sobbing and then the sound of deep swallowed breath. "I'm sorry. It's just this one got to me, you know. I liked Rick. He was trying. I understood his desire to keep his daughter safe and I appreciated his willingness to fight for that."

And I could understand that; I had liked Rick, too, as far as it went. "So what happened?"

"He was called out on a job, but it must have been a set-up. He went out to his truck in his garage where someone was waiting for him. His neighbors found him this morning with blood everywhere. He'd been knifed. The EMTs got him to the hospital, but apparently he never really stood a fighting chance. They tried to put him back together but it didn't work."

Another sob while I thought about all the families I'd investigated over the years. They were like a long line of humpty dumpties and none of them were ever going to get put back together again. I couldn't cry about Rick anymore than I could cry for the others. Damned parents fighting each other and using their kids as weapons. The flipping courts played right into it.

"Where does Natalie fit into this?" I asked. "Why's she in jail?"

"I hear the cops like her for it. She might not have plunged the knife herself, but she had the street connections and just last night she was seen at Rick's place. Apparently they got into a huge argument about custody and the cops had to be called because of the noise."

Typical Natalie. She never could do anything low-key—at least that was what Quinn said. I thought a moment longer. "So what happens now?"

Merissa sniffled a little and then a deep breath came through the phone. "I guess it's over," said quiet and just a little too sad.

"So mom just takes the kid then?"

"I guess."

A sick feeling hit the pit of my stomach and I felt like retching all over the puke-brown carpet in my stupid pale-green office. "You guess? You guess? You let that little girl go with her mother she's going to be in government care in a matter of days."

"And welfare will place the child with her grandparents."

"Possibly," I said.

"Yeah. Possibly."

"Or they could just believe Natalie is cleaning up her act and leave Savanna with her."

"Yes." Merissa sighed. "They could do that, too. They have before. Listen, I really have to be going, Casey. It was nice working with you on this case."

And then she hung up and I sat there feeling violently ill, or maybe just plain violent at the idiocy of the system. I took a long look out my office window at the small pine tree growing in the garden. I'd planted it there, five years before after tearing it from a back corner of my garden where it didn't have any room to grow. Here it had filled out and grown about two feet taller—my legacy to the court house.

I inhaled deeply and let the rush of air out my nose calm me. There was no place for anger at Savanna's situation. I was neutral.

I was.

* * *

And I was there in criminal court the day that Natalie was brought in to have her bail hearing. A sadder place you didn't want to see. Where family court reeked of anger and fear and defeat, here it was all about despair and no one looked more desperate than Natalie Hunt.

She sat hunched in her spindle-backed chair beside her legal aid lawyer, her black hair a tangle around her face, her arms skinny and scabbed again as if all the badness in her veins had tried to come out overnight. She'd been chipping again, it was pretty clear to see.

It didn't go well for her, though for me it went fine. No matter that she had parents who could offer her a stable place to live. No matter that she had a child. What mattered was that she had a record for drugs and solicitation. She'd been known, before meeting Rick, to travel to the US and Calgary to ply her trade. The Criminal Court judge just listened to Crown Counsel's litany of past transgressions and Defense didn't stand a chance. Natalie was bound over in custody. The judge's gavel rang out nicely, hardwood on hardwood bench.

As the Sheriffs were leading her out of the glare of the court, she caught sight of me and an incandescent ray of hope entered her gaze.

It was wrong, but I couldn't help myself.

I went to see her. Court holding cells are painted grey. Grey floor, grey walls and ceilings and in Natalie's case it seemed they'd painted her flesh as well. In the puke-scented cellblock she sat on the edge of an iron cot with a musty grey vinyl mattress and looked at me out of frightened eyes the color of mud. Her hands shifted and moved like two frightened, trapped animals as she scratched, scratched, scratched at her forearms and at her thighs.

"Hey," I said, through the bars. "How are you doing?"

"How's it look?" She said bitterly and shook her head. "This isn't me. I wouldn't kill Rick. They've got it all wrong."

"I guess you'll have to prove it in court," I said.

Then her eyes filled with tears and she buried her face in her hands. "What's going to happen, Casey? What about me and Savanna? What about our dreams?"

Her dream. It was sad really. She hadn't a hope in hell of ever achieving that dream. At least not in this lifetime.

"The court is going to have to make some sort of finding, Natalie. It has to make a decision that'll be in Savanna's best interests."

"But I'm her mother. I'm her best interests!" Her voice rose and I could smell the sour coffee and cold toast she'd had for breakfast in custody. "The court has to find for me. She hasn't got anyone else!" there was panic in the movement of her hands now. Those ragged fingernails were digging through the fabric of her orange prison uniform.

"Well she doesn't have Rick anymore, that's for sure. She'll probably end up a ward of the state."

She glanced up sharply. "It wasn't me who killed Rick. I loved Rick once upon a time. I could never hurt Rick."

Which was a lie and we both knew it. She'd been trying to crush his balls in her hand since the whole separation began. She had even threatened to take Savanna and run.

But I let the lie sour the air between us and the sounds of the other prisoners disappeared so I swear I could hear her quick breaths and the serious pounding of her heart. "There *is* one thing we could do," I said into the quiet. "So the state doesn't take her."

She looked up at me with another of those faint glimmers of hope so I could almost feel sorry for her. Could almost feel guilt.

* * *

It wasn't really that hard.

As a Family Court Counselor I could draw up papers for custody and access when the parties were in agreement. I stayed late at the office the day I visited Natalie, and really it didn't take that long to write up a Consent Agreement between Natalie and her parents. Quinn and Jeffrey McGuire would become the sole custodial parents of Savanna, and her guardians. Natalie would have access as long as she could produce drug tests proving she was clean.

The next day I took the papers to Natalie in the City lockup, and she signed them and then stood up and hugged me, assailing me with the scent of institutional laundry and the bristle of her unkempt Nix-treated hair. She felt thin and pointy, comprised of all the sticks and stones that had been thrown around in Family Court. But that was over now. I set her aside, and smiled.

"It'll get better. You'll see. And just think, you don't have to worry about Savanna now. You can have your life to do with as you want. You can even clean up your life and get Savanna back if you want."

She nodded. "I can, can't I?"

I left her like that, living in hope while I knew that the likelihood of her getting off of the charges was relatively slim. The police had the witnesses and the motive, even if it was circumstantial. And even if she did get off, the likelihood of her cleaning up her act was somewhere between slim and none. Addiction is like that.

So I took the papers back to my office to where Savanna's grandparents were waiting. They preceded me into my office and we sat down and looked at each other, before I turned the signed papers around to them.

"It's done," I said.

Quinn looked up at me almost disbelieving. "But how? Grandparents don't have any rights under family law. You told us that when we wanted to apply."

It was my turn to smile and I met Jeffrey McGuire's deceptively slow shifting gaze. He nodded his head.

"Sometimes miracles happen," I said, looking out at the small pine tree shifting in the breeze and thought of Savanna with room to grow and run and play like a child. Miracles with a little help from an ex-cop's friends to do the deed and fix the evidence.

King Solomon is always touted as the wisest of kings, but he had it all wrong when he wielded the sword. It wasn't the innocent babe that should be chopped in two. It was the two arguing parents who should feel the blade.

That's what neutrality should really be about.

Many years ago, Dean Wesley Smith and I started an anthology magazine series called Pulphouse: The Hardback Magazine. *The first author I invited to be part of that series was Kate Wilhelm, and she graciously accepted. I decided to continue that tradition when we started Fiction River. Kate was the first person I thought of when I began my invitations. The question was: should I request one of Kate's science fiction stories, since she's won three Nebulas and two Hugos, and is an inductee in The Science Fiction and Fantasy Hall of Fame? Or should I ask for a mystery story, since she's written—by my count—at least 23 mystery novels?*

Fiction River's lineup answered that question for me. I'm not editing an sf volume solo for some time, but I knew I had a crime issue upcoming. So I asked Kate to participate.

About "Plan B," she says she mused over "how often classic mysteries involved heirs apparent scheming to kill off elderly Auntie Bertha, or elderly Uncle Thaddeus, before one or the other could rewrite a will. A little twist on that comfortable theme came to mind."

———

Plan B

Kate Wilhelm

Jackson met Ruth Leary late one Saturday afternoon at the Garden Lane Manor, where he was delivering a box of sweaters, a donation from his aunt for the patients housed there. The foyer was as dismal and institutional as he remembered. It smelled medicinal, of harsh chemical cleaners, Lysol. Elephants' graveyard, he thought with disgust. At the sound of a musical voice, he paused at the doorway to a large common room. There were seven or eight residents in sight, several in wheelchairs, others in rocking chairs, grouped before a gray-haired woman who was reading. He couldn't see her face, just the back of her head, the rest of her hidden by the chair she sat in.

She had a good voice with clear enunciation, some drama, a touch of a lilt. Her audience was unmoving, listening with rapt attention. He moved on toward the office, where the manager, Dottie Mason, met him.

"You have a new patient?" he asked, motioning toward the common room.

"Oh dear, no. That's Ruth Leary, a volunteer. She comes in every week and reads to our guests. Poor dear, she's lonesome, and I guess this gives her something to do. And we certainly do appreciate her. Those who listen to her for an hour or so are relaxed, as good as a tranquilizer for some of them."

Jackson's interest spiked and he lingered longer than he had planned, asking questions. Ruth was a widow who had lost her husband nine months earlier. He had suffered from cancer when he was sixty-four, too young for Medicare. Nine years later the cancer had returned. This time he lost the battle.

"Oh, they had such medical bills, you wouldn't believe," Dottie said. "Had to sell their ranch out by Pendleton. She was a librarian, retired now, of course, and when she brought him over here for treatment, she decided to stay. The ranch gone, no job for her, nothing much to do, I guess, Portland must have seemed a pretty good choice. But she hasn't had time to make many friends. Like I said, she's lonesome."

She had been removing sweaters from the box as she spoke and now said, "I'll just get a receipt for your aunt."

After accepting it, he hesitated, then said, "Have you done any kind of background check on her, on Ruth Leary? Do you do that for volunteers?"

He listened attentively as Dottie talked. She knew people in Pendleton who knew Ruth Leary and had only good things to say about her. In the end he met Ruth. They sat in the manager's office and talked for half an hour.

She was seventy-one years old, with gray hair, milk-chocolate-brown eyes, hardly a wrinkle except for smile lines at her eyes, and a melodious, lilting voice.

"What we need is someone to be companionable, maybe read to her," he said. "No medical care, nursing, no cooking or cleaning, nothing like that. A couple of afternoons a week if it works out."

Ruth smiled and murmured, "From what you say, it may not work out. Have you tried others who failed to meet your needs?"

Jackson felt uncomfortable under her gaze and he shifted in his chair. "Aunt Margaret can be difficult," he said after a moment. "She's impatient, not used to being an invalid, and she resents it. Yes, we've had a few other people in, but they were nurses or professional care givers, and that didn't work. I think you'd be different. I heard you reading, heard that group laughing."

Ruth's smile broadened. "Mark Twain. He can be very funny." Gently she added, "Mr. Loomis, I'm really not looking for a job."

Jackson leaned forward. "Please, Ms. Leary. Give it a try. It may be for a few weeks, or if it goes well maybe for an indefinite time. Five hundred a week. From about noon until about six, two days a week to start. Will you do it?"

Ruth drew in a sharp breath. "That's a lot of money, Mr. Loomis."

"If you can alleviate her discontent, make her happier, just help her find laughter once in a while, it will be worth every cent." He wanted to take her hands, even shake her, make her understand how desperate he was. "I love my aunt," he said. "She has an inoperable heart condition. She's weak and she couldn't stand a shock, or great stress. Her heart condition isn't curable or even very treatable. A heart transplant is what she needs, but she's too weak to undergo such surgery. She isn't suffering physically, but emotionally, psychologically, she's in pain and anything I can do to make her life easier would be worth any price."

Driving home, he kept hearing the phrase in his head: Elephants' graveyard, and along with it something the manager had said, something about his aunt clearing things out. As if getting ready to die? Was that what she had meant? He bit his lip and drove faster. His aunt had a bad heart, but people lived a long time with heart problems. She was getting excellent care. She wasn't any worse now than she had been the past few months. He found himself reciting the silent, reassuring litany and bit his lip again.

"But she is worse," he muttered, stopping the flow.

The house where his father and his Aunt Margaret had grown up, where he had grown up, was several miles out of Portland in a wooded, hilly section where the lots were an acre or more, and the houses, built a century ago, were large and comfortable, lavish by many standards, and for the most part well hidden by old-growth shrubs and trees. By the time he turned in at the long, rhododendron-lined driveway, he felt almost frantic because the elephants' graveyard phrase, the dismal nursing home ambience, and the worry that Aunt Margaret was getting ready to die all continued to darken his thoughts.

He put the car in the garage and entered the house through the back door, deposited a bag of groceries on the kitchen table and went looking for his wife and his aunt. He found them in the library, Aunt Margaret in her wheelchair, and Sheila on a ladder at the book shelves.

"I'm home," he said. "What are you doing up there?"

Sheila Loomis looked like a model, slender to near emaciation, with long blonde hair, and the face of an ideal beauty who posed for turn-of-the-century cameos. The last few months had taken a toll on her with weight loss, dark hollows under her eyes, restless sleep that left her tired. They were both tired. This situation was wearing them down.

Sheila's smile was wan as she motioned toward Aunt Margaret. "We're looking for a box of photographs. She thinks it was up here."

"I know it was up there. That's where I kept it," Aunt Margaret snapped. "Down farther, closer to the chimney." She was almost concealed by a shawl around her upper body, a throw over her lap down to her feet. Her hands were bony, her face bony, and that day her gray hair was frowsy as if she had not brushed or combed it. As sharp as her bones were beneath colorless skin, her voice was sharper.

"Come on down," Jackson said to Sheila. "I'll look for it."

"Did you get that flaxseed bread I asked for?" Aunt Margaret asked. She turned her wheelchair around and started to move toward the doorway.

"Yes, I did. And I delivered the sweaters."

His aunt was already out the door and on her way to her room. The whisper of her wheelchair motor was the only response. He went to hold the ladder as Sheila came down.

"How's it been this afternoon?" he asked.

She closed her eyes before answering. Then, in a measured voice she said, "Aunt Margaret was not amused when she couldn't find those damn pictures. She thinks we might have thrown them out. And she's afraid the hospital is mistreating Dad. She said we're to take her out there tomorrow so she can see for herself how he's doing."

"Forget that," he said. "It won't happen. Let's go to the kitchen and talk. I found a woman today that I want to tell you about. I think, hope, she's the answer to some of our problems."

"Jack, it's really too much. Your father dying a little more every day, Aunt Margaret getting worse all the time. It's just too much!" She looked near tears.

"I know," he said, putting his arm around her, steering her toward the hall and the kitchen.

His father, Aunt Margaret's brother, was in hospice care, suffering from late stage Alzheimer's disease, and daily Jackson expected a phone call informing him that his father had died. And Aunt Margaret... She was furious at herself and the world because she felt cheated, suddenly stricken with a heart attack, now with a heart condition that had turned her into a complaining, miserable old woman. She had always been vital, always on the go, busy, now confined to her childhood home that had become her prison. Jackson felt as if he and Sheila were like the filling of a moldering sandwich, caught between the two old people who had only death to look forward to.

He sat at the kitchen table while Sheila finished the dinner preparations she had interrupted in order to search for a box of photographs. He told her about Ruth Leary.

"She'll come on Tuesday to meet Aunt Margaret and we'll see how it works out," he finished.

Sheila stopped stirring something in a pot and said, "It had better work, Jack. I don't think either one of us can take much more of this."

"A few more weeks," he said. "Dad's fading so fast, it won't be much longer." He looked down at his hands on the table and added in a low voice. "For all our sakes, I hope to God it won't be more than a few more weeks."

It was less than that. The call came from the hospital the next morning. Jackson listened, mumbled something and closed his cellphone. "Dad," he said in a low voice. "He's gone."

Involuntarily he looked at the tray Sheila was preparing for Aunt Margaret. Poached egg on toasted flaxseed bread, juice, milk, tea. "Try to get her to eat it all."

"You know how that works," Sheila said. "Jack, you'll have to go, make arrangements for the cremation."

He nodded, then crossed the kitchen to stand before a wall calendar. He took a pen from his pocket and made a small X on the date November 8. Thirty days from now. Aunt Margaret had to live for at least thirty days. He bit his lip as the thought came that if he could put her on a life-support system, tubed, plugged in, the works, he would do it.

On Tuesday Jackson opened the door when Ruth Leary arrived for her interview. She was gazing at the front garden with a faint smile. Dahlias and roses were in bloom, and fuchsias overhung many hanging baskets on the front porch.

"Ms. Leary, please come in."

"This is so lovely," she said motioning toward the roses. She smiled her gentle smile and said in a low voice, "I'm so sorry about your father, Mr. Loomis. I read about his death in the obituaries. My deepest sympathy for your loss."

He swallowed hard and nodded. Then, after a quick look behind him at the foyer, he said, "Ms. Leary, I know this may sound strange, but you mustn't mention that to Aunt Margaret when you meet her. She doesn't know, and we'll hold the condolence cards and phone calls until she's a little stronger. I'm afraid it might shock her, or send her into a depression. She was devoted to him and consoles herself with the belief that he is getting better."

Ruth reached out and patted his arm. "I understand, Mr. Loomis. Of course I won't say a word."

"Thank you. Come on in and meet my wife. We'll tell you about the arrangements here, what your duties will be, and so on." He led her through the wide, bright foyer to an open door to the library, where Sheila came forward with her hand outstretched. Jackson introduced them and they moved on into the library.

Ruth Leary gazed at the walls of books with undisguised pleasure. "It's so rare to see a private library," she murmured. "What a wonderful room."

"Aunt Margaret, my parents, we all love books," Jackson said. "Aunt Margaret was always an avid reader until recently. Her eyesight isn't very good these days, and holding a book tires her. She'll love being read to."

Then, with them all seated in comfortable chairs near bay windows, Sheila said, "Our routine is pretty simple. Jack or I prepare Aunt Margaret's breakfast and take it to her room. She has a bath and dresses herself. She isn't bedridden, but she's terribly weak. Anyway, she watches television or listens to music. We prepare her lunch. Afterward, she might nap. A housekeeper comes on Mondays and Thursdays, and she's a little company for Aunt Margaret, and there's a cook for dinner Monday through Friday. She seldom sees Aunt Margaret. The kitchen is on a lower level and Aunt Margaret can't manage the stairs. Most often we take a tray to her room for dinner. So she's alone much of the time. Jack and I quit our jobs in Seattle to be here, but we're not good company for her. We think someone nearer her age, a reader, a lover of books is just what she needs to keep up her spirits."

Jackson leaned forward and said, "Ms. Leary, we both love Aunt Margaret and we want to help her get well. Her doctor said we have to keep her spirits up, not let her sink into a depression. Mentally she's sharp as a razor, but her body is failing, and that's hard for her to take. She came here to help out after my mother passed away six years ago. Dad went to pieces and couldn't cope, and Aunt Margaret took care of him right up until she had a heart attack last spring and we had to hospitalize him. Now it's our turn to take care of her and we need help. Your help."

"Cut the crap," Aunt Margaret said from the open door. She rolled into the room, looking at Ruth Leary with a cool appraising gaze. "George, his father, is bonkers," she said, nodding toward Jackson. "And his mother, Anna Marie, covered for him for years, hiding his dementia. I moved from Salem to keep him out of the loony bin as long as possible. And they came," she added, nodding toward Jackson and Sheila, "in order to keep me alive for at least thirty days after George dies. Our father, George's and mine, tied up a fortune in a trust. It pays for all this," she said, waving her hand generally at the room, the house. "And it pays for them, for my keep, for George's keep in the loony bin. It's a ticking clock that keeps Jackson and Sheila in fear that I'll die too soon, before George, or before thirty days after he kicks. The whole schmear goes to the Audubon Society if that happens. If I survive his death for thirty days, the trust is ended, I inherit, and since Jackson is my only living relative, when I bite the dust, he gets it all. Damned if I'll see a fortune sent off to Audubon and I don't give a shit about how Jackson and Sheila use or misuse it after I'm gone. Jackson would be a damn fool if he didn't do whatever it takes to keep me alive. That's the situation you'll walk into, if you decide to take the job, and if I decide I can put up with you twice a week."

No one moved or spoke for an awkward moment until Ruth said softly, "Oh, dear, it appears that it's for the general good of all of us to make certain you recover your health."

Aunt Margaret laughed. "You're wondering why my father wrote such a trust, aren't you?"

"Well. . . . Yes, I am."

"Because he was a grade A ass. He got mad at my crazy brother because everything he touched, every deal he tried to make turned to mud. And he got mad at me because I married a man who worked for the Oregon Tax department and would have nothing to do with the Loomis Forest Products Corporation. Our father had the trust written to teach us a lesson, and he had every intention of revoking it in due time, but he outfoxed himself and died first. So we're stuck with an angry man's insane desire to punish his wayward kids." She wheeled her chair around and started to move toward the open door. "Come along, see where I hibernate and contemplate an imminent death, or a life of luxury depending on the mood of the day."

Ruth caught up with her at the door and Jackson followed a few steps behind. He could hear Aunt Margaret's voice until she entered her own room.

"I like mysteries," she said. "Puzzle mysteries, not the gore, slash and burn kind. Clues. Mysteries should have clues, puzzles. I don't care how horny the detective is, or if he schlepps every pretty young thing who comes along, but I don't want to follow them into the bedroom and watch them roll around like dead things washed up by the tide."

"I know exactly what kind of mysteries you're talking about," Ruth said. "I like them, too."

"Good. Now, close the door and let's get down to it."

The door closed with a click.

Jackson unclenched his hands and tried to release the tight muscles in his neck before he rejoined Sheila in the library.

"I think Ruth Leary will work out fine," he said in a stiff, unnatural voice.

"I think we can both use a drink," Sheila said. "Little point in pretending any longer, is there? Aunt Margaret knows damn well why we're here, and so does your timid little Ruth Leary."

* * *

Two weeks later Jackson was in the living room cradling a strong bourbon and water. He had not turned on a light, and the light from the foyer was dim, casting the room in deep shadows. He jerked in startlement when Sheila spoke as she entered the room.

"For God's sake, Jack! It's three in the morning!"

"I couldn't sleep."

"You never sleep any more. Every night, two, three times a night, checking on her. She'll outlive you if you keep this up."

"I keep thinking of what's at stake. Dad got sixteen million in cash when he sold out his shares of the company! Sixteen million! And God alone knows how much it's increased, how much in stock. There was a split again this week."

"Ruth is helping. You were right about her. We should have her more days a week. Aunt Margaret was laughing like a school girl this afternoon over those old pictures. They spent an hour putting pictures in the scrapbook."

"She didn't even get out of bed two days this week. That's what I know."

"Two more weeks, Jack. Just two more weeks and it's over. Come on, get some sleep."

"I'll look in on her first. I haven't yet."

"Oh, sweet Jesus! Finish your drink. I'll go." She walked out swiftly, angrily.

He was still sitting on the couch, still holding his glass when Sheila returned. She came to the couch and sat next to him. She was shaking.

"Jack, she's dead!" she whispered.

His glass slipped from his fingers. It didn't break, he thought with wonder. He felt as if he were watching the glass, watching himself jump to his feet, watching Sheila cover her face with her hands, watching himself hear her say, "It's over. We've lost."

He ran from the room, through the foyer to Aunt Margaret's room, where, at her bedside, he stared down at the wasted face. He felt her hand, as cold as ice. Her face was waxen, white. Dead white, he thought distantly. He backed away from the bed, all the way to the door, left the room and closed the door softly, as if afraid he might waken her.

Sheila was standing by the library door when he crossed the foyer again. "I was going to call someone," she said. "I don't know who to call. Nine-one-one? What's the point? Her doctor? The police? Who do we call?" Her voice was shrill and tremulous.

"No one," he said harshly. "No one. Not yet. We have to think. Let's go make coffee and think."

* * *

The following Friday Jackson opened the door for Ruth Leary at twelve thirty, her usual time. He was carrying a cup of coffee when he ushered her in.

"Mr. Loomis," she said in concern, "are you ill? You don't look well."

"I'm fine, fine," he said. "But we've had a few bad days. In fact, Sheila had to take Aunt Margaret to see her doctor and she just called to say they want her in the hospital for some tests."

"Oh, I should leave," Ruth said. "She'll want to rest in bed when she comes home. Tests can be so tiring."

Jackson shook his head. "Actually, I was going to ask you to do something special today. I want to go shopping for Aunt Margaret. Get something nice for her, a surprise for when she returns. I was thinking of a beautiful new robe, something like that. Would you go with me, pick it out, make sure the size is right? You know, things women have a knack for that render us guys almost helpless." He laughed and swung around in such a way that he spilled coffee on Ruth's coat.

"Damn it," he said. He hurried to put his cup down on a side table, then whipped out a handkerchief and began to dab at her coat. "That's no good," he said. "It's soaked."

"It's quite all right," Ruth said, backing away from his hands. "It's an old coat, as you can see. No harm done." It was a dark-red raincoat with a hood, the only coat he had ever seen her wear.

Ignoring her soft-spoken protests, he said, "It's not all right. I'm a damn fool, not sleeping enough, worried. Here, let's get it off. I'll have it dry cleaned, and meanwhile you can use one of Aunt Margaret's coats. God knows, she has more than she can use." He slipped the coat off her shoulders as he talked. Then, holding her by the arm, he guided her through the foyer to Aunt Margaret's room.

"Things are a little messy," he said in the bedroom, as he walked to one of the closets. "Our housekeeper quit on us this week and we haven't had time to find her replacement. Here, I think this one will do nicely." He pulled a black cashmere coat from the closet and handed it to Ruth. "Try it on. I bet it's a perfect fit. She was just about your size before she lost so much weight."

"Mr. Loomis, I can't take this. It's too expensive. And that brooch! It must have cost more than a dozen of my own coats." The brooch was gold with emerald gemstones.

"It's just a loan," he said. "I'm afraid the brooch stays with the coat. She's particular about things like that."

Hesitantly Ruth put on the coat, and it was a perfect fit. She looked almost frightened.

"Okay," Jackson said. "Let's go. Be thinking of robes, what would be appropriate for her, something warm, beautiful, luxurious. The best. That's what we're after, the best."

He took her to Nordstrom's in downtown Portland and stood aside as she began to look over the racks of robes. She chose an iridescent, dark blue, raw silk robe embroidered with silver and gold flowers on the sleeves and a sash with gold tassels. It was the priciest one in the store. Ruth's face was flushed when she handed it to him and watched him pay with his credit card.

"That's a first for me," she said softly as they walked from the department. "I mean not looking at the price tag."

"You're not done yet," Jackson said. "I saw a woman with a fur hat on, and I want to buy a fur hat for Aunt Margaret. Something to go with that coat. Black fur."

Ruth caught in her breath. "Sable," she said. "It could be sable."

When they found a sable hat, he insisted that she wear it. "Why not?" he said. "It goes with the coat. You look great in it." The smiling saleswoman nodded in agreement.

"One more real quick stop," Jackson said when they were again in the car. "I have some papers I have to drop off in our safe deposit box. It won't take more than a couple of minutes. Do you mind?"

"Of course not," Ruth said. "I feel like Cinderella in these clothes. I'm in no hurry for the clock to strike twelve."

He glanced at her. She was stroking the sable hat, a faint smile on her face.

At the bank he insisted that she go in with him. "You can't wait in the car," he said. "What if you got car jacked or something. I don't want to leave this either. Too tempting." He picked up the Nordstrom bag.

They entered the large lobby and he glanced around. There was a line at one of the teller's windows, people were sitting with bank employees at several desks beyond a glass wall. No one paid any attention to them.

"Oh, there he is," Jackson said. "Wait here a minute. Someone I want a word with." He hurried off, waved to a man beyond the glass, and was ushered through. Ruth continued to stand in the lobby gazing about. Jackson and the man exchanged a few words, shook hands, and he rejoined Ruth.

"An old friend," he said. "The safe deposit desk is this way."

He took her arm and they approached the desk, where he signed in, and very soon they were escorted to the vault with the boxes. As he had said, it took only a minute or two to remove the box, for the bank employee to leave, for him to open the box, take papers from his pocket and deposit them. He replaced the box.

"Now we're done," he said and pushed the button for the door to be opened again.

Neither spoke during the drive back to the house. When he pulled up behind her Camry parked in the driveway, Ruth said, "Mr. Loomis, would you mind if I pick up a library book or two. I can return them in the morning and I think I know just the right kind of thing to check out. Margaret will be exhausted from a strenuous day today. Something light and amusing is what she should have tomorrow." She took off the fur hat, stroked it one last time and handed it to him.

"Good thinking," he said.

* * *

"She's late," he said angrily on Saturday. It was twenty minutes to one.

"Ten minutes," Sheila said. She looked frightened, sounded nervous. "Maybe she got stuck in traffic."

"She's never late," he snapped. He was pacing back and forth through the foyer.

"Today she's late," Sheila snapped back at him.

"I'll call her," he said yanking his cellphone from his pocket.

"For God's sake, stop it! She'll know something's wrong. Just calm down. Give her ten more minutes, fifteen minutes."

He scowled at her, but he replaced his phone and went to the door, opened it and looked out at the long empty driveway. He banged the door shut.

He called Ruth's number at one o'clock. There was no answer. He called at one fifteen, and again there was no answer. At two o'clock a message came on to say that number was no longer in service.

"She skipped with the coat and the brooch," Sheila said dully. "You shouldn't have let her keep the brooch."

"Shut up!" He stamped to the living room and poured a drink. "She didn't skip," he muttered more to himself than to Sheila, who had followed him. "She's too frightened to try to get away with stealing. She knows I'd bring charges. Something's happened to her. Maybe she had an accident or something."

Sheila brushed past him to pour herself a drink, then crossed the room to sit on the couch. "What are we going to do now?" she asked, not looking at him.

"Wait out the weekend. I'll go find her on Monday, find out what happened. Maybe she forgot to pay her bill, got a different phone number, lost her phone. There could be any number of reasons."

"Right," Sheila said. "Or maybe she skipped with the coat and the brooch."

* * *

On Monday at Ruth's apartment building he talked to one of the tenants. The woman said, "She told me that the lady she was sitting with let her go, and there wasn't any reason to hang around. She said she sold her car, and I think she planned to travel, head down to California to visit family or friends. I don't remember, just someone down in California."

It would have worked, he told himself when he started driving. Sheila would have driven Ruth's car to her designated parking space at the apartment. She would have gotten out, dressed in that old mangy raincoat with the hood up over her hair. She would have been carrying a shopping bag, and instead of entering the building, she would have walked down the street, around the corner toward Safeway, and in the parking lot there she would have gotten into his car and they would have gone home. Ruth would have been tucked away in the basement room they had prepared for her, there to fast on bread and water for a week or so to lose a few pounds, until Aunt Margaret could officially die in her bed. The cardiologist would have signed off on the death. He had told them it could happen like that at any time. No one would have questioned Jackson's identifying her as Aunt Margaret, whose death had been expected. It would have worked.

He realized he was eyeing middle-aged-to-old women as he drove slowly through town. It could still work, he told himself. They just needed a slightly built, brown-eyed woman without attachments to play one of the parts.

* * *

"Tonight," Jackson said as he entered the house with Sheila. It was the afternoon of November twelfth. "It's good that it's raining. No one will be out walking around. All you have to do is drive. I'll get her inside the car and you take off. That simple. Nothing to it."

"What if she starts screaming? Puts up a fight?"

"Shut up!" Jackson said, grabbing her arm. "What's that?" Music. Someone was playing the piano. The cook playing music? He shook his head. It was coming from Aunt Margaret's room, not the distant kitchen.

He pushed Sheila aside and ran through the foyer to Aunt Margaret's room, and came to a dead stop in the doorway. She was standing across the room, no more than a silhouette against the window. She was wearing the blue robe with the silver and gold embroidery. Jackson felt the world spinning around him and he clutched the doorframe for support. He heard Sheila's gasp behind him, heard her moan.

"Good afternoon, Jackson. I thought you'd never get here."

The woman turned to face him. Ruth Leary!

"What the fuck are you doing here?" he demanded. "What are you doing, wearing my aunt's clothes?" He took a step forward, his fists clenched. "How did you get in?"

She laughed softly. "One at a time, Jackson. I used my key, of course. I picked it up the day you were showing me off. And I'm trying to decide if I should take this with me." Her voice sharpened when he took another step forward. "Stop right there, Jackson. I think you'd better hear what I have to say before you do something rash. I want to tell you about my busy days this past week or so."

He stopped moving. Nodding in approval, she took off the robe and tossed it down on the bed. She was wearing a handsome pearl-gray pantsuit. On the bed were the black cashmere coat and the sable hat, and an open suitcase. Another closed suitcase was by the bed.

"It was very helpful that you paraded me in front of Mr. Drummond at the bank," Ruth said. "I approached him with my request to talk to the trust department vice president, and he recognized me and arranged it expeditiously. Of course, the bank was trustee and it was to their advantage that I wanted to have all of the trust funds transferred to my newly opened account as soon as the thirty-day period expired. That was accomplished with no complications whatsoever. The trust is now dissolved, my separate account opened, and all credit cards and bank accounts with you as a registered signatory have been cancelled. My lawyer was equally accommodating with the arrangements I made with him. He actually came to the bank where we had our conference and he drew up a preliminary will on the spot. I signed it today." She began to fold the robe. "I think I shall need it for several days, at least," she said, and placed it in the open suitcase, which she then closed. "The day I picked up the key, I also picked up a few other things. I have a passport, a driver's license, cash, temporary checks, credit cards, everything I'll be needing in my new life as Margaret. The resemblance is close enough, considering that official photographs are always so awful."

"You think I'll let you get away with this?" Jackson cried. His voice was hoarse, harsh. His fists were clenched again and he felt his head pounding with an insistent hard beat.

"You won't say a word," she said softly. "I wrote a will, Jackson. It's complicated, but the gist of it is that for as long as I live you will be provided with one hundred thousand dollars a year. You will be permitted to reside in this lovely house, which will be maintained by funds set aside for that purpose. Household help will be your responsibility. If you choose not to live here, the house will be turned over to the Audubon society, for them to do with as they choose. You will not have my address and any correspondence will be conducted through my lawyers." She drew a business card from her pocket and placed it on the bedside table. "Their names. She glanced about the room, then picked up the cashmere coat and put it on. She moved to stand in front of the mirrored dressing table and put on the sable hat.

"Jackson," she said, regarding his image in the mirror, "the other part of my will expresses my intent to honor my father's wish to enrich the Audubon Society. When I die, my assets, everything, will go to that group in his memory. I wonder. Did you have Plan B in mind from the start? Or, did you improvise it when Margaret died too soon? No matter," she said, waving it away. "I devised my own Plan B the day you proved to the world that your Aunt Margaret was still alive. Add me to your prayers, dear. Pray that I might live for many, many years." She turned to face him again. "Now, please take my bags out to the car I ordered for three o'clock. I told the agency to have the driver wait if I'm not out yet. I believe he must be waiting."

She walked past him into the foyer without a glance at him or Sheila, who looked haggard, pale, and disbelieving. After a moment Jackson went into the room, picked up the bag on the bed, grasped the handle of the roll-on, and followed Aunt Margaret out to the waiting limousine.

M. Elizabeth Castle pulled off something I thought impossible. She's written a cozy mystery in haiku form. When asked about this fun little piece, she sent her answer in haiku form.

She writes:

Deadline looms, panic!
Current project off the rails.
Wait…an idea.

I can crank haiku
out like nobody's business.
Hey look! A story!

———

Gas, Tan, Video

M. Elizabeth Castle

Gas—Tan—Video
Jan's Place, small Southern beach town.
Summer comes early.

Ralph, Jan's ex, and for
a simple reason: asshole.
(Look—his monster truck!)

Jan's dog Edgar barks
mostly at stupid tourists.
Today? A body.

Ralph's current girlfriend.
Squished behind the propane tank,
Looks like she's asleep.

But no, she's quite dead.
Strangled with someone's big hands.
Hmm, Ralph has big hands...

Ralph's the suspect but,
Slammed into the town pokey,
He claims innocence.

He *was* an asshole.
He's not (Jan knows) a killer.
And they were young, then.

Town cop? Off fishing.
Or maybe drunk again, or
more than likely both.

It's up to Jan to
figure out who killed LynnAnne.
She bikes around town.

Old Pete the mailman:
Tobacco juice and sweat stains,
Noncompliant shirt.

He saw something weird
that night (staggering home drunk).
Might have been a ghost.

No, really! Flowing
white figure, hazy midnight ...
Um ... maybe not? ... shrug.

Super Tanning Gal,
In her store every day, not
enough sun outside.

Says she saw LynnAnne
crying in the trailer park.
Brother, Harve, was fired.

Delivery Dan:
Spotless truck, ordered life, don't
Deviate from path.

Truck has a dinged front.
Cleaned up, but ... just a bit missed.
Brown and crusty ... hmm.

Yeah, he hit a deer.
Damn things, jumping in the road.
Oops, look at the time.

Harvey worked for Dan.
Different route, a different truck.
Ran around with Ralph.

Westside trailer park:
Jan ignores the stench, and learns
Big Harvey is gone.

His trailer's a mess!
No, it wasn't rifled through—
It's always that way.

Jan finds Harvey's truck.
Bleah. Bigger mess than his place.
Harvey inside, dead.

Looks like Dan lost it—
Harvey's truck (and life) too much.
Bashed him on the head.

What about LynnAnne?
Cellphone message, Harvey knew
Dan was gonna snap.

Dan attacked at night.
She squeezed out the window, ran!
He caught up at Jan's.

Jan calls state PD.
Dan arrested, Ralph set free.
Exonerated!

Ralph has seen the light
(lots of time to think upon
old indiscretions).

Maybe (just maybe)
he deserves another chance.
And his truck *is* cool...

Gas—Tan—Video
Jan's Place, summer sun beats down
Edgar at Ralph's feet.

"Jackrabbit DMZ" marks Annie Reed's fifth appearance in Fiction River. Since we've only had seven volumes so far, that's impressive. Even more impressive, she's managed to sell a story to each of our editors, publishing fantasy, science fiction, and mystery in these pages.

Annie's a native Nevadan who often writes stories set in her home state. Her novels Pretty Little Horses *and* A Death in Cumberland, *as well as her short story collection* Fight from the Silver State, *focus on the wide variety of people who choose to live in a desert state infamous for wide open spaces, legalized gambling, and other less savory pursuits.*

"As someone who's worked in the legal field for more years than I care to remember," Annie writes, "I'm fascinated by people who think they can beat the system. Jill Jordan, my rule-bound sheriff from A Death in Cumberland, *would never put up with that kind of hubris, but Jill wasn't always the sheriff. The invitation to participate in* Crime *gave me the perfect opportunity to tell a story from Jill's past as a patrol deputy on the Jackrabbit DMZ, a lonely desert highway where no one thinks they have to play by the rules."*

Jackrabbit DMZ

Annie Reed

Highway 50 stretched from Fernley to Cumberland across a wide expanse of flat Nevada desert populated by more free-range cattle, jackrabbits, and rattlers than people. Long before Deputy Jill Jordan had been assigned to patrol those lonely miles, a burned-out Vietnam vet who'd seen too much action near the demilitarized zone had come back to Cumberland and decided to take out his post-traumatic stress on the rabbits. He'd told everyone who'd listen that Highway 50 was the Jackrabbit DMZ, and any of the little buggers that came near it better watch out. The name had stuck.

The Vietnam War had been her dad's war, not Jill's. Her generation's war would be the one in Iraq. Two of the younger deputies in the Sheriff's Department had resigned to join the military after the towers fell. Jill had a five-year-old daughter and a marriage she was trying to salvage, so she'd stayed with the department, a patrol deputy just like her dad had been before a speeding car plowed into his cruiser.

The guy who'd killed her dad had been drunk, no doubt just like the guy in the lemon-yellow GTO Jill had just pulled over.

She approached the GTO as cautiously as she would have if there'd been a bear in the driver's seat. She held her flashlight in her left hand. Her right hand touched the butt of her service pistol. Her holster was already unsnapped, just in case. The department didn't have enough deputies on staff to patrol the hundreds of miles of roads in the county. Only one cop at a time patrolled this stretch of Highway 50. Jill was on her own out here. Her nearest backup might as well have been on the moon. The old cliché "better safe than sorry" was a damn good thing to remember for a woman alone in the desert, even if that woman was a cop.

Technically, Jill didn't need the flashlight—it was only a little after seven and still twilight—but she wanted the intimidation factor. *Shine a light in the driver's eyes and he can't get a good look at you*, her dad always used to say. This guy had been doing ninety when he zoomed by Jill's patrol car, and he'd hit nearly a hundred once Jill started chasing him.

She'd been heading the other way, cruising and looking for motorists in trouble. As soon as the GTO sped by, she'd flipped a U and floored the cruiser. The thing had a heavy-duty engine—all the patrol cars in Cumberland had as much horsepower under the hood as anything Detroit manufactured—and Jill wasn't afraid of speed, not even at twilight.

The GTO and her cruiser had been the only two cars on the highway. Siren wailing, the red and blue lights on her cruiser strobing the desert, Jill had chased the GTO's taillights. No county roads intersected with the highway until the outskirts of Cumberland proper, still a good twenty miles away. If the driver had tried to turn off into the desert, he would have flipped the car. The speedometer on the cruiser had topped one-hundred ten, then one-hundred twenty, GTO's taillights growing closer, and Jill had prayed the driver wouldn't try to rabbit into the desert.

He didn't. After a chase that felt longer than it probably had been, the driver had slowed and pulled the GTO onto the shoulder of the road.

The GTO didn't have plates, just a dealer proof-of-sale sticker in the rear window and an empty Cumberland Dodge license plate holder on the back bumper.

That pegged the driver as one of Hal Taylor's customers. Hal Taylor's Cumberland Dodge was the reason the Sheriff's Department had souped-up engines in all its cruisers. Hal's dealerships—he was up to three now—were the biggest businesses in Cumberland outside of the local casino, drawing customers from as far away as Reno some sixty miles to the west, which made Hal an important man in local politics. Jill hoped the driver wasn't one of Hal's good buddies. Unofficial department policy was to let Hal's good buddies off with a warning unless circumstances warranted otherwise.

Jill hated that policy. She'd gone to school with Hal Taylor, and she hadn't thought he was anything special back then. She still didn't think he was anything special now, but she wasn't in charge. This was rural Nevada, and the good old boys still ruled the cow counties. They sure as hell ruled the Sheriff's Department. If Jill's dad hadn't worked with the current sheriff, she'd probably still be filing reports and answering dispatch calls. She was keenly aware that her promotion to patrol deputy hadn't been a popular decision with most of the department.

Gravel crunched beneath her boots as she approached the car. The stench of hot oil and grease from the GTO's over-worked engine mixed with the dusty smell of sagebrush coming off the desert, but Jill didn't smell the sharp, sweet tang of marijuana. At least that was something. In her experience, drivers who tried to run from a traffic stop were either high or drunk or stupid, drunk coming out on top more often than not.

She aimed the flashlight beam at the back seat of the GTO, looking for empty beer cans or a poorly-stashed bottle. The back seat was clean, not even fast food wrappers on the floorboards.

When she shifted the flashlight beam toward the driver, the light reflected back at her. The driver still had his window rolled up.

"Roll your window down, sir," Jill said, projecting her voice so the driver could hear.

Instead of rolling the window down, the driver turned the music up louder on his radio. A rock song that had been a classic before Jill was born blared at her even through the closed windows. She could almost feel the deep bass thrum from the speakers. The guy had definitely paid for an upgraded sound system.

She rapped on the window with her flashlight, not really caring if she marred the glass. The driver was looking straight ahead like he was studying the desert illuminated by the car's headlights. Looking for jackrabbits, maybe. Trying to figure out how many he could turn into road kill.

He didn't move, so Jill rapped on the window again, harder this time. He glanced at her, his expression bland, and she made a *roll it down* signal with her hand.

The driver smiled before he went back to staring straight ahead.

The guy was in his mid to late thirties, dark haired with a high forehead that was a precursor of baldness yet to come. He was clean shaven, although he had a pretty good five o'clock shadow going. He wore a light-colored golf shirt. He had his left hand on the wheel, and Jill could see an expensive watch on his wrist and a plain gold wedding ring and fancier pinkie ring on his fingers. He hadn't turned the engine off. He looked like a guy sitting at a red light, patiently waiting for it to turn green.

Jill stepped forward just enough to be in his peripheral vision. Although she'd already unsnapped her holster, she made a show of unsnapping it while she kept her hand on the butt of her gun. With the flashlight, she made another *roll it down* gesture.

The driver rolled the window down a quarter of an inch.

Music from the car radio escaped into the desert twilight. It was loud enough the farmers probably heard it back in Fernley.

While the crack was big enough to let her smell tobacco smoke, she couldn't tell whether the driver smelled of alcohol.

"Turn the music off, and shut off your engine," Jill said, making sure her voice was loud enough to be heard over a screaming guitar riff.

The driver killed the engine but twisted the key so the music would keep playing. After a beat, he turned the volume down.

"Now roll the window down," Jill said.

The driver lifted one eyebrow and shrugged his shoulders.

What the hell? Passive resistance out here in the middle of the desert? Or was the window broken? Not likely on a newly-purchased car from one of Hal Taylor's dealerships. Not even a newly-purchased used car like the GTO. Hal Taylor was a jerk, but he was a jerk who sold only quality products.

To other jerks, apparently.

Jill decided to see exactly how much passive resistance she'd get from this guy.

"Slide your license, proof of sale, and proof of insurance through the crack in the window," she told him.

She expected more non-compliance, but this time he actually passed what she'd asked for through the crack. The license and insurance identified him as Clifford Chester. The car wasn't registered yet, but the name on the dealer's report of sale matched his license and insurance information. According to his license, he lived in Fernley and he'd purchased the GTO from Cumberland Dodge last weekend.

Jill made a show of moving the flashlight beam from the paperwork back to his face. "Mr. Chester, I'm going to need you to step out of the car."

She saw him sigh. Instead of getting out of the car, he just sat there, staring straight ahead.

She needed him to get out of the car so she could perform a field sobriety test. "Sir, get out of the car."

He ignored her.

If something like this had happened in pretty much any action movie starring Bruce Willis, Bruce would have shot out the guy's back window, said something witty, and the driver would have scurried out of the car before the next bullet went through his skull. Real life cops, especially female deputies in Cumberland, did not go around discharging their firearms unless absolutely necessary.

"Sir, if you don't get out of the car, I will place you under arrest for failure to obey a law enforcement officer. Is that what you want?"

In response, he turned up his radio. The thrum of the bass vibrated Jill's fillings. He must be going deaf in there.

There were days Jill really wished she could trade places with Bruce Willis.

She walked back to her car and radioed dispatch. "Elaine, I need a tow truck."

Static crackled on the radio before the dispatcher answered. "Your cruiser break down, Jill?"

She wished. She pinched the bridge of her nose. "No. I pulled a guy over for speeding and suspected DUI, and now he's doing a Gandhi impersonation."

"What?"

Elaine might be a great dispatcher, but obviously history wasn't her forte.

"Passive resistance," Jill said. "He won't get out of his freaking car."

At this point, Jill didn't care whether Clifford Chester got out of his car when the tow truck showed up or stayed in his car for a leisurely drive on the back of Ted Magnuson's flatbed. He'd have to get out eventually, and Jill intended to be there when he did.

To her credit, Elaine didn't chuckle on the air. She said she'd see if she could find Magnuson or one of his kids. Jill gave Elaine Clifford Chester's name and driver's license number and asked her to run the guy for any outstanding warrants. Somebody who'd pull a stunt like this might have more problems with authority than just refusing to get out of the car when ordered to do so. At least Jill hoped so, otherwise she'd never live this whole thing down.

She stood by her cruiser watching the back of Clifford Chester's head through the GTO's back window. Her husband would call a car like the GTO a muscle car. Privately, Jill thought so much horsepower under the hood was compensation for guys who didn't have a whole lot of horsepower elsewhere.

Her radio crackled. Jill expected Elaine, but instead she got Oren Michaelson.

Chief Deputy Oren Michaelson. Her supervisor.

"What's the problem?" he asked.

Oren was an officious little man, but he was also a dangerous little man. Everyone expected him to run for sheriff one day. Oren Michaelson was one of the good old boys in Cumberland, and not only that, he was good buddies with Hal Taylor. The guy who'd sold Clifford Chester his lemon-yellow GTO.

Jill gave him a brief rundown of the situation, just like she was giving any other traffic incident report.

"You suspect he's drunk?" Oren asked when she was done.

She'd just said that. "I do," she said again, keeping her voice level.

"What's your probable cause? Besides speeding."

Probable cause for DUI was erratic driving. Jill gave every speeder she pulled over a DUI test if the situation warranted it, and this situation damn well warranted it.

"The guy couldn't keep to the line," she said. Chester hadn't swerved much, given how fast he'd been driving, but if push came to shove, it would be enough for the D.A. to make a DUI charge stick. Provided Jill could get Chester out of the damn car to administer the test.

"You said he was doing nearly a hundred. I bet you didn't keep to the line either while you were trying to catch up to him."

Jill kept her mouth shut.

"What else you got?" Oren asked. "You smell alcohol? See any open containers? Any physical signs of intoxication?"

The man's eyes hadn't looked glassy. He'd sat still in his seat, his movements normal—frustrating, but normal—not the over-exaggerated carefulness of a drunk. She would have been able to tell better if she'd been able to make him walk a line.

"No," she said.

"So what you've got is a speeder."

"What I've got is speeding, reckless driving, and resisting a law enforcement officer," she said before she could stop herself. "I'm pretty sure I also have a drunk who's trying to get away with it by not cooperating."

"No, what you've got is a no-win situation. If I send Ted out with his tow truck, it's going to be an hour and a half, maybe two, before we get your suspected drunk driver back here. *I* suspect by the time we finally talk him out of his car and give him a breathalyzer test, he's going to blow below the legal limit. The D.A.'s not going to want to prosecute based on a theory of what his blood alcohol might have been at the time you pulled him over. So at that point the county will have incurred a tow bill for no good reason and tarnished the reputation of its newest member of the bar."

Shit. Clifford Chester was an attorney. If he was opening up shop in Cumberland—not exactly a hotbed of legal activity for a lawyer looking to make a decent living—and he was driving a GTO from Cumberland Dodge, that meant Chester was one of Hal Taylor's good buddies, maybe even his new lawyer. Jill was willing to bet Chester knew any good buddy of Hal's also had a good buddy in the sheriff's department.

Oh yes, Mr. Clifford Chester *Esquire* knew exactly what he was doing. He was beating a DUI arrest, and there was nothing Jill could do about it.

"You want me to drop it," she said.

"No," Oren said. "I want you to issue a citation to Mr. Chester for the charges you can prove—speeding and reckless driving—and get back on patrol."

"What about resisting?"

Static crackled on the radio, and for a moment Jill thought Oren wasn't going to answer. "No probable cause to order him out of his car," Oren finally said. "He knew it, you didn't. Let it drop. Unless you want to find yourself up on the stand explaining yourself to Judge Gibson."

Jill shut her eyes. Gibson was one of two district judges who covered trials in Cumberland as part of a three-county circuit. Gibson could be a bastard when he wanted to. Oren had mentioned the judge by name, which was his way of implying that Gibson knew Clifford Chester personally. If Jill pressed the matter and Chester fought the ticket, which he no doubt would do, Jill wouldn't have to worry about a defense attorney beating the hell out of her probable cause. Gibson would do it for him.

Was she letting what had happened to her father influence her more than it should have? Not every speeder was a drunk. She had a gut feeling that Clifford Chester had been drinking, but he was sober enough to know how to beat the charge. She doubted it was the first time he'd pulled a Gandhi routine.

"Got it," she said, and clicked off the radio.

She wrote up Mr. Clifford Chester for the citations she knew she could make stick, including failure to wear a seat belt. He nodded politely at her when she handed him the ticket along with his license, insurance card, and report of sale through that maddening quarter-inch slit in the driver's side window.

"Drive carefully," she said.

To his credit, he didn't leave two smoking trails of burnt rubber on the road. Instead, he drove the GTO away at a sedate rate.

Jill had meant what she said. She hoped he'd take his close call seriously and drive like his life mattered.

He didn't.

She was headed back to Cumberland when she got the call. A trucker had reported a single-car rollover accident ten miles west of Cumberland. A lemon-yellow GTO upside down off the side of the road.

Jill turned on the siren and the lights, and punched the gas. She needn't have bothered.

Clifford Chester was dead before the trucker even spotted the wreck. When Jill aimed her flashlight toward the busted-up driver's side window, his vacant eyes stared back at her. The safety glass was long gone, scattered over the hard-packed desert dirt. Chester's body was crumpled against the roof of the car. He hadn't put the seat belt on before he'd driven away.

At least he hadn't taken anyone else out with him. Jill wished she could feel more for the man than that, but she couldn't. He was one of those guys who thought the rules didn't apply to him. Too bad for him that gravity didn't give a damn who his good buddies were.

While she waited for the ambulance to transport Chester's body to the morgue, Jill put additional flares on the highway to supplement those the trucker had placed behind his truck.

"Think he blew a tire?" the trucker asked.

Jill shook her head. Hal Taylor wouldn't have sold a car with bad tires, especially not to an attorney. The last thing anybody wanted was to give an attorney a reason to sue.

"No." Jill had seen skid marks as she drove up to the scene. It was too dark now to take pictures. She'd come back tomorrow during the day and take a couple of shots to supplement her report. "He swerved trying to miss something on the road."

Something bigger than a jackrabbit. Besides jackrabbits, coyotes, and free-range cattle, wild mustangs roamed the desert, and so did deer. While the horses weren't normally a traffic hazard, cows and deer got stupid when they got caught by headlights.

By the time Jill made it back to Cumberland, Elaine had gone home and the first of the day shift deputies were coming on duty. Oren had gone home hours ago. Jill had radioed him to let him know about the fatality. It had been all she could do not to tell him that he should have let her haul Chester in. Clifford Chester might have gotten mad, might have complained to his good buddies Hal Taylor and Judge Gibson, might have even sued the county and Jill personally, but he'd still be alive to do it.

It took less than a week for someone else to try Chester's get-out-of-a-DUI stunt. This time it was Marc Freeman's seventeen-year-old son. Marc was the sales manager at Cumberland Dodge, and his kid was a punk who thought his daddy was someone important. The kid actually giggled at Jill when he refused to get out of his car.

The fact that the kid knew what to do meant that Clifford Chester must have taught Hal Taylor his clever trick and Hal had passed it on to Marc, who'd told his son who'd told who knew how many of his football buddies. That meant every jerk who'd had enough to drink to put them over the legal limit was going to stonewall her and risk a resisting charge instead of a sure-fire arrest for DUI.

Whether they thought they could get away with it because Jill was a woman doing what everyone thought was a man's job or simply because they thought they'd found a flaw in the system, she didn't care. She wasn't about to give anyone else a chance to kill themselves and maybe take someone else—an innocent someone else—with them.

She made a show of unsnapping her holster. Marc's son giggled harder.

Jill drew her gun. The kid made a pretense at being shocked.

Then she shot out both front tires on his car.

Before the car finished settling on the rims, the kid was out the door and in Jill's face.

"What the hell do you think you're doing?" he screeched at her, all acne-faced and football-player huge. "Do you know who my father is?"

He was close enough to her now that she could smell the alcohol on his breath, but his eyes weren't glassy and his gait was steady. He'd probably had just enough to drink that if she'd let him stay in his car for the trip back to Cumberland, he could have passed the breathalyzer test. The alcohol was making him brave, and Jill was glad she still had the gun.

"You just threatened a sheriff's deputy," she said, her voice calmer than she felt. "Turn around and place your hands on the hood of your car."

"Or what?"

She gave him a steady look. "I already shot out your tires. Want to see what else I can hit with this thing?"

The staring contest was short. The kid gave her the finger before he turned around and put his hands on the hood. The sun was an hour away from setting in the west, and already the kid had been out drinking. A lot of the high-school football players drank, not the Jill had ever been able to catch them. She wondered if the only day he stayed sober was game day.

He sputtered and complained when she cuffed him and put him in the back of her cruiser. He'd failed the breath test, just like she knew he would.

"You probably won't believe me, but I'm trying to help you out here," she said as she got in the front seat of her cruiser.

The kid cursed at her then turned his face away, and Jill didn't say anything else.

No doubt Marc would go to Hal Taylor, and Hal would pressure the D.A.—the man was an elected official just like the sheriff, and that was how small-town politics worked—and the kid would cop to a lesser charge. Jill's father had fought against crap like that, but he'd never risen above the rank of patrol deputy. He'd been a hard case who never let anyone off with just a warning.

She'd just become a hard case herself. She'd shot out the tires on a car to make her point. Bruce Willis would have been proud. She liked to think her dad might have been, too.

She'd fight like crazy to make the charges stick, even if she had to explain to Judge Gibson why she shot the kid's tires. Oren could suspend her for using her firearm when she had no just cause. He might even make her pay for the tires. She didn't care. She couldn't make the good old boys like her for invading their turf, but if nothing else, she could make them respect her.

Whether the kid knew it or not, she'd done him a favor. He was still alive. Clifford Chester had played the same game and lost. The kid might hate her for the rest of his life, but on the Jackrabbit DMZ, where road kill was more than just bunny rabbits, Jill would take that as a win any day.

Dean Wesley Smith also gives us a story set in Nevada. "Eyes on My Cards" is the first short story Dean has written about professional poker player Doc Hill. The second, "The Road Back," appears as a standalone, and is part of a promotion that WMG Publishing has done to encourage people to buy Dean's amazing thriller Dead Money, *which came out last fall.*

About the story, Dean writes, "Way back in 2005 I wrote a thriller with the name Dead Money. *It starred Doc Hill, a professional poker player. I had every intention when I wrote the thriller to continue to write more Doc Hill stories, but because of the strangeness of publishing at the time, I put the novel in a drawer and pretty much forgot about it. Fast-forward to 2013 and a meeting with the publisher of WMG Publishing, Allyson Longueira, and my wife, Kristine Kathryn Rusch. Kris brought up* Dead Money, *the long-stored thriller, and suggested I take it out, dust it off, and sell it to WMG Publishing."*

Let me say categorically, as the wife in question and as an award-winning editor, I did not say this to stroke my husband's ego. I said it because Dead Money *is a fantastic book.*

Now, back to Dean's "about the story," he says, "So, after rereading Dead Money *and coming to remember and like the characters again, I decided to write a new Doc Hill story for* Fiction River Special Edition: Crime. *This story is the first of many to come."*

Thank goodness. Doc Hill is a special character. You'll see that in "Eyes on My Cards."

Eyes on My Cards

Dean Wesley Smith

One

I pushed back from the table and stood, disgusted.

I needed a break.

I left my chips in my spot indicating to the dealer I would be back. I wasn't down any of the five hundred I had bought in for, but I sure wasn't up either.

But for a change, winning money wasn't the reason I was at that table.

Around me the noise and lights of the Grand Casino and Hotel on the Las Vegas strip seemed muted and flavored by the slight smell of popcorn, like I was walking in a carnival instead of a casino. I moved between the empty poker tables, away from the no-limit game, and toward the larger part of the casino and the gaming tables.

To my right three tourists in shorts and bright shirts stood, laughing at something, and beyond them Webster stood in his dark silk suit, his hands crossed over his chest, his eyes missing nothing on the gaming floor around him.

B. B. Webster, the head of Grand Casino operations was the man who had hired me. He was the reason I was sitting in this mid-level no-limit game in his casino. He had asked a favor and I had agreed to help.

He had a suspected cheater working his poker room, a guy in a dark golf shirt and Reds' baseball cap. Webster wanted me to tell him how the guy was doing it.

And after an hour at the table with the cheater, I had no idea.

Not one, which had me totally frustrated. I had spent all that time at the table and couldn't spot a thing. Yet I too was convinced he was cheating.

I walked past Webster without even a nod and headed to the left of the gaming tables and toward the huge, ornate front lobby of the hotel and casino. Giant marble pillars dominated the lobby and it never seemed to be empty or quiet, no matter the time of day. And the popcorn smell faded in the big space as well, replaced by the faint smell of lilacs. Over the sounds of the people talking I could hear the fountains that lined two walls, water flowing over rocks and into pools.

A dozen tourists stood along the large front desk on the left, talking with smiling front desk clerks, clearly checking in. Suitcases were scattered behind them like deer droppings along a trail in a forest.

Right now it was just after midnight on a Thursday night.

As I went around the corner to my left and out of sight of the poker room, Annie Lott joined me, tucking her arm in mine and matching me stride for stride.

She had on a black pants suit with an open-neck white blouse and low heels that clicked lightly on the marble floor. Her long brown hair was pulled up tight on her head. She looked stunning and just having her walk with me, her steps matching mine perfectly, made me calm down a little.

We had been together now for over a year, living together for the last six months, and I had loved every minute of it.

And sometimes, like tonight, we worked cases together as favors for friends. She had been a former Las Vegas detective before becoming a full-time poker player. I saw things on poker tables she didn't see. But she saw things in the real world I never noticed. It was one of the many reasons we made such a good team.

Since our first meeting while investigating the death of my father, we had become known for being able to figure out some darned strange crimes in and around casinos. We didn't take every request for help that came our way, but if the friend really needed help, or the problem was weird enough to get our attention, we would try to help out.

"He's cheating all right," Annie said. "I can see that from beyond the rail. You figure out how?"

I shook my head. "Not a clue and it's driving me nuts."

"Yeah, me too," she said.

Poker was a difficult game to cheat at in a monitored casino. But it did happen, usually with some sort of collusion between a dealer and a player. This guy clearly wasn't working with any of the MGM dealers, since three dealers had gone through the table in the hour I had been there. And Webster had made sure the dealers tonight hadn't worked or dealt to the guy last night.

And two of the dealers had actually looked at the guy funny a couple of times, as if they were picking up on something being wrong as well.

We walked in silence past the front desk and down a very wide hallway that headed toward the parking garage. A few paces down the hall we went through an unmarked door on the left and into a reception area with a large desk.

We moved toward a lounge area on the right that had bottled water and soft drinks in a fridge and tea and coffee on a counter. The room was comfortable, with three overstuffed couches on three walls that seemed to be from an earlier MGM Grand décor. A very red one, including strange red paintings of desert land-scapes on the walls. It seemed like it would have been too much, but oddly, I found the room comfortable.

I grabbed a bottle of water and dropped onto one couch and Annie worked to make herself a cup of black tea.

We didn't say anything. There was nothing to say until one of us came up with an idea as to how this guy was cheating.

The door opened and my childhood friend and business part-ner, Fleetwood Korte, entered, followed by Webster. Fleet's silk suit rivaled Webster's and together they looked like they belonged on Wall Street, not in a Vegas casino.

At six-two, Fleet was two inches taller than me and thicker around the waist than I was. His hair had thinned since our col-lege days ten years earlier, but he made up for that with a huge handlebar moustache. Every time I kidded him about how Carol, his wife, liked his moustache, he would just smile and nod, a dis-tant look in his eyes that told me far, far more information than I actually wanted to know.

"You got anything, Doc?" Webster asked, his voice deeper and filled with a sound like gravel being washed together. He clearly had smoked far, far too many cigarettes in his day.

"He's cheating all right," I said.

"That much is clear," Annie said as she moved over beside me and sat down with her tea. "I could see that just watching from a distance."

Fleet took a bottle of water and sat on another couch while Webster sort of stared at the three of us.

"Doc, I think he's got spotters," Fleet said.

I glanced at Fleet and nodded. I had thought the guy had spotters as well, but I hadn't been sure. That's why both Annie and Fleet were here, to scout around the table and the poker room area. "Guy in the blue tee-shirt who is pacing the hall?"

Fleet nodded.

"What about the woman in the green sun dress and long black hair," Annie asked, "sitting in the room to the back reading?"

"Possible," I said. "But she came in with the big guy who called himself Big Ed two seats to the right of our target."

"And what good is a spotter going to do him?" Webster asked. "They can't see your cards or anyone else's cards. I've watched some security videos and everyone is playing down on the felt, no flashing at all."

I shrugged, because I honestly didn't know.

Webster shook his head at our silence. "Strangest damn thing I have ever seen. And that's going some considering how long I've been in this damn business."

He headed back out the door and left the three of us sitting and thinking.

Finally, I broke the silence. "Let me lay out what I've got and see if we can put any theories together before we go back in there."

Fleet and Annie nodded, so I went on.

"He's a decent player. Nothing fancy, like he has played a lot of hours in a low-level casino somewhere in a three-six game."

"He doesn't know how to bet in a no-limit game," Annie added.

"That's right," I said. "But somehow he knows the cards in other player's hands."

"Or he's manipulating his own cards to make sure his cards are the best," Fleet said.

"He's not a mechanic," I said, shaking my head. Beside me Annie shook her head as well as she sipped her tea.

I went on. "The guy can barely hold his cards at times. And he's not playing hands when he doesn't have the best cards. But when he does play, he almost always wins. Or drops when his hand gets beat on the last card."

"Maybe he can read minds," Fleet said, shrugging.

"That would explain a ton of things," Annie said, laughing. "But my guess is that this is some sort of very ornate scam we just can't see yet."

"I agree," I said, the frustration coming back. "The guy played for five hours last night and didn't lose a hand he played to the end. And tonight he has kept that streak up, at least for the hour we've been watching."

"You know, if he were better at hiding what he was doing," Annie said, "Webster or any of the rest of us would never have picked up on this."

I glanced at Annie and smiled. "I think you might have given us a clue. He's a mid-level poker player, so this winning and high-stakes game is unusual to him. He flat doesn't know how to hide what he's doing yet."

Fleet shook his head. "And that's going to help us how?"

I ticked off three items on my fingers. "He can't manipulate cards, he isn't working with dealers, and he isn't used to these levels of games. What's left?"

Both Annie and Fleet shrugged.

"Mechanical," I said. I pointed at the ceiling.

"He can't be working with anyone in the security room," Annie said. "I doubt that would be possible. And Webster would have checked that first, before even calling us."

"The guy's not working with anyone in the casino staff," I said, standing. "I'm sure of that now. But I've got an idea how to take this guy and expose him."

"And how are you going to do that?" Annie asked, as she stood to join me.

"If he's not used to this level," I said, smiling, "I bet he's never dealt with a blind player."

Annie laughed, the sound wonderful to my ears while Fleet just looked puzzled.

"I'll show you," I said to my best friend. "You just keep on eye on the spotters. Especially that black-haired woman in the back."

"Got it," Fleet said, looking even more puzzled. "I think."

Two

I waited until Annie and Fleet got back into positions so they could see the table, then I joined it again.

The cheater with the Reds' baseball cap had a stack of chips in front of him that looked to be a few thousand large and there were two new players in the game.

I glanced at my cards a few times, tossing away garbage, then when the button came around to me, I decided it was time to really see what was happening.

One guy in early position made a slight raise, the cheater called, and I re-raised just enough to not scare anyone.

Big Ed folded quickly as did others.

I had not looked at my cards at all. In fact, I hadn't even touched them.

And I knew for a fact that the cheater hadn't noticed I hadn't looked at them.

The guy in early position called my raise, but the cheater was looking puzzled, shaking his head slowly.

Finally he folded.

The flop came and I pretended to look at my cards again, then folded to another bet from the player in early position.

The next hand the cheater limped in again with just a call and I raised. Again I had not looked at my cards. I was playing blind.

By the time the other players folded around to him, he looked very, very confused. Since I had not looked at my hand, he didn't know what I had either.

This sort of made sense if he was reading minds, but I doubted that was what he was doing.

Finally he again folded and I knew I had him.

As the dealer was washing the deck and putting the cards in the shuffling machine imbedded in the table, I pretended to play with my chips as I felt the underside of the rail in front of me. It took me a moment to find them, but I did.

Very slight bumps just under the rail in the leather.

My guess was that they were very, very tiny cameras, no larger than the size of pins stuck into the leather of the rail.

I looked around at the other seats. I honestly couldn't see the tiny camera heads at all, they blended in so well on the underside of the edge of the table.

I was impressed.

In major tournaments there were what were called "button cameras" to allow television viewers to follow along with the play. This guy and his team had cameras so small and perfectly matched with the table that they couldn't even be seen. At least three per spot to make sure that no matter where a player looked at their cards, the camera would pick it up.

This must have taken him and his partners a long time to set up. Days carefully installing the tiny pin cameras without seeming to do anything strange at the table.

Webster would have to go back over a lot of footage to catch the people who had installed the little pin cameras.

I just shook my head in disgust. Even a monkey could win at poker if he knew what everyone else held for cards. The idiot in the Reds' baseball cap was worse. I hated cheaters, almost more than anything else.

I made myself calm down and sit back and try to think. I had found the cameras, but how was this guy getting the information relayed to him?

I played the next hand normal, looking at my cards and playing them like a normal mid-level player. When I did that the cheater seemed to relax again and I studied his face when he didn't know I was watching.

I couldn't see a thing.

I could read the best players in the business and this guy was a blank slate. I doubted he had a good poker face. He just didn't think he needed to hide anything from anyone.

In other words, this guy was not trained well and I was starting to doubt he was in charge of this.

It took someone smart to figure out how to do all this.

People had always tried to cheat casinos. Over the years, people had put in signals in their shoes, small electrodes on their arms, and so on to help them count cards in blackjack or get information from spotters. But this guy didn't seem to have any of that and the Grand Casino's normal security systems were designed to block most electronic signals, or at least spot odd ones.

And from what little I knew about tiny cameras like these, they didn't have a very large broadcast range. In fact, they were so tiny, I couldn't imagine them broadcasting much beyond the edge of the table, which would guarantee that the signals from that many small cameras would not be picked up by casino electronic scanning.

The dealer took the cards out of the shuffling machine, cut and started to deal.

I glanced over at the woman with the long black hair sitting in the back of the room. She was reading on some sort of tablet and she had it turned so no camera over her could see what she was reading.

Suddenly I knew I had it figured out. And I had a sinking feeling it was a lot larger cheating scam than anyone had first figured. A lot more than one bad player winning too many hands.

I mucked my cards without looking at them and stood up. "Back in a second," I said to the dealer.

Then I again turned and headed out of the poker area and toward the casino. Again the popcorn smell filled the air and shouting from the direction of the craps table seemed to cover almost everything.

Out of sight of the table, Fleet and Annie and Webster caught up with me.

"So that's playing blind, huh?" Fleet asked as we stopped near the hotel lobby.

Annie laughed. "Doc drives people crazy doing that in tournaments when he spots someone who really cares too much."

"He drives a lot of us crazy like that," Fleet said, shaking his head.

"Well, Doc?" Webster asked.

"I got him," I said, smiling. "When did you switch out those shuffling machines?"

Webster looked puzzled. "A month or so ago, if I remember right. But they are carefully checked."

"I know," I said, nodding. "That's why this is so amazing, more than likely there's more teams involved in this working other casinos right now."

"Oh, crap," Webster said.

Annie squeezed my arm and smiled.

Fleet just shook his head as he often did when I said outrageous things.

I just smiled. "Get security to surround the entire area and hold that woman in the back with the tablet as well. She's the spotter, so you had better take that tablet away from her quickly before she erases anything. And my sense is that the guy who calls himself Big Ed is also in this, since he never played against the guy in the cap. He's just a better player is all and harder to notice."

"You're sure about all this?" Webster asked, his voice sounding even more full of gravel than normal.

"Positive," I said, smiling at the frown on the casino manager's face. "I'll show you. It's actually pretty damn smart system. Just get your people in place and keep a lid on this until you can warn other casinos."

Three

It took Webster five minutes to carefully put his men into position around the poker room without anyone seeming to notice. His guys were good.

"Introduce me when we walk up to the table would you? I want to see their faces."

He laughed. "Gladly."

"Just make sure your guy gets that tablet quickly."

Webster nodded at his guy standing behind the woman and I smiled. She wouldn't even see that guy coming.

Fleet and Annie followed us a few steps back.

As we neared the table, Webster signaled for the dealer to stop play.

"Folks, I'd like to introduce you to Doc Hill, the top ranked Texas Hold'em player on the planet."

I did a slight bow, smiling at how the guy in the Reds' baseball cap had gulped and his face had gone white.

The guy named Big Ed just shook his head and muttered something about how he thought he recognized me.

Webster's man had taken the woman's tablet and was holding it and blocking her escape.

"I asked Doc to join this table," Webster said, "because it felt like something was wrong with the play."

I reached forward, under the edge of the leather near my chips, and pulled out a tiny pin and held it up.

"Camera. Three at each spot," I said to the table. "Pretty nifty, huh?"

All the regular players except Big Ed and the guy in the Reds' cap started feeling under the edge of the table in front of them and pulling out camera pins.

"The cameras all relayed their data to a small device inside the shuffling box," I said.

With that the dealer looked shocked and actually moved back from the box like it might bite him.

"The shuffler then sent the image of all our cards as a phone signal to the woman in long hair sitting back there."

Everyone looked around at her and she just sneered.

I went on. "She would then relay the information about the cards to our two friends here also by phone signal, which is not blocked in a casino or monitored."

I turned to Webster. "You'll find tiny ear bugs in their ears set to receive the phone signal from the woman's tablet."

"You can't prove that," the idiot in the baseball cap said.

Webster only snorted and motioned for the guards to take them away. Then he had the dealer split the cheater's chips among those of us at the table and broke the game.

"You had better be informing the other rooms around town and up in Reno," I said to Webster.

"I'm going to, as soon as I take that box apart and figure out how we missed the phone device in there. But I know you are right. This is a big ring and these three are going to suddenly vanish into some deep parts of this casino for a short time so that we don't alert everyone else."

He stuck out his hand. "Thanks, Doc. Fleet. Annie."

"Check's in the mail?" Fleet asked.

Webster snorted. "Not so much a check, but a lot of free dinners from here and I'm betting other casinos in town."

"Sounds even better," Fleet said, laughing.

"Come to think of it," I said. "I am hungry. That popcorn smell has been driving me crazy."

"It does that," Webster said.

"Steak?" Annie asked.

"I love steak," Fleet said, smiling at Webster.

"Maybe I should write you a check. Might be cheaper."

Then in his gravelly voice he laughed. "Head on over to the steak house and I'll tell them you're coming."

He turned and walked away.

The three of us laughed as I tossed the small pin camera on the table and racked up my chips. Then we turned and headed for a late meal.

It felt great to help protect the game I loved. Poker is a game of skill, but there will always be those who look for shortcuts in anything that takes skill.

I just hoped Webster kept these three "lost" for a very long time before turning them over to the police.

And that thought just made me laugh, so I told my friends what I hoped Webster would do and they laughed as well as we headed for dinner.

Even Annie, the former Las Vegas detective.

"In Vegas," she said, "casino justice can be much worse than police justice. Always has been, always will be."

"Especially for cheaters," I added and they both laughed again.

M. Elizabeth Castle returned to traditional prose format for her second story in this volume. "Jokers" comes from life, she has worked with maps on computers before.

She writes, "Every map tells a story, and every map lies. Even if maps could capture every single feature in a geographic area, the world is always changing. What to include, what to leave out, the exact position of features—these are part of the cartographer's art. Jokers, on the other hand, are just flat-out fabrication. I've placed my share of them on retail maps (mostly in Florida and North Carolina if anyone wants to go hunting)."

She now works and lives in Washington State, for those of you scanning maps.

———

Jokers

M. Elizabeth Castle

Stanley leaned forward, the piece-of-crap office chair squeaking under his weight. He put his elbows on either side of his keyboard and studied his huge monitor. At least the Boss didn't pinch pennies when it came to the workstations and software. The displayed map's streets and text were apple-crisp, as his mother used to say. (Huh. Dear old mom hadn't been the first, but he'd finally dealt with her.)

He enabled the StreetName layer. Twenty years in the business and the problem labels stood out like hookers in a suburban neighborhood, begging for him to fix them. None of the interns could even see the problems, most of them had to be shown every single time what needed to be done. They got stupider by the year. He tweaked a few names, making them curve properly along their street linework. Abbreviated "276th Place Northeast" to "276 Pl NE" so it would fit the tiny cul-de-sac. It felt almost feng shui, setting things right in the map, making the whole correct and orderly before it got sent to the printer.

The notion of people using his maps to find their way gave him a little buzz of satisfaction, like a distant version of the big buzz he indulged in when he had to.

And this particular street map was even more satisfying. This was Crawford County. The home port. The mothership. Took the Boss long enough to produce a road map where he ran his business.

Stanley scrolled to the far west point of the county. No highways here, just woods. Forest and fields and rural streets leading to nowhere.

He contemplated a particular private road off a particular far-flung street. The reference air photo showed the private road winding into the forest and petering out to a dead end. This would be good. Poetic, in fact. He activated the street centerline layer. Sketched in five new streets, his fingers slick on the mouse. Considered giving them womens' names, then settled on African trees. Placed the labels perfectly. Activated the schools layer and added an elementary school. A tiny neighborhood of his own making. This was good. Just maybe needed a pocket park and—

"Morning, Stan! Boss said you're working on Crawford? Cool. Nice to do something in Georgia, isn't it?"

Stanley jerked, the chair squeaking. "Stanley," he muttered as he turned to glare at the intruder. This was the latest intern, Britney, some silly design major from Atlanta or maybe Augusta, it didn't matter. He wished the Boss could hire a decent cartographer. But the ones that didn't get sidetracked into mapping analysis or programming headed for the big outfits, Rand or Thomas or even the USGS. So he got stuck with training flighty little design majors. But this one seemed to be catching on, not quite as stupid as the rest. Much more obnoxious, though.

"Sorry, Stan, didn't mean to startle you." She was wearing shorts and some sort of cropped, sleeveless top that didn't even try to conceal her midriff. Flip-flops, long blonde hair in a ponytail and far too much makeup for a nice girl to be wearing. She'd been here a month and he'd yet to see her wear anything appropriate. She pulled a chair around and sat down, leaning close. He could smell her perfume. Again, far too much. "Dude, you're sweating," she said.

"It's hot out today." The late spring sun heated up the warehouse, which in turn heated the attached map production offices. The little fan he'd attached to his monitor couldn't keep up.

"Not that hot." But she wiped her neck and chest with her hand, running it down her cleavage, and he had to look away. Not a nice girl. He felt the ember deep within him flare, and despised her for it. Despised himself. It was too soon, and he didn't have vacation saved up, which meant that if his mind exercises failed— and they always eventually failed—he'd have to deal with it here, on his home turf, like he had years ago before he'd gotten smart.

* * *

Every time Britney got near Stanley Hargrove, she could feel the maggots in his brain turning toward her and breathing heavy. Now he looked like she'd caught him surfing porn instead of working, but if she knew one thing about Stanley-not-Stan, it was that he was a mapping machine. Eight hours a day, minus one break for lunch and two for cigarettes, he sat in front of his gigantic screen in the warehouse's stuffy production office and he made maps.

Now every time she thought about paper road maps, she pictured an army of sweaty Stanleys churning them out. After this was all done, she'd never touch a paper map again. Thank God for Google and Bing. And fine, Apple too.

She leaned away from him. He looked like he was about to have a stroke and she didn't want that. Not yet, anyway. "How does it feel?" she asked him.

He jumped a little. No, not guilty at all. "How does what feel?" He'd turned back to the screen and panned away from the area he'd been sketching. She'd gotten a glimpse of his brand-new streets laid on top of the woods.

"That you'll be out of a job in a couple of years. There's hardly any market for paper maps. One day—soon—they'll go the way of eight-tracks and buggy whips."

"There'll always be a market for maps," he muttered, zooming into the gigantic city of Roberta. All dozen streets fit on the screen at once.

"Sure, but they'll all be digital. On phones and in cars. No need for paper."

He pointed at the screen. "There," he said. "That section between Crusselle and Agency Streets. Tell me what needs to be cleaned up."

Oh for crying out loud. She sighed, steeled herself, and once again leaned closer to him. She let her breast come within a finger's width of his shoulder and saw him tense. "That one," she said, pointing. "Move it to the bottom of the street so you can move the other two next to it into better position. And scoot the fire station icon away from the corner and break its text label there so it stacks better." She pulled her finger back but not her shoulders. She wanted him uncomfortable.

"Humph," he said, and she knew she'd gotten it right. Let's hear it for preparation. He turned to her. "Where do you think those digital maps come from? Those ones on your smarty-phone? Somebody has to make them. Somebody has to check the automated labeling programs and fix the errors." He was leaning into her now, forgetting himself, almost touching her breast with his shoulder without knowing it. She suddenly couldn't help herself and moved away from him.

"Sure, there'll always be a need for human eyeballs," she said. "But no more for what you were doing. You—" and she stopped.

He'd flushed bright red from his damp collar to his hairline. What the hell? Placing jokers was a common practice in the paper map business to combat plagiarism. Stanley had explained it on her second day.

So why did he look guilty about it?

He was already uncomfortable and twitchy. She didn't want to push him. Not yet. So she stood and said, "I've almost got the Collier County map done. I'll print a draft out this afternoon."

Stanley blew out a breath and said, "Good."

* * *

Stanley watched her pass through the door and turn up the steps to the upstairs offices. It was sweltering up there in the summer, bad enough in the old days when he had to bend close over the Mylar sheets, laboriously placing sticky-back street labels with an X-Acto knife. He thought of her sweating up there as she worked, how it would bead on her forehead and mess up her makeup, she wore too much makeup, not a nice girl not—

He shook himself. Eventually he'd have to deal with Britney. But for now he had work to do.

* * *

Britney *was* sweating. She'd be more than happy to leave this inferno once she was done here. The Boss had warned her about Stanley—not saying he was a perverted serial killer, nothing like that, just that he was a bit weird and had hard time dealing with the rest of the human race. But he was harmless, the Boss had said.

Britney knew better.

She figured that Stanley was the reason that Map Resources couldn't keep a second cartographer—anyone with half an ounce of sense could see that Stanley was off.

Yeah, he was good at what he did, that was obvious to even her hastily-trained eye. But still. The Boss must owe him.

And speak of the devil... she could hear the Boss's heavy foot-falls coming up the back steps to the loft.

"Britney!" He was breathing hard from his exertion. Every time he came up here, she expected him to expire from the effort, or the heat, or both.

She met him by the big plotter, close to the top of the steps where it was a couple of degrees cooler. He leaned his weight against it, then reconsidered as it slid against the wall.

Grover Carson was a big man, a florid man, a man who reveled in fine cooking, and, as he had told her on her third day, a man whose aorta had come within a couple cells' thickness of bursting in his chest. The near-miss hadn't seemed to change his outlook or habits.

He considered himself the world's foremost retail mapping marketing expert, despite the fact that his business did less than a fraction of the sales of the big companies and he had no digital products whatsoever. "Britney! How's Collier!" Even standing at the edge of the room, he still managed to fill the space with himself.

"I just told Stan I'll have a draft printed this afternoon."

"Good, good. Glad to see you're coming along. He says you may have an eye for this."

"Really? He's never said that to me."

"He wouldn't."

"I make him nervous, I think." She made him nervous, she *knew*.

"Well," said the Boss, with a glance at her legs, "As hot as it gets up here, I'm not going to make you wear slacks and an Oxford shirt. He can just learn to deal with it until I can get the new workstation set up downstairs."

She didn't plan to be around for that. Nor did she plan for Stanley to be around. She almost felt guilty at taking the Boss's cartographer—basically his entire production unit—away. But not really. Stanley had worked at Map Resources for nearly twenty years and the Boss was too blind to see what was under his roof.

* * *

Stanley worked mechanically, letting his eyes and fingers move of their own accord to straighten and re-place errant street labels.

Something about that Britney, especially when she stood close to him like she had earlier, something about her made him think. But he couldn't pin it down.

At 11:45 he heard the big plotter warming up above him, heard her come down the stairs. Probably going to eat an early lunch while Collier County printed. He'd put off his own lunch until she was done.

And it was Thursday, so he'd drop his homemade pies off at the retirement center on the way home. It'd be safe—the old ladies didn't trigger his ember.

* * *

She stood on the loading dock and finished her Coke, looking out into the dusty woods beside the warehouse and letting the warm breeze cool her. She could feel the weight of the rows and shelves of boxed road maps behind her, many of them outdated by ten or more years. Incredible to believe they still sold those things.

Robert, the back-end guy, had taken the truck into town to get the oil changed. The Boss was in his office, making lunchtime sales calls, and Stanley had finally come out of his lair for his Thursday lunch outing to McD's. She had the place to herself.

She dialed her cellphone and the other end rang three times before it picked up. "Pratt." He sounded out of breath.

"Deputy, it's Britney Cole. Did I catch you at a bad time?"

"Britney. No." He took a deep breath then said, "What's happening?"

"He's on edge. I'm afraid he's going to bolt. I think I have to do it tonight."

"Oh for—Don't. Just don't. It's too short notice."

"He's going to bolt. I don't know what it is, but he's super twitchy and every time I look at him he acts like I caught him surfing porn."

"How do you know it's you?"

"I can see how he looks at me, it's different. It's ... God, it's just creepy. He's looking at me like he wants to eat me or something. Like he's holding himself back."

"Can you at least push it to tomorrow? We can put surveillance on him tonight."

"Like that worked the last time." She heard his little intake of breath and knew the barb had stung.

"Goddammit," he muttered. "What the hell did you do to him?"

"I don't know. I'm not even sure it was me. But it's me now, and he's gone over some edge."

"Look, we're short-staffed tonight. I can't keep you safe," he said. "Tomorrow I can have half the force out there."

"He might be gone in the morning and we won't know where and another girl will die," she said.

"Christ, Britney. I just don't have the manpower tonight. It has to be tomorrow."

Stanley might bolt before tomorrow. He might do something else before tomorrow. But Deputy Pratt had a desperate edge to his voice. And he'd accommodated her, heck, defended her, and most likely against his better judgment. She listened to him breathe while she considered.

"Just don't spook him," he said. "I trust you. You can do that."

Don't spook him. She probably already had, and she didn't even know how. She found herself pacing up and down the loading dock and forced herself to stop. She could be careful. "Okay, tomorrow," she said.

"We'll be there. I'll talk to you tomorrow."

"Thanks, Deputy."

* * *

Lieutenant Mike Pratt poked the disconnect button and wound up like he was going to throw the phone across the Sheriff Office's tiny parking lot. Damn that girl to hell and back. He let his arm drop to his side.

Bad enough that every cop in the county suspected they had a serial killer living in their back yard. Bad enough that he was a suspicious, paranoid sonofabitch and they couldn't get near him. Bad enough that said paranoia extended to a lack of ownership of a computer, a cellphone or a car with any sort of electronic chip in it so they couldn't track his internet usage or use his GPS to watch him. Bad enough it had been going on for two years. All that bad enough.

Worse was Britney Cole.

She'd contacted the Sheriff's Office out of the blue two weeks ago, come down to the station to talk to him. He'd taken her to one of the small conference rooms, didn't bother to sit as he asked her what she needed. She said she'd taken a job at Map Resources for the express purpose of getting close to Stanley Hargrove.

He hadn't even let her continue. Told her to quit, get the fuck away. She'd smiled and politely—but firmly—refused.

At that point, he'd begun reconsidering his initial blonde airheaded beach girl assessment of her.

Fifteen minutes later, when she stopped talking, he'd sat down in one of the worn conference room chairs and just stared across the table at her.

She'd done her research, the same research that his department had done. They'd correlated six of Stanley's vacations to missing young women in other parts of the country. She had all those, plus five more they didn't.

One of whom was her older half-sister in San Diego, seven years ago. Britney had gone to the police there, but they'd shooed her away. She'd gone to the police in Boise, where two girls had gone missing over a ten-year gap at U of Idaho. Again, dismissed.

So she'd come to the source. And, wary of a third dismissal, had decided to act first and apologize later.

Except that she'd fucked up his life and hadn't yet apologized.

His people didn't have enough evidence to bring Stanley in. Neither did anyone else. It was all circumstantial, and weak at that. And they couldn't get near him. They'd tried a year ago, but he'd spooked and disappeared for a week. They'd scoured their feeds, made innumerable calls, but there were no college girls missing that week. None that anyone knew of.

And now this—this idiot vigilante girl was trying to set the guy up.

But not an idiot. After his initial denial, he'd grilled her for an hour about what she was doing, what she intended, where her head was, what her contingencies were, a dozen other topics. Looking for chinks in her armor, gaps in her knowledge, soft spots in her resolve. And then he found himself defending her to the Sheriff, saying that she was their best and likely only chance at catching Stanley Hargrove. That as much as he hated to admit it, Britney Cole was tough and smart and tenacious as hell.

The Sheriff hated the idea. But the Sheriff was a smart man, a political man, and he saw all the possibilities. And he'd eventually agreed. But he'd put Mike in charge to take the fall if the possibility of disaster was the one that won out.

And even after promising—*promising*—that she'd work with him every step, she'd pulled the trigger and made Stanley so nervous that they had to move now. Now, with the Sheriff gone to some glad-handing conference in Sacramento. Christ on a stick.

He sighed and stretched his arms across the top of his unmarked. Then pulled back from the heat. He thought of his own sister, living in Atlanta with a husband and two kids. What he'd do if it were she who had been killed seven years ago as a college sophomore. Or had insinuated herself in the killer's world today. Goddammit.

* * *

"Uh, what?" Stanley wasn't sure he'd heard right. The summer rain drumming on the warehouse roof was muffled here in the offices, and he wanted to make sure.

"My family has a place, off Porter Road," she said. She dropped her eyes. "I'd like to show it to you."

She'd like to show it to him. He'd heard right. The ember inside him had ignited in the night, and now it blazed like a beacon, burning him with a fire that wouldn't be quenched until ... until. Well. Until.

And she was making it easy. No need to take vacation, no need to pick another city, no need to wait.

But it was his own back yard. First rule was don't do your business in your own back yard. He'd learned that early with a couple of close calls. "I thought you said your family was in Atlanta."

"I did," she said. "They are. My parents grew up here, and the place was my grandmother's. My folks only come up here a couple times a year."

Nobody local to miss her, not until it was far too late. And he could fake a letter to the Boss. It wouldn't take much. It'd be easy.

But still dangerous. "No, uh, that's okay. I've got something to do tonight."

She raised her eyes and looked at him. He'd seen that look, the one that said come with me, I'll make you feel good. But it was a lie, it didn't make him feel good. It was bad and he felt bad and he didn't like when he had to do what he did, but he had to do it and—. He resisted the urge to close his eyes as he fought for and regained his control.

"Okay, Stanley," she said. "Too bad, though. It's a neat place." And she turned to go.

She'd called him Stanley. Not Stan. The fire blazed. Insistent. "Wait!"

She paused at the doorway, turned and said, "You'll come?"

"Yeah, okay, I'll pick you up."

She shook her head. "I'd rather meet you there. I have some things to get. Food and such."

He started to argue, but realized that if she met him there, that would take care of her car. "Where off Porter?" he said, trying to keep his voice from betraying his thoughts.

"Pretty far out. You'll have to go through the gate. I'll draw you a map," she said. She walked back to his desk and picked up his pen. And she smiled a whore's smile at him as she drew.

* * *

In the dingy ladies' room in the back corner of the warehouse, Britney leaned over the bowl and tried not to throw up. "What am I doing?" she muttered.

She'd tiptoed around Stanley all yesterday afternoon. And then she'd thought she'd lost him when she gambled just now and let him turn her down.

But he'd agreed. And she knew he'd be there.

She took a deep breath and stepped into the muggy warehouse, the sound of slacking rain on the metal roof nearly deafening her.

* * *

Stanley turned his VW Rabbit onto Porter Road, ticked off eight miles as the road wound up into the low rural hills, then began to look for the cutoff road Britney had drawn on her map.

He'd prepared carefully. Showered and dressed and arranged his tools in their nylon bag, each one velcroed in its proper place. The bag in the trunk, along with his rope and shovel and pickaxe. And duct tape. Never go anywhere without duct tape.

Once he'd decided to treat this like any other outing in any other place, he'd calmed down. Matter of fact, maybe he was too calm. No matter, he was overthinking.

He found the cutoff and turned onto the overgrown gravel road. A hundred yards ahead, just like she said, was the gate. And just like she said, it was unlocked.

He got out and squished through the grass to push the gate open. At least the rain earlier had been brief. Made the evening that much more humid, but it washed the dust off the trees and everything smelled nice.

Then again, he was getting mud on his shoes. He'd have to clean them well when he got home.

Once he'd driven the car through, he closed the gate behind him.

He checked her map again. Second drive on the left, it would dead end. If he drove past instead of turning, then past another dead-end drive, the unnamed gravel road would loop around and meet back up with Porter Road east of where he'd come in.

He put the VW into gear and eased up the gravel road. A hundred yards and he saw the break in the trees on the left, just where she said. The drive wasn't even graveled, but the trees were so thick, the leaves so huge that the dirt was hardly wet from the rain.

It opened up and there was her little Subaru sitting next to a tiny honest-to-gosh log cabin. A log cabin in the woods. He liked that.

He pulled up behind her car and got out. The cabin door opened and she stepped onto the rough porch, smiling at him.

Glad to see him.

The fire in him raged.

* * *

Britney didn't dare let Stanley see her nervousness. If he caught even a whiff of oddity, he'd run. Or worse.

Cops in the woods, their cop cars hidden along the far drive, which was little more than an overgrown stub into the undergrowth. No cabin back there. Mike Pratt in the van hidden down the first drive, listening to the wire taped to her chest and stomach. The tape itched.

The cops had debated on the van, whether to park it in the first drive. If Stanley turned there by mistake, he might see evidence of its passage and flee.

But they'd taken the chance. The first drive was closer than the one further down. He could hear better, respond faster.

Wine cooler. That was her safety phrase. Mike had told her to use it in a sentence if she got uncomfortable for any reason, and his team would swarm out of the woods. He'd stressed that her safety was more important than getting Stanley.

She disagreed. But she hadn't told Mike.

She smiled at Stanley as he got out of the car, and stepped off the porch to meet him on the moist grass of the clearing.

* * *

"This is it, people," Mike said. He listened to the soft assents as his officers checked in.

The van, two cars, and six officers, not including himself. Macon's SWAT team was supposed to come, but they were dealing with a gang-related home invasion and standoff.

He had everyone he could muster. Him in the van, the remaining six officers in the woods. He didn't have enough bodies to have anyone ready in the cruisers. And he hadn't dared put anyone in the cabin.

It wasn't enough. He knew it wasn't enough. And if anything happened to Britney it would be his fault.

Christ.

* * *

The girl was dolled up just like a whore. Not even a possibility of a nice girl remained on her. Her shorts were shorter than anything she'd worn to work (and he'd paid attention, oh yes), and her top strained against her breasts, gapping almost obscenely.

"Stan!" she smiled, her red lipstick and dark eyes just wrong in this place. In any place.

"Stanley," he said automatically.

"I'm sorry. Stanley. I know that," she said.

"I've, uh, got something I want to grab out of my trunk, is that okay?" Something about her was making him tongue-tied. Something pinging the back of his brain.

"Sure, no problem."

He popped the trunk and retrieved his bag of tools. Adjusted the strap carefully over his shoulder. Only then approached her.

"What's in the bag?"

"Uh, just stuff. Can we go inside? I'd like to see the inside." Smaller space inside. More control.

"Sure, Stan. But in a moment, okay? I'd like to talk out here for a few minutes."

This wasn't how it should go. He should be in charge. And he would be, once they got inside. Let her talk for a moment, though, he had time, plenty of time. They were out here alone. "Okay," he said.

She paused for a moment almost studying him, disconcerting. Her eyes—they were green, he'd noticed that before but hadn't really remembered—seemed to harden. Her smile slowly faded. He shifted his weight. This felt wrong, he should be in control and he wasn't. He could feel sweat trickle between his shoulder blades.

"Stan, do you know a woman named Victoria Efferman?"

He frowned. Definitely out of control. But, "No. Why? Should I?"

"She was my sister. You killed her seven years ago in San Diego."

* * *

FuckfuckFUCK! What the fuck was she *doing*? Mike slammed his palm on the console. She was supposed to be more subtle, they had discussed it at *length* over the past week, run through all sorts of scripts and scenarios and role-playing until she could deal with anything.

Accusing Stanley with her first godforsaken breath was *not* the script.

Send them in, now. Take him down before he went for her. Or, for that matter, she went for him. Because he sure as hell couldn't trust her now. Mike's hand hovered over the radio switch. One word and his team would go in hot.

But it would be for nothing. Nothing had changed, except that Stanley would certainly disappear from Crawford County for good, turn up somewhere else, and more young women would die.

God *damn* it all to hell.

He pulled his hand back. His decision had taken less than a second to make.

* * *

Stanley's blood seemed to turn to ice all at once. All he saw was her, all he heard was her voice. Seven years ago in San Diego. Seven years ago in—

Then he saw it. Saw *her*. Dressed exactly like the one before him, but a different face. A sister's face. Felt the echo of heat of the unusually warm California night as he killed her, using some of the same tools that were in the bag that hung heavy on his shoulder.

San Diego had smelled of the sea. Crawford smelled of green. It had always smelled of green, from the very beginning.

"You killed other girls too, didn't you, Stan? In Idaho, and Illinois. And other places, too. Why'd you kill them, Stan? What sort of sick, perverted, twisted piece of shit of a man does that sort of thing? Huh, Stan?"

He opened his mouth, closed it. He'd lost control. He'd lost control and he had to get it back.

"What sort of man, Stan?" She closed the gap between them, in his face now, she was as tall as he was, and he smelled her perfume, too much for a nice girl, too much. "Tell me, Stan!" she was shouting at him and he heard his own voice shouting back even though he didn't realize he had even taken a breath.

"Stanley! It's *Stanley*, you stupid whore!"

She took a surprised step back and he seized control, the inferno inside him consuming him. "Your sister screamed as I killed her." He didn't shout, he was done shouting. Shouting was for people who lacked control. He saw her flinch. Good. "They all screamed," he said, taking a step toward her. She took a step back. "They all cried. They all begged me. Begged me to stop. All those places. All those women, not just girls. Even my fucking mother begged me. But I got her too. I got—"

Her lips had curled into a snarl, her hands clenched into fists at her side. "You son of a bitch," she murmured. She advanced on him and he saw the murder in her eyes.

He recoiled in shock. What had he done? This was not control. He had never had it, not for a single second since he got out of the car and saw her on the porch.

She took another step. And as sure as he could list the tools in his bag, he knew she was going to kill him.

He flung his bag at her and fled toward his car.

* * *

"Crap! Mike, he's running! Wine cooler! *Wine cooler!*"

Mike keyed the switch. "He's running! Everyone in!" He scrambled to the front of the van, cranked it up and floored the gas. The back wheels spun dirt then caught and the van roared down the drive and onto the gravel road. He slewed to the left, barely missing a thick trunk on the far side—oak, a tiny detached part of his mind said—and the van rocked back the other way as it righted.

In front of him, fifty yards up the road, Stanley's Rabbit shot backwards out of the drive. It slid to a stop in a shower of gravel. Mike saw Stanley's pale face turn toward him for an instant before he turned the car the other way and fishtailed away from him.

* * *

Even in the midst of his panic, his utter *failure*, his mind clicked with facts and possibilities. Six cops had come out of the woods, at least one more in that van. All were local boys. If they hadn't called anyone else in—but they would have come from the woods if that were the case.

The entire department had turned out. Which meant nobody on the road. Most likely.

He kept the gas pedal mashed, his little VW protesting on the gravel, fighting him for control. He passed a drive on the left.

The road would be curving around any second now. Looping back toward Porter Road.

Movement in the rearview. A police cruiser behind him, another one coming out behind that. That was okay. He could lose them, he knew it. He just had to get to Porter. The road would curve to the right at any time, and his little car would cut through the woods, go where the cruisers couldn't and he'd lose them.

The road didn't curve. The trees closed in. This wasn't right. He eased off the gas, peering ahead to—

—nothing. Green and trees in front of him where the road ended.

* * *

She was already out there, standing in the middle of the gravel road so that he had to brake hard or hit her. Christ on a stick. She jumped in and slammed the door as he floored it.

"Goddammit, what the fuck were you thinking!" he shouted, fighting the ungainly van on the gravel.

She laughed. It had a hysterical edge. "Hi Britney, thanks for getting Stanley to confess on tape." She turned to him. "You did get it on tape, didn't you?"

He'd left the tape running, so he didn't say what he wanted to.

* * *

Britney didn't even let the van stop completely before she jumped out. She heard Mike cussing behind her as she ran past the two cruisers, toward the steam rising from the smashed front end of the VW.

Mike's deputies surrounded the car, guns drawn. Two of them had yanked the door open.

A strong hand pulled her back. "Goddammit, I said *stop*," Mike said.

"We're secure, boss," said one of the officers. Jim Something. "He isn't going anywhere."

Mike's hand on her arm relaxed and she pulled it away.

"He alive?" said Mike.

"Unfortunately," said Officer Jim.

Britney moved forward to stand next to Officer Jim, who had his gun trained on a bleeding and groggy Stanley sitting inside.

"You fucker," she said to Stanley.

He turned his head to her and gave her a puzzled, almost far-away look. "Your map," he said. "The road should have curved. It should have gone back to Porter Road. I don't understand."

"Jokers," she said, a ferocious satisfaction making her voice rough. "You showed me yourself, remember? When I first started. You showed me how maps can lie. My map lied, asshole."

Jokers. She remembered his reaction from yesterday. There was a connection there. "What's out Hilltop Road?" she asked him. "Why did you pan the map?"

"Britney, what the hell are you talking about?" asked Mike.

"Yesterday, he was placing jokers on the new Crawford County map." At his questioning look she said, "Fake streets. There's always a couple on printed road maps. But he got all flustered when I saw him doing it. Tried to hide the location."

"Fake streets," said Mike. "Huh." He leaned down toward Stanley. "What's out there? Huh? Should we go and check? Think we'll find bodies? Maybe the three local girls you killed twenty years ago?"

"Bodies," muttered Stanley, his eyes glazing. "All the pretty bodies, with jokers on top. It's poetic." His eyes closed.

"I'll be godddamned," said Mike.

* * *

Britney sat in her little Subaru in front of Map Resources, poking her cellphone, the AC running full blast against the heat that rose off the asphalt parking lot.

"I still can't believe that asshole worked under my roof for twenty years and I didn't know," the Boss had said.

Britney couldn't believe it either but she hadn't said that.

"I heard that the FBI is coming in to help figure out who all Stanley killed and where he stashed the bodies."

"He was at it for a long time. They've got a lot of work ahead of them." She didn't mention that Mike had kept her filled in on the developments over the past week. Once Stanley had figured out he was caught and not ever, *ever* getting out of jail—served him right, the bastard—he was talking. A lot.

"Sure you don't want to stick around?" the Boss had said. "Apparently I'm in the market for a head cartographer."

"I'm sure," she'd told him.

He'd shaken her hand and wished her well, and she'd parted ways with the map industry.

Now she was trying to figure out where the Java Bean in Macon was while the car cooled down.

Somewhere along the line Deputy Pratt had become Mike. She was meeting him for coffee in thirty minutes.

The Boss had given her a map of Crawford County on her first day—one of the old ones. It was under the seat, never unfolded. She'd use her smartphone to find her way, thanks very much.

"*Photo World*" marks JC Andrijeski's second appearance in Fiction River. She appeared in Moonscapes *with a literary science fiction story. She provides a historical mystery for* Crime.

It's not unusual for Julie to write in a variety of genres. She's currently writing a new adult series called Allie's War *that's romantic alternative history, a dystopian series called* The Slave Girl Chronicles, *and the* Gateshifter *series about shape-shifting aliens and a tough-girl PI from Seattle. In addition, she writes nonfiction for such places as* NY Press *and holistic health magazines.*

Like Megan in "Photo World," Julie worked as a senior photo printer in high school and college, and in that job, printed photos for the police departments in Santa Cruz and Los Gatos, California.

"Of course, these jobs don't exist any more," she writes. "With the advent of digital, that whole industry went the way of the dodo. At the time, however, we had more work than we could handle….We did get murders, along with suicides, break-ins, overdoses, drug deals, motor accidents…and a heck of a lot of birthday parties and weddings."

Photo World

JC Andrijeski

"Blue roll," Devin said, handing her the roll, his voice indifferent. "Five of them, this time. Looks like a doozy..."

"Today?" She grimaced. "You've got to be kidding me."

A sardonic smile touched Devin's lips when he saw her wince. "Jeez, Meg. Since when are you squeamish?"

"Was Dave here?"

"Yeah. He asked about you. You guys screwing or what?"

Rolling her eyes, Megan DeLaney didn't dignify that with an answer.

"You were out back...mixing. Esteban didn't want to bother you," Devin added, still grinning like a fool. "Next time I'll come get you when you've got a gentleman caller..."

Meg only nodded to that, too. Maybe it was the egg sandwich she got through the fast food drive-thru that morning. Or maybe (more likely) it was the six or seven tequila shots she'd downed the night before, cushioned by five cans of cheap, Black Label beer. Whatever the reason, nothing was sitting in her stomach right at the moment, not even the coffee she practically lived on as a student at the local UC.

She really should have called in sick today, but Megan figured Laurie, her manager, would have completely lost her shit if she'd tried it. Not only was it New Year's Day, so a dead-giveaway for a fake sick day, but Laurie would have heard all about the crazed festivities in the UC dorms the night before.

The big bash to signal the end of the 1980s and entry into the 1990s had been posted in flyers all over the college town of Santa Cruz for weeks.

Unfortunately, it would probably be a busy day in this crap-hole of a job. People would still want their holiday and party pictures developed today, even if most of the world got to spend it moaning over Bloody Mary's—or their toilets, if they'd really let things get out of hand night before.

Or, in the case of Santa Cruz, lying facedown on the beach, hoping the January sun would burn away the worst of their hangovers.

They'd probably all want one-hour rush jobs, too.

Frowning a bit as the doorbell rang to signal another incoming customer, Meg turned up her portable cassette player rebelliously, mainly to drown out the sound of piped Muzak in the other room. She knew no one would complain since she was the head printer and the queen of this—admittedly crappy—domain.

Really, she probably could have called in sick and not gotten more than an irritated tongue lashing and a lot of guilt trips about lost customers and the lack of decent printers on staff. They couldn't afford to fire her. All of the local photo jerks would throw a fit if they lost their favorite printer.

Sighing again, Meg picked up her lukewarm coffee in its chipped, 'Santa Cruz Beach Boardwalk' mug with the picture of the Coconut Grove on the front and the beach in the background. She took another grimacing sip before tackling the blue roll, blowing on the surface of the brown liquid absently despite the absence of steam and glancing around the lightless cave that formed her primary hangout when she wasn't in school or studying at the UC Santa Cruz library.

Cracked linoleum covered the floors, what had been white but now looked like a camouflage pattern of stains and dug in dirt from their shoes. The low, painted ceiling shone with bare bulbs in a few places, but the hulking printing machine blocked a fair bit of light, giving it a blue-tinted cave vibe, even in the dead heat of summer when yellow sunlight streamed through the glass front doors of the customer service area that started a few feet away from where Megan sat.

The printing room smelled sharply of chemical developer and bleach from where they had to scrub the floors and the mixing vats every night.

You had to be careful with both, because if you used the wrong solvent you could end up with a poison gas that might knock you out or even kill you, if you were stupid enough to do it without all the fan vents open. Even then, it probably sucked at least a few hours or even weeks off Megan's life every time she did it. She might only be in her early twenties, but she wasn't too keen on ending up with emphysema—or sterile, for that matter.

Especially not from something that wouldn't even give her a decent buzz before it knocked her down for the count.

She knew she was lucky, though, really.

This was a temporary gig for her, only there to provide gas, beer and grocery money while she finished up her degree. Devin, even though he was still only a senior in high school, was probably in for a longer haul, since he barely managed to remain un-stoned long enough to make it to class.

He'd already told her he wasn't bothering to apply for colleges, but would just take a few classes at the local JC so he could keep sponging off his parents and surfing.

Taking a final sip of tepid, bitter coffee, Megan made a face, plunking the mug down on the counter by the color buttons for the printer, which was already stained with similar, coffee-colored rings from countless other times she'd left the same mug in rough-ly the same spot...even though she wasn't technically supposed to have any liquids near the machines at all.

Giving an internal sigh, she resigned herself, clicking her fin-gers for Devin to hand over the first reel of the cop's evidentiary roll.

The printer was a hulking monster of a thing, and took up the vast majority of the room, leaving only a small corridor all the way around it. That corridor existed mainly to feed chemi-cals in at various times when the beeper warned that this or that mixture was running low, but also to re-program the thing or adjust the overall settings, which she did on occasion, mainly because she'd figured out how and the maintenance guy took forever to get there. Waiting for him could back them up for hours, even days, during the summer crunch months, so she'd gotten in the habit of doing a lot of things herself, even though she'd nearly been electrocuted twice, and no one had ever actu-ally *trained* her on any of it.

Megan did 70 or 80% of the actual printing that came through, too, and more like 90-95% of the difficult stuff, which the other printers would leave for her between shifts, at least when they could get away with it.

She also got stuck with 100% of the 'blue rolls,' meaning the rolls they got from their contract with the local police, which had them processing most of their crime and other evidentiary shots. The local police department was too small to have their own dark room, and they often couldn't wait for the time it took to send it out and back to the San Jose cop labs, so Photo World got stuck with anything they needed in the interim.

Anyway, the cop rolls were often tricky to print, too.

Not everyone had the eye for this kind of work. Megan did, a fact for which she was grateful, mostly because it meant she didn't have to work in the crappy restaurants around town, like most of her friends. It also meant she could crouch in the back room of Photo World and blast the college radio station and her own mixed tapes, instead of having to listen to that zombie music out front and worse, having to deal with any actual customers.

Of course, they still dragged her out there to deal with one of their 'difficult' people, who seemed to think their crap-tastic pictures were somehow the fault of the people who printed them. Which yeah, okay, sometimes that was true, but most of the time they wanted Megan to make a Van Gogh out of a pig's ass, which wasn't going to happen, no matter how good she was.

She actually had some jerk complain at her the other day because the heads were cut off in his photos. She had to show the guy the missing heads in the actual negatives before he believed that it hadn't been her doing. Even then, he seemed to think she could have magicked the missing heads out of her asshole if she'd been remotely competent at her job.

Morons.

Ironically or not, the worst ones were usually the 'professional' photographers, mainly jackasses who hung out a shingle with zero credentials, then charged suckers an arm and a leg for underexposed wedding pictures with half the heads cut off. Those same 'professionals' then came to Photo World and other cheap-o printing shacks and screamed at people like Megan to make their crap viewable before going back and charging those same suckers a 400-500% mark-up before they'd cough up so much as a wallet-sized image from their lousy prints.

Megan knew most of those jokers on sight by now. Every time one of them came in and smugly handed over another ten rolls of crap, for which they were probably making more money than Megan saw in six months, she couldn't help thinking she was in the wrong end of this stupid business.

Sighing a bit, she lifted the metal mask around the main light of the printer and threaded the negative strip through, past the first few junk frames until she got to the first real print. Lining it up with the metal frame, she frowned down at all of the cyan in the image, assessing it clinically.

The reason they called them 'blue rolls' was that red showed up as a kind of turquoise blue in negatives before they got printed.

So yeah, Megan had a pretty good idea what she'd been seeing when it popped out on the other side. Motorcycle accidents, like Devin said, were the worst. This didn't look to be one of those, but it still had an awful lot of cyan in most of the frames that passed under her eyes.

Pushing aside the probable content of the images, for now at least, she squinted down at the negatives, hitting plastic-coated and only slightly-raised buttons to correct for the excess of red, which the machine itself would over-compensate for and wash out with too much cyan, thus tinting the final print with a bluish hue. Jacking up the contrast levels a touch and adjusting the color to compensate for that, too, Megan darkened the whole thing with a plus five on the overall print exposure to clean up the main subject from where it had been washed out by the bright flashes of the police cameras.

Devin hung around, bored probably, but more likely mor-bidly curious.

Megan's suspicion was confirmed when he peered over her shoulder, unable to see much because a boulder-like hunk of the machine protruded out over the bright rectangle of light of the printer. It mainly gave Megan a place to rest her forehead as she stared down at each frame.

"That a body?" he queried.

"Yup," Megan said, without looking up.

"Dead?"

"Shit if I know," she said, sighing a bit. "Probably."

Her fingers started clicking through color-corrections faster, almost by rote now that she had the basic spectrum down. She stayed roughly within the same set of adjustments for most of them, a plus five red and a plus five exposure with a minus one yellow for good measure, adjusting here and there for frames that were more or less exposed, or that didn't have the same wash of cyan as a lot of those in the beginning of the roll.

"You sure it's not another motorcycle accident?" Devin ventured.

Megan shook her head, her fingers still hitting keys as she tugged the negative strip through after each click of an ex-posed print.

"No," she said. "I don't think so."

"What's with all the blood then?" he said.

Megan paused long enough to give him a flat look, hiding her irritation badly. "Don't you have some rolls to develop?" she said. "Or some envelopes to stuff? I just did the whole Johnson order..."

"I thought you said you needed to go through those your-self?" he said. "You said she set her camera wrong, didn't you?"

Shaking her head in irritation, Megan took another sip of cof-fee then crouched back over the roll. "Whatever."

Truthfully, though, Devin made a lousy spotter.

It had taken Megan months to figure out why, but at one point, when they were smoking out together in the back room after hours and cleaning the vats, he confessed to her that he was red/green color-blind.

At the time, Megan had burst out in a surprised laugh.

"You're color-blind?" she snorted, handing back the joint. "Seriously?"

He grinned at her, taking another hit for himself and nodding. "Yup," he said, with that sucked-in-breath voice of the experienced stoner. He motioned at her, waving smoke out of his face. "Totally. Can't tell if that shirt you're wearing is puke green, or puke purple..."

Megan glanced at her shirt, then stared at him again. "What the fuck would make you think you could work as a photo printer, when you're color-blind?" she said, still stuck somewhere between amusement and outrage. "Are you totally stupid?"

"Maybe," he grinned, handing the joint back to her. "Hey, don't tell on me, okay? I need this job."

Irritated, Megan only shook her head.

She'd kept his secret, though.

Thinking back on it now, she wondered why.

She clicked through keys in almost a uniform pace, only hesitating on one or two where the contrast seemed worse, or the splashes of cyan brighter. Within a few more seconds, she'd programmed prints for the last frames on the roll. Handing it to him for cutting, she said,

"Thirty-eight. Let me check them out before you chop it."

Megan meant before he cut up the negative into five-frame chunks to fit the plastic sleeves they'd eventually give the police, just like any other customer. It was a pain in the butt to drag out those little pieces of negative to reprint something. Really, she should have done some test prints, first, but she didn't really want to go through this whole thing twice, not if she didn't have to.

Even so, she knew she couldn't scrimp for the cops. She needed to make sure her base corrections had been okay before she let Devin cut up the negs, and before she started printing the rest of the rolls in the five-roll order.

Luckily, the other rolls looked pretty much the same as this one, in terms of color and exposure spectrum. Night time, heavy flash, lots of cyan and pale skin, which showed up nearly black in the neg itself.

Whatever she did here should apply to all of them, more or less.

Standing up, Megan dumped the remains of her shitty coffee in the plastic-lined trash bin jammed to the brim with throwaway prints and wandered to the back of the machine.

There, a conveyer belt ran in a long oval directly to the packing station, where the printer spit out the actual prints and stacked them neatly behind plastic dividers that delineated each individual roll. Picking up a handful of the prints coming out from the roll she'd just done, Megan flipped through them to get a sense of the color and exposure work she'd done.

She sighed a bit when she saw the first few, satisfied that she'd compensated about right for the flash, and that the whites were actually white and the blacks, black, rather than being some varying shade of cyan or dirty yellow from the machine's hyper-sensitive sensors.

The images themselves made her wince a bit, but she didn't concentrate on any of them well enough to make total sense of them, not at first. Vague was better when it came to the blue rolls, at least for her...at least lately.

Megan found her stomach couldn't take a lot of graphic images these days, whether at work or in movies or whatever. She used to think she was immune to that kind of thing—a dozen years of crappy horror movies and fake blood could do that to a person—but not anymore.

Just then, her eyes caught hold of one of the prints and Megan stopped.

Pulling the image that had caught her eye to the top of the stack and flipping the rest behind so she wouldn't get them out of order, she stared at the face of the girl in the flash-bleached frame.

She knew her.

"Lily," Megan muttered.

Devin leaned over her shoulder. "Hey, she's kind of hot."

Megan felt her shoulders clench.

It's not like she'd never heard the dicks in printing say that kind of thing about a blue roll before. She knew why they did it, that it was a form of whistling in the dark, like bad doctor or cop humor, making light of things they couldn't really deal with in a more straightforward way. Still, to have him say it so close to her, given the contents of the picture in her hand, made it hard to stay silent.

Megan bit her lip anyway, and flipped through the next few pictures.

"Damn, she *is* hot," Devin grinned.

That time, Megan shoved hard on his shoulder to get him away from her, glaring up at him.

"Asshole," she said. "You're not even supposed to be looking at these!"

"Jeez, overreact much? They know we have to see some of this stuff. They just want you to print them because you do the best job..."

Megan knew that was true, too, but she didn't answer him.

Her eyes went back to the picture of the girl.

Well, part of the girl, anyway. Her body had been dismantled, cut into pieces with a cleanness that some part of Megan found fascinating, even as it made the bile rise abruptly to the back of her throat. The first image she'd stopped on was that of Lily's head without her body. The second had been of Lily's torso missing its arms, legs and head. Flipping back to the image of the decapitated girl's face, Megan studied the features, trying to make sense of them, or maybe to convince herself that she was wrong in what she already knew.

No, it was definitely Lily.

Megan knew that face. Hell, she should know it.

Someone had set the stump of the girl's neck on what looked like a dirty oil drum before snapping the photo.

In a weird sort of fluke, the drum itself had been painted red, with splatters of black that looked like oil or tar bleeding down the sides.

The red color of the painted drum had actually provided most of the cyan in this roll, unlike the cyan that splashed the frames of the more-common motorcycle accidents that Devin had referenced earlier. Megan got a lot of those from the cops, and on the whole, they were ugly. Highway 17, which ran from Santa Cruz over the mountains to Los Gatos and then San Jose, was a known death-trap of sharp turns, narrow lanes and drunk beach-goers returning to the valley after a day or more of baking their brains in the sun. They lost a few people just about every weekend between 17 and the heavily-trafficked Highway 1, which ran along the beaches itself and consisted of two lanes of fog-drenched, blind corners up and down a few hundred miles down this segment of coast.

The corpse in these images looked strangely bloodless, though, unlike those more ripped apart highway deaths.

It looked almost as if someone had already preserved the thing in formaldehyde, or maybe cleaned it before photographing it for posterity. The light blue eyes that Megan remembered alive and shining just a few weeks before had gone a milky gray with death. The girl's lips and teeth sat strangely ajar, as if she'd been choking in her final minutes, or perhaps never closed her mouth after exhaling her last breath. Otherwise, her face looked exactly as Megan remembered it, if a lot smoother and distinctly lacking in expression.

There was no doubt about it. It was Lily.

"Shit," Megan muttered under her breath.

* * *

Dave Ruiz leaned against the glass counter of the Photo World customer service area, rubbing the back of his muscular neck with one sun-browned hand.

"You knew her, huh?" He squinted at Megan's face, his eyes lingering on her long, black hair before giving her a sympathetic frown. "That's tough, Meg. I'm sorry. I would have warned you, if I knew..."

Megan waved off his words, leaning against her side of the glass counter.

No other customers were in the store, and the front counter worker, Esteban, was in the back, probably toking up with Devin since they knew they could leave any customers to Meg for the next ten or so minutes while she talked to Dave.

Knowing Devin, he'd fished for the rejects out of the blue roll to show Esteban, too, just for shock value.

Guys, Megan thought disgustedly.

She hated working with these jerkoffs sometimes.

Dave was okay, though. He wasn't an idiot, at least.

"Hey," she said, hesitating, before she decided to go ahead and say it. "I noticed something...thought I should give you a head's up."

"Noticed something?"

Dave's head shot up. A sharp look rose to those dark hazel eyes, a look that Meg only saw on him every now and then, even though they'd known each other for over a year now. She remembered, seeing the look living there, that he'd been made a detective at his age for a reason.

She'd clearly pricked his cop ears now.

"Noticed what, *querida?*" he said, smiling at her.

That harder, more intense look, never left his eyes.

She rolled her own eyes at his pretense of casual, but leaned over the counter anyway, pushing a piece of paper towards him where she'd done her best to scrawl a symbol from memory, and blowing her bangs up from her face.

"This," she said.

"What am I looking at?" he said, frowning as he glanced down at it.

"A tattoo Lily had," Megan said, pointing to the top of her own thigh. "There."

"I didn't see no tattoo like that," Dave said, shaking his head. "I've been on the docks all morning, Meg—"

"I know," she said impatiently. "Look."

Taking the stack of prints off the counter where it lay between them, above a full-color ad for Fuji film with a picture of a smiling, toothless baby through the glass counter, Megan opened the paper envelope and shuffled through the stack, finding the image she was looking for. Setting it down on the counter over the baby, she held its place in the roll with her fingers, pointing at the image of the girl's severed left leg with her free hand.

"See? It's gone."

Someone had cut the skin off that part of Lily's thigh.

Dave's eyebrows rose as he stared at the image. He looked at her, and that time, the cop's gaze was in full force.

"I think you'd better come in with me, Meg."

"*In* with you?" she said, alarmed. "In with you where?"

"To the station," he said. "We should take a statement, *querida*."

* * *

On the ride over, Dave had her sit up front, instead of in the caged back-half of the vehicle, where she'd asked to ride. He did let her play with the siren on top of his black and white, though. He laughed when she asked, but humored her regardless, laughing again good-naturedly as she waved away traffic, even as he rolled his eyes in open exasperation as they whipped through two red lights with the sirens blaring.

"You'll get me written up," he said. "What are you? A wannabe criminal?"

"Who says I'm a wannabe?"

He smiled at her appreciatively that time, glancing at her arms in the stretchy, black tank top, and the baby-doll skirt she wore beneath. "Is that what's up with the goth crap?"

"Punk," she corrected. "Not goth. Punk. Get it right."

"Punk is like 1970s, chica." At her surprised look, he grinned. "I know my discs, girl. Don't doubt it."

Laughing again, she shook her head. "The fact that you just called them 'discs' totally ruined whatever cred you got for knowing the heydey of punk...and it's revival time, my friend. Get with it."

"That was the 80s."

"So I'm retro," she laughed. "It's been 1990 for what...ten hours?"

Dave shook his head again, slapping her hand away when she reached down and flicked the switch on the siren a second time. He turned it off after only a short burst, giving her another mock stern look.

"You're like a big kid. What are you, twenty-five?"

"Seventeen," she lied, watching him wince. Laughing, she stuck her head back out the window, calling back to him through her streaming hair. "...Ah, but you made a small-town girl's dream come true," she sang out, slumping back in the seat when he burst out in a laugh. "Pretending to be the man, like that..."

"How old are you really?" he pressed.

"Twelve?" she tried. When he shoved at her arm, she said, "Thirteen?"

"I know how old you are, chica. You're twenty. I checked."

"So why ask? Is this an IQ test?" She grinned again, sticking her head back into the wind through the open window. "Isn't that illegal? Stalking your police printer to determine if she's of drinking age?" She waggled her eyebrows at him, glancing back. "Or was it something other than drinking you had in mind, officer?"

He burst out with another laugh.

"You're a weird one, Megan."

"And you're a stalker pervert, Officer Ruiz..."

He laughed again, but she saw his tanned cheeks color a bit that time.

"Maybe you've been sniffing those chemicals too long in the back," he suggested, rearranging his fingers on the leather-wrapped steering wheel and gripping it tighter with both hands. "Lost a few brain cells in the process...eh, chica?"

"Maybe," she agreed cheerfully, sticking her face back into the wind. "Probably more than a few..."

He grinned at her when she glanced back in his direction, though.

Megan even forgot her stomach for a little bit.

It wasn't as formal as she'd feared when he brought her inside. A lot of guys and even a few chicks in cop uniforms rushing around, a lot of them holding files or staring down at typewriters, and even the occasional computer. The latter had gray screens curving out in front, covered over in yellow text, and a back end that jutted out kind of like a smaller version of the crappy television set Megan had in her dorm room up on the hill.

Dave led her back to one of the conference rooms, plunked down a styrofoam cup of even crappier coffee than what they had at Photo World, and started firing questions at her.

Most of them were pretty easy.

Like, how long and how well she knew Lily, when she'd last seen her, when they'd lived together in the dorms, when Megan had seen the tattoo, what she knew of any acquaintances or other friends of Lily's, boyfriends, ex-boyfriends, teachers, family, anyone who might have a grudge, anything about the tattoo itself, the last time Megan had spoken to Lily, and so on.

Megan couldn't tell him much, but she'd already warned him about that on the drive over. Dave said it was okay, that it would at least give them a few more leads to chase down at the UC, and they'd have the thing about the tattoo down somewhere in writing, until they found a picture.

That was his big interest in what Megan had to tell him. The tattoo, and why anyone would bother to cut it off a dead girl's thigh.

"Dunno," Megan said again, taking another sip of the crappy coffee and grimacing. "Maybe they don't like mediocre body art with lame, Renaissance-Faire Celtic symbols of cheesy hearts?"

Dave frowned to himself, not answering, but clearly, Megan's smart-alec response didn't do much to add to his own theories.

He drove her back to Photo World about an hour later, not talking on the drive itself that time. She left the siren alone, too, lost in her own thoughts.

She'd kind of forgotten about Dave entirely, figuring he was done with her on this Lily thing, but when he got to the parking lot of Photo World, he turned off the car's ignition and swiveled in his seat to look at her directly. He made it clear he had more to say right off, probably so she wouldn't take off the second she managed to unbuckle herself from the seat belt and open the door.

"Hey, Meg," he said.

The tone of his voice made her stiffen that time, and glance over at him warily. Something about it was troubled-sounding, but also more intense than usual. When she looked at him, he rearranged his leg on the seat so he could more-or-less face her.

"I'm going to tell you a few things, okay?" he said, that serious thing still in his lightly-accented voice. "But you have to honor the confidentiality thing this time, okay, chica? For real this time...not like with the pictures, okay? I know those stoner *pendejos* in there usually dig through the trash to see the prints, but they really can't know this stuff, okay? For real, this time, Meg..."

Megan leaned back in the seat, frowning a bit, but nodding.

"Okay. Sure," she said.

"We have a suspect for this thing," he said. "The guy alibi-ed out, but we still think he might have paid someone else to do it. He's got that kind of money, and the psych guy says he fits the basic profile. We're working to bring him in now, but there's some chance he might rabbit..."

Megan gave him a puzzled look, and Dave waved it off.

"He's out of the country," he explained, his eyes still distracted as he watched a kid on a skateboard coast by on the curb. "...That's his alibi, too."

"Who is he?" Meg said.

"Older guy she was sleeping with. Married. Big mucky-muck at some software firm, over in Germany doing the big handshake deal for the past week. He's got witnesses and everything, so I'm not doubting the story. I still think he's our guy. But I can't figure how the tattoo fits in..."

Megan frowned a bit, staring at the glass front of Photo World. She watched a woman walk in, holding the hand of a toddler in bright orange, corduroy coveralls. Mrs. Johnson, there for the birthday party photos, Megan thought absently. She hoped Devin bagged them up right, and wasn't in the back room, blasting Sonic Youth and messing around with her machine.

It had taken Megan an hour to do all the color and exposure corrections on the Johnson order, given that the dumb bitch had the ASA set wrong on her camera. She'd cried and pleaded about how important the pictures were, though, so Megan tried her best to do right by her.

"I don't know," she said finally, looking back at Dave. "Maybe he thought it would be harder to ID her?"

Dave shook his head, sighing a bit. "No. He'd cut her face first, if that was his goal. Or get rid of the hands...or the teeth. Burn her. There are a hundred other things that would make more sense. This guy might be an amateur, but he's not an idiot." Frowning harder and shaking his head a little, Dave looked at her again, laying an arm on the window of the cruiser and exhaling before he glanced back at the passing cars on the highway.

"...It was a fluke they even found the body, Meg," he added. "Someone knocked over one of the oil drums, and it came spilling out...the guy called the police. It was a big fucking mess, but it was decent of the guy to call it in. He was an illegal, so a lot would've just hidden the evidence in his position. We found pieces of her scattered in drums all over the shipment..."

Megan winced, wishing again that she'd cut out the drinking about two hours earlier the night before. Wishing maybe she'd kept her mouth shut about the tattoo, and maybe about the fact that she'd known Lily at all. Taking a lung-full of ocean-tainted air from the open window, she only nodded.

"Gotcha," she muttered.

"Those drums would have been gone, in twelve hours," he added, still watching her face. "Someone might have found her eventually, but..."

"Yeah, I get it."

He made a vague motion with his hand.

Megan did get it, though.

Illegal dumping. That kind of crap went on all over, from what she knew. They'd just done a whole piece on that in the *Mercury*, about busting people for dumping off the coast to save the money from the EPA regs.

They got audited at stupid Photo World now and then, too, because of all the toxic chemicals they used. Thinking again about the tattoo, Megan glanced up, saw blue sky starting to emerge as the fog burned off the coast. Must be getting close to eleven. Still six hours more of her shift, even with the trip downtown.

Sighing, she wished again that she'd called in sick with her hangover. She could be lounging on the beach now with her friends. More to the point, she could have read about Lily in the papers like everyone else, not had to see Lily's face like that, with those dead, gray eyes.

"I don't know, Dave," she said finally, looking at him. "Maybe, if it was a contract thing, like you said, he got it for proof? For the boyfriend?"

Dave grimaced, but looked doubtful.

"Maybe *he* got her the tattoo?" Megan said, trying again. "The boyfriend. Maybe he thought it tied her to him?"

Dave shook his head again, letting out a breath. "No. That's the damnedest thing." He gave her a hard look. "Now this is a real secret, chica...he put his wedding ring on her. His damned *wedding* ring. Why would he do that?"

Megan shrugged again, her face blank.

"Because he's batshit crazy?" she said, when Dave didn't speak.

Dave gave her a thoughtful look at that, but only nodded, not answering.

After another pause, where they both just sat there, he patted her leg with one hand, smiling at her.

"Thanks for your help, *querida*..."

Megan smiled at him, realizing that was finally her cue to leave. Snapping the latch on the door, she climbed out, letting him see her roll her eyes at him teasingly as she stepped out.

"Pervert," she told him good-naturedly.

"Go out with me," he smiled back. "A real date...Miss 'Pretending to Be Jailbait.' I'll take you to the drive-in. Buy you an ice cream..."

Megan only snorted, rolling her eyes again.

"Ask me sometime when you haven't just dragged me into the station," she countered, slamming the door on his white-toothed grin. "Or given me nightmares with stories of boyfriend-slash-serial killers..."

"Would you say yes?" he said, peering up at her with a smile through the open window of the passenger side.

"Maybe I already got a boyfriend, *pendejo*...?"

"Do you?" Dave pressed.

"Wouldn't you like to know?"

"I would."

Glancing over her shoulder, Megan gave him a last wave and a wink, sticking her tongue out at him instead of answering.

Then she pushed her way back through the glass doors, into the air-conditioned insides of the cave that was Photo World, to count down backwards through the next six hours to when they'd set her free.

* * *

Devin handed her the last roll of the day with an apologetic grimace. "Rush job. Esteban told her we'd get it to her before close...I guess the lady was totally freaking out or something..."

Megan glanced at her watch, then at the clock on the wall, feeling her irritation rise. "That's in five minutes..."

"So you better do it now, right?" Devin grinned.

From the blood-shot condition of his eyes, Megan figured it wasn't worth arguing with him. Snatching the negative strip out of his hands, she held it up and eyeballed it using the overhead lights, trying to get a sense of what she was in for on the overall before she threaded it through the machine.

"Top the levels," she told Devin. "Do it now, so we can get the hell out of here as soon as this comes out..."

Her voice had lost some of its tension, though.

The roll looked pretty normal, and evenly exposed. No weird flash contrasts or splashes of one color over another, the whole thing was kind of the normal reddish-brown with darker and lighter variants. Outdoors. 200 ASA. Mostly people shot outdoors. Some basic color corrections for the beach and sunset, but Megan had those down by now, working in Santa Cruz.

Whoever the last-minute-Nancy, she at least knew how to work her camera.

Truthfully, most people couldn't tell if a roll needed a basic color correction anyway. Most people, when they got their crappy photos back, blamed the camera, or their own photography skills, or some fluke of the image. The average joe almost never blamed the actual printer, who could fix a hell of a lot more than they usually let on...or knew themselves, more likely. Megan usually had more pride than to let rolls go through the door like that, and would do her best to make masterpieces even out of the dullest of subject matter.

But this chick handed her an end-of-the-day rush order after Megan had already worked behind this stinking machine for ten hours. She had another think coming if she thought Meg was going to do test prints at five minutes to close on a Saturday. Meg would take her best guess, but she was doing the whole roll in a single shot, and if it happened to be off-tint a little or she missed a few keys in either direction on the exposure adjustments, then so be it.

It's not like she got paid much more than minimum wage, anyway.

Meg suspected that was the real reason most of these photo labs churned out so much crap. You pay a bunch of stoner college and high school students to do a fairly technical job, then spend five minutes having other untrained bozos train them, and you pretty much get what you'd expect to get...that is, if you weren't a cheap weasel living off churn, like Photo World's owner, Mr. Anstead.

Sighing a bit, Meg lined up the first negative and began systematically knocking them back, hesitating only a bare second over each exposure before punching it through. When she'd gotten through the last frame of the roll, she grabbed hold of the reel and walked over to the packaging station to process the prints herself, since, for once, Devin was doing what she'd asked and topping off the levels.

The latter consisted of using a footstool and opening the lids to plastic vats behind the machine, peering at where they matched up with the line someone had etched in permanent marker on the outside, and pouring in the various mixtures that had been lost to evaporation and whatever else wherever needed.

Stopping first to chop up the negatives, Meg fed the roll into the sleever in five-frame increments, lining up the cutter between frames and chopping down on the separating line before tugging down another row. The sleever itself was basically a modified paper-cutter, with a simple cutting arm and handle over a grid-engraved slab of metal, fed by a roll of plastic sleeving material with the words 'Photo World' stamped on them in blue letters.

Meg had done this job so many times by now, she barely had to look at what she was doing. She cut through all seven segments in about thirty seconds, cut off the end tab of the film with its identifying sticker and tucked that into the last sleeve over the black lead, and folded the sleeves up, accordion-style, to stuff into the paper envelope. Fitting the whole thing into the front pocket of a new one on the stack, she walked the few steps over to where the printer was spitting out glossy, 4X6 images against the dividing line of plastic on the conveyer.

Picking those up once she got close enough, she began to flip through them, pausing on a few that probably could have gone a bit darker or lighter, but not finding anything glaring enough that would force her to re-do one of the prints. She focused on faces briefly when she got to a group of shots of a beach party down by the wharf, then stopped cold, knocked once more out of her usual focus solely on the exposure and the varying tints of color.

She gazed down at the familiar face among the orange-splashed, edging-towards-the-end-of-the-day sunset pictures that finished off the last eight frames in the roll.

"Lily," she muttered, for the second time that day.

This was a picture of Lily alive, though.

Lily grinned into the camera, her brown, curly hair wet and hanging on either side of her heart-shaped face. More muscular arms circled her from behind, gripping her where she sat on the sand, their legs stretched out in front of them on the warm-colored sand. She wore a bright teal bikini and her pale blue eyes shone bright in the late-afternoon sun above that wide-lipped smile, making them almost white against her deeply tanned skin.

Megan couldn't help staring at Lily's left thigh, and the tattoo that stood there, the same one Megan had first seen in the dorms, the one and only time Megan saw Lily heading for the shower. Lily had been wearing a frayed purple towel, faded nearly to gray with countless washings, obviously a hand-me-down from her parents for her first time living away from home.

She'd stood there in that towel, chatting away to Megan, but Megan had found her eyes glued to the tattoo for most of it, oblivious to most of Lily's actual words. She remembered fragments though. Stuff about some party, a band she'd gone to see, her new boyfriend, since she talked about him pretty much incessantly those days, like a broken record.

"Oh, do you like it?" Lily had said, shifting her leg under the towel to show off the bright colors, which had barely faded from the clearly-new ink. "Me and my boyfriend got them together... just a few weeks ago. Hurt like a bitch, let me tell you...but I swear *he* complained more than I did..."

Megan remembered that laugh.

Lily laughed a lot, Megan remembered now.

The guy holding her in the photo had an identical tattoo, on the exact same place on a distinctly more muscular and hairy leg, although there wasn't a ton of hair around the tattoo area itself. The same cheesy Celtic heart, though, with connected loops of green and red. With the tattoos next to one another like that, it was clear they were connected designs, since the reds and blues had been reversed on each to make them mirror images of one another.

Sleeping with married guys. Jeez.

From what she knew of Lily, Megan wasn't exactly surprised. Still, it was a shock, seeing Lily there, for the second time that day.

Megan deliberately didn't spend time looking at the face of the man in the photo. She didn't dwell much on either of them, really, not after seeing the tattoo and what was unmistakably Lily's face. Stuffing the photo back into the paper envelope with the rest of them, Megan went to the wall telephone in the back of the lab, instead, picking up the white, hard-plastic handled receiver. The phone was stained blue and brown in parts with chemicals, too, just like most things back there, including the linoleum floor, which had off-color splotches pretty much all the way around the hulking printing machine.

Pulling a card out of the pocket of the men's shirt she'd thrown over her tank top, Megan rested the receiver against her shoulder and punched in the white buttons according to the number on the card.

It only rang a few times.

"Yeah...Dave?" she said, still holding up the card, but without focusing on it anymore. "I think you'd better come down here..."

* * *

The person who came to pick up the photos hadn't been who Megan had been expecting. Instead of the middle-aged woman with the bleached-blond hair that Esteban described to her, a guy about Megan's age showed up. It only took Megan a second to realize it was the same face she'd just seen in the photo with Lily on the beach. The new boyfriend. The same new boyfriend Lily had been so gushy about, all the while she was playing hide-the-sausage with some rich, married dude on the side.

Jeez, people were fucked up.

Once Megan saw him standing there, she receded behind the door jamb of the entrance to the back printing room, letting Esteban do the customer interaction thing. She watched, just out of sight, while Esteban made a show of giving Lily's boyfriend his prints and charging him the eight dollars or whatever it was for the finished roll and handing back his change from a ten.

Once money exchanged hands, Officer Ruiz walked into the store, making the little bell do its trill over the door and looking more cop-like than Megan had ever seen him. She grinned a little, in spite of herself as Dave kind of walk-swaggered up to where the boyfriend stood.

"Christopher Harmon?" Dave said. "I'd like to have a word with you."

Megan just watched, Devin peering from over her shoulder. Devin bounced on his heels a bit while the whole thing went down, grinning like a kid who was about to be handed an ice cream cone, as Ruiz led the now scared-looking boyfriend out the front door of Photo World. All three of them, Esteban, Megan and Devin, just stood there, silent, until Dave got the boyfriend to his police car, which now had its lights flashing although the siren remained silent.

"You think he did it?" Devin said, pushing at Megan's back. "You think he did it, don't you?"

"I don't know," she said, noncommittal.

"But you think he did, right? Don't you, Este?" he asked the other guy, who only held his hands up in an indifferent shrug. "You think so, right Megan?"

"Shut up, Devin."

Megan couldn't help thinking about how scared the boyfriend had looked, though, as he got into the back of the vehicle.

Almost like he knew the gig was up, that he was fucked, good and proper.

Almost like he knew he was guilty.

She didn't feel about that the way she'd thought she'd feel.

Instead of feeling relief, the whole thing just made her angry.

* * *

The next day, it was all over the papers.

Lily's face, the twin tattoos...Megan even came up as an 'un-identified witness' around the photos. Photo World was on the front, mentioned in a sting operation, although, of course, they didn't mention anything about the fact that the police got their photos done there, too.

Megan paged through the photos of Lily and her crying parents, scanning through where the article talked about the evidence they'd found in the boyfriend's dorm room, including a saw covered with Lily's skin and blood, with serrated teeth that matched the marks left by the one that had been used to cut up the body.

Grimacing a little at the gory details written to the easily-titillated masses, Megan closed up the paper and tossed it down on the back counter, not far from her crappy coffee from the broken machine in the back.

Devin didn't even look up. He was sitting on one edge of the counter in the packing station, next to the negative sleever, his own newspaper spread out in front of him as his eyes scanned the small print as if to memorize every detail. A faint smile still lived somewhere on his face, and his expression held a trace of excitement even as he absorbed all the sordid details.

"Bastard did it," he said, as if he'd known he'd done it all alone. "Son of a bitch. He really did it...and he was here, in our store..."

Internally, Megan rolled her eyes, but she gritted her teeth a little, too.

Guys...jeez.

Leaning back in her printer's chair, she paused long enough to pull her thick dark hair back in a messy ponytail, using one of the rubber bands they used to collate prints to hold it back out of her face. Glancing up at the strings of negatives waiting for her on the rack, clipped to their customer bags with the ID tags showing up front, she found herself thinking through some of the details that the police hadn't shared with the press.

Like the fact that the tattoo, and the skin it had been left on, had been found in Chris' dorm room, too. Dave told her that part. Megan was kind of wishing he *hadn't* told her that, but Dave seemed to feel like he owed her more information than he usually gave the average joes. Or maybe, now that the case was solved, they didn't have to worry so much about keeping that stuff secret.

The day was longer than usual for some reason, even with all those images and Dave's words from their brief phone call the night before still rolling around Megan's mind...or maybe because of it. She couldn't help thinking about Chris, and why anyone would do something like that. She considered asking Dave that, too, see if he had any theories or whatever, then decided maybe she was better off not getting too close to that particular type of mind.

Heck, the police seemed to think this kind of shit just happened sometimes, boyfriends going nuts when they found out about second boyfriends, and then panicking and trying to hide the body after things got out of hand. Apparently, Chris was just a little more creative than most when it came to the actual body-hiding part. And the tattoo thing, which must have been an attempt by Chris to hide his connection to her, too. The wedding ring thing was pretty weird, but Dave explained that when Chris confessed, he told them he'd been trying to pin it on the new boyfriend. It hadn't even been the guy's real wedding ring, it turned out.

So yeah, pretty dumb.

But Chris seemed to think the death part itself had been a kind of accident, and Dave said his confession matched the forensic evidence they'd found in the dorm room after the fact. Lily and Chris had a big fight about her new guy. Chris had shoved her at some point, and she'd cracked her head on the edge of his wardrobe, snapping her neck and killing her instantly.

So yeah, not first-degree murder, but still murder.

A crime of passion.

It was still pretty weird to think he might have gotten away with it, if it weren't for the clumsy illegal worker guy on the docks that night, leaning against the wrong barrel, or tripping, or what-ever he did to knock over the first one and spill out part of Lily all over the docks.

Bad luck on Chris that the guy ended up being honest, too.

Grimacing again, Megan tried to shove the whole thing from her mind.

She almost succeeded. She managed it well enough to get her through to lunch, and then the rest of the afternoon. She finished the last of the prints at quarter to five.

She was sprawled out in her chair reading a comic book, boots propped on the flat surface of the printer, when the bell jangled from above the door in the other room. A now-familiar sound of rubber-soled leather shoes walked steadily across the main store just outside her printing cave.

"Megan?" Dave called through the open doorway. "You ready?"

Hiding a grin, she let her boots drop to the floor, rising to her feet in the same smooth motion. Tossing the comic book back on her vacated chair, she tipped a finger salute at Devin as she shoul-dered on a red, vinyl jacket.

"Try not to set the place on fire while I'm gone," she said.

Then, glancing around, she pursed her lips, amending her words.

"...On second thought, knock yourself out. There's a book of matches in the drawer by the sink..."

Devin looked up from where he was pretending to read a photography book, one of those big, coffee-table type things that he and Este used to camouflage the pin up magazines they shoved in the crease of the spine. Megan didn't know why he bothered. No one was there but her and Este.

Looking Megan over in her black skirt and boots, the spa-ghetti strap tank top under the white blouse she wore above, Devin smirked, setting aside both the magazine and the book.

"You going to let him use his handcuffs on you?" he said.

"Only if he asks nicely," she said.

"Ask him about the guy," Devin called after her, his voice rising an octave as he remembered the murder. "Ask your Officer Dave if the guy's shitting himself yet, waiting for the day they put him behind bars..."

"Ask him yourself," Megan shot back.

She was already forgetting about Devin, though, as she returned Dave's grin, seeing his eyes widen in appreciation when he got a good look at her legs in the shorter-than-usual skirt. Pushing dead girls and psycho ex-boyfriends and lame, poser-Celtic tattoos out of her mind, Megan decided to be an optimist, at least for tonight.

She kept her eyes on Dave's when she finished answering Devin.

"...*We're* going to the drive-in," she said, with a finality that surprised her. "So don't wait up."

Acknowledgements

This project wouldn't have gotten off the ground without the Kickstarter support from these wonderful people:

Anthony Cardno
Gary Dockter
Sandra Hofsommer
Tony James
Michael Stackpole

Thank you!

About the Editor

Kristine Kathryn Rusch is an award-winning author and editor. Her short mystery fiction has won the *Ellery Queen* Readers' Choice Award twice, and has been nominated for the Edgar, Shamus, and Anthony Awards. Her mystery novels also appear under the names Kris Nelscott and Kris Rusch. For more information on her work, go to kristinekathrynrusch.com.

FICTION RIVER: YEAR ONE

Missed a volume from Fiction River's first year?

No problem. Buy individual volumes anytime from your favorite bookseller.

See why *Adventures Fantastic* calls *Fiction River* "one of the best and most exciting publications in the field today."

FICTION RIVER: YEAR TWO